a twin falls

A High Sierra Mystery

Terry Gooch Ross

For information:
Diane Eagle Kataoka
Two Birds Press
P.O. Box 7274
Mammoth Lakes, CA 93546
email: publisher@two-birds-press.com

a twin falls

my heart grows by half again

Mary lives there

Dedication

To Mary Gooch Wallis and Robert Wallis

Mary was my twin. Her brain died suddenly on January 7, 2001, of an aneurysm. We turned off her life support the next day. I did not believe I could ever survive without her, and there are days when I am surprised I have.

Mary's husband Bob died ten years before Mary on May 11, 1991, of non-Hodgkin's Lymphoma. His death was not sudden. Mary's hair turned from lush brown to almost completely white during the two years of his illness. She loved him more than life.

A few months after Mary died—in the aftermath of 9/11—as I was flipping through TV channels, I happened upon a talk show of sorts called something like "twins who lost twins on 9/11." As hard as I tried, I could not turn the TV off or change the channel. I sat there mesmerized and sobbing, listening to twins—now singles—speak about their tragedies. To this day I think about a comment one twin made when he was sharing his story, because it has proven so true. He said that when his twin was alive, they spoke often; now that he has lost his twin, he speaks with him every day.

My dialogue with Mary begins every morning when I choose a memory that will be with me for the day. I picture it, savoring every detail. I have relived many of our memories multiple times. So… on the seventh anniversary of Mary's death, I decided I would make new memories with Mary. This is why I have written *A Twin Falls*, and why I dedicate it to Mary and Bob.

Prologue

I fell into a deep funk on my 35th birthday—the kind of depression reserved for major life milestones. When I phoned Mary, my twin, to commiserate she couldn't understand why I was upset. I guess I shouldn't have been surprised that she didn't get it. After all, Mary was a successful marketing executive, happily married to a software/hardware genius, living in an Architectural Digest–type home in Northern California where her personal masseuse came twice a week to give her and her husband Bob a massage. So, of course, perhaps she hadn't noticed that we turned thirty-five. When stubbornly I listed what I believed to be the obvious drawbacks to turning thirty-five, including competing with twenty-to thirty-year-olds for work, dates, and attention by a bartender to order a drink, she had no clue what I was talking about. Dismayed at how different our lives were, I got off the phone feeling worse than I had before I phoned Mary. A phenomenon that rarely occurred.

This is why, when later in the day I saw an ad in our local weekly newspaper announcing a Mid-Life Crisis Support Group being held that evening at the Mammoth Lakes Community Center, I decided to attend.

About twenty minutes before the session was scheduled to begin, I parked in the Community Center parking lot next to the main entrance so I could scope out the other pathetic individuals who shared my melancholy. After ten minutes I decided there must be several different groups meeting at the center that evening because I saw nearly twenty people walk in—from twenty-somethings pushing strollers to eighty-somethings pushing walkers.

About two minutes before the session was scheduled to begin, I pulled down the make-up mirror on the back of the sun visor of my Subaru Outback station wagon and checked my hair. It was light brown with a few highlights of sun regularly placed there by Michael, my hairdresser. Before I could take out my brush and start primping, I returned the visor to its original position. If I were late to the meeting, everyone would stare at me. So my messy hair and I climbed out of the car and walked to the front door of the center.

Community Center construction had been completed about four weeks prior, and this was my first time there. Through the doors, I discovered one big room—not a number of smaller meeting rooms as I expected. *Everyone* who had passed my car was seated in folding chairs with their attention focused on a slight, gray-haired woman standing next to the podium. I could immediately tell that she was one of those serene, yoga, health food, La Maze types who had met each one of life's milestones with a smile on her face. I hated her.

When I turned to make a quick and quiet exit, she said in a calming, Zen-like voice, "Don't be shy, dear. Come in and join us. I am sure our lives will be made richer by your participation."

At this point, everyone, including children in strollers and impatient little old ladies, turned to stare at me, some shouting encouragement—some giving me the thumbs up sign, a few just telling me to sit down. I had no choice but to find a chair. Of course, the only vacant chairs were in the front two rows.

I took a seat next to a woman dressed in Chico's latest casual wear who appeared to be in her early fifties. As I sat down, she took my hand and squeezed it.

"You will be so happy you decided to stay," she said.

Her hand was damp and she smelled like garlic was one of her daily staples. I gave her a forced smile, withdrew my hand as quickly as I could, and breathed through my mouth.

As if things couldn't get any worse, the meeting leader, who announced her name was Cassiopeia, asked me to introduce myself to the rest of the group since this was my first time. Trying my best not to embarrass myself, I stood and blurted out, "Hi. I'm Janet Westmore," and quickly took my seat.

"Oh no, dear," sang Cassiopeia. "We need to learn all about you so you can become…" she glanced around the room opening her arms, "…part of our family." She pointed to a corner, where a flip chart posed a long list of questions.

"The points you need to cover are on the list," she soothed. "And, please, take as much time as you need. We care."

Before I could bolt from the room, the fifty-something woman next to me reached for my hand again and gave me a supportive nod. Believing my hands were already damp enough without taking hers, I took a step forward just beyond her reach. I read the list. I couldn't believe it. They wanted my whole life's story and all I wanted were some hints on how to get through a midlife crisis. The list read:

What's your name? Do you have a nickname you prefer?
How old are you?
Where do you live?
Do you have a spouse? A partner? A special friend? Does he or she know that you are here?
Do you have children?
Do you have pets?
Do you work? What do you do?

Why are you here?
What are your passions?

I checked to make sure I didn't know anyone in the room—after all, Mammoth Lakes is a community of only 8,300 permanent residents—and seeing no means of escape, I began:

"My name is Janet, but my friends call me 'J' since I have always hated my given name. My age and the reason I am here are the same: Today I turned thirty-five and realized my life is almost half over and I haven't really done much with it."

I heard some sympathetic murmurs, someone called out happy birthday, and the woman next to me say under her breath, thirty-five! What does she have to complain about?" Cassiopeia made a humming sound and everyone quieted down.

I continued, "I have a boyfriend. We tried living together but that didn't work so we just see each other a lot. I don't have children or pets."

This time the woman next to me harrumphed, so I added, "But I have several bird feeders. I like watching the different variety of birds change with the seasons."

I peered again at the list and said, "I work for myself. I help organizations mediate employee conflicts. I also conduct trainings and provide coaching for organizations to help people become better managers."

I stopped, gave the list one more glance, and focused on a spot just above Cassiopeia's head. "My passions are cross-country skiing, running, and living in the mountains away from the cities."

With a pause, I added, "And my twin, Mary."

I ended with, "Since I have already told you why I'm here, I guess that's it."

As I reclaimed my seat, perspiration ran freely off my face. I sat down deliberately on my hands so the woman next to me couldn't grab one. The blood was pounding so loudly in my ears that I only vaguely heard Cassiopeia thank me for my candor and welcome me to the family. Then she started to check in with other people in the room. I surreptitiously took the announcement I had torn from the newspaper out of my jeans back pocket, quietly unfolded it, and confirmed that I would be in the room for another seventy-five minutes.

While the meeting droned on, I decided on a plan of action on how to get through my crisis. As soon as it ended, I bolted for the door before anyone could detain me with pleasantries or words of advice.

I would do what I always did when faced with a disappointment or life problem. I would go see Mary. She might not understand what I was feeling, but I knew I would feel better just seeing her. I always did.

Chapter 1 — Three Years Later

The bed feels all wrong. The room is cold yet I can't feel the fresh air on my face from the window next to my bed, which is always open. I try to open my eyes, but they feel glued shut. I either have to stop wearing eye makeup or remember to take it off before I go to bed. Then I hear muffled voices and really begin to freak out.

I try with all my strength to open my eyes, but they won't budge. Where was I last night? Did I drink too much? Did someone drug me? I finally manage to open my eyes a millimeter. I see two people standing at the foot of my bed. Although it is dark, one appears to be a man in a white jacket. Huddled next to him is a woman in a blue smock. They are whispering to one another. Gradually, I make out a few words or think I can, because what I hear doesn't make sense. "Crash, broken clavicle, no brain injuries," some medical terms I don't understand, then "twin and her husband killed instantly."

I can't breathe. Mary couldn't, she wouldn't, die and leave me alone. I am being sucked into a dark hole. There is someone else in the room, standing to the side. It's Mary. She is smiling at me. I relax. I am just having a bad dream. I drift back to sleep.

I'm not sure how long I slept. After a while I began to understand that I must be ill or injured, because I seemed to be in a hospital room, and I could only stay awake for a moment or two at a time. Sometimes it was light in the room when I surfaced, sometimes dark. But every time I woke, I saw Mary—either sleeping in the chair next to my bed, looking out the window, or lying next to me with her head on my pillow. Each time I saw her, I knew that whatever was wrong, *everything* would be all right. Then I would give in to the overwhelming desire to close my eyes.

The first day I could stake a claim on consciousness, I woke up early in the morning. No one was around. I assumed Mary had either taken a break from my bedside or returned home. Between a demanding job as a marketing research executive for a top Bay Area firm, and her marriage to Bob, who loved to play, she had little time to spare. That Mary was not at my bedside was a good sign. It must mean I was doing well. I was healing from… *what was I doing in a hospital?*

When I tried to sit up, I realized my left arm was strapped to my chest and felt useless—the slightest movement sent a spasm of pain throughout my entire body—and I was dying of thirst. As I was about to see if my vocal cords still worked, a nurse walked into my line of sight. Attractive, athletically built, she was tending to an IV I hadn't noticed. When she realized I was awake, she started a little.

She said with a warm smile, "Good morning. I didn't realize you were awake. I'm your R.N., Erin."

She paused to see if I understood her, and continued, "The doctor will be in shortly. Let me get you some water."

She brought in a cup with a straw and held it for me to drink. "Slowly. Just take a small sip."

But I was thirsty and took a big gulp. I nearly choked to death. Whatever was wrong with me included broken ribs.

By the time I was able to breathe normally again, a doctor had entered the room. The nurse moved to the end of my bed. The doctor introduced himself as Dr. Paul, and after some requisite poking and prodding, he set his face in an oddly sad smile and began.

"Do you know who you are?"

"Janet Westmore?"

"Do you know where you are?"

"In a hospital?"

My eyes told me this was true, but I still couldn't remember coming here or even needing to come to a hospital, for that matter.

"What's the last thing you remember?"

I hesitated. What was the last thing I remembered? I had gone to see Mary and Bob in Portola Valley after concluding a sexual harassment investigation for one of my clients in Mammoth. I had been anxious to leave town before the results of the investigation became public. Fortunately, a neighbor was driving to the San Francisco Bay area, so I hitched a ride with her. Portola Valley is an upscale rural community, halfway between San Francisco and San Jose, which meant she wouldn't have to go too far out of her way to drop me off. When it was time to return I was hoping I could convince Bob to fly me home in his recently acquired single-engine plane.

My stay followed its usual pattern. In the mornings Mary and I ran just a block from her home on Alpine Road—a scenic route that borders the Windy Hill Open Space Preserve—a favorite of cyclists and joggers. We went shopping for clothes and other items I couldn't afford. The three of us went out to dinner every night and drank too much wine. It had been easy to talk them both into coming home with me. They loved the Eastern Sierra, especially skiing on Mammoth Mountain this time of year, with its more than 3,100 vertical feet and 3,500 skiable acres of sunny California early spring skiing.

Bob was flying us to Mammoth in his Cessna Turbo Skylane Mary and he had named Oscar. Mary and I named all our vehicles; Bob's plane was no exception. The only thing Bob loved more than his plane, fast sports cars, skiing, and anything by Mozart, was Mary.

Bob was at the controls next to Mary, listening to Mozart's Grosse Messe, looking at peace with the world. Mary was trying not to fall asleep. I was in the seat behind her alternately trying to figure out how to use the Smartphone she had talked me into buying and feeling airsick. Small planes are not my favorite things. Then… I felt a sudden rush of nausea. "What ?!?!"

I hadn't noticed her move. Now the nurse was standing next to my bedside holding my hand gently.

That was when Dr. Paul, clearly concerned, but with little inflection in his voice, said: "The airplane crashed. Both your twin and her husband were killed instantly. You were thrown from the plane. Fortunately, some backcountry skiers saw the plane go down, and Search and Rescue was able to get to you within an hour or so of the crash. That was two days ago. You suffered multiple injuries mostly along the left side of your body, but none are life threatening, and you will recover over time. I'm sorry."

I protested, explaining Mary had been by my bedside every time I awoke over the last couple of days; that she had even lain next to me while I drifted in and out. I must have become hysterical, because as I was trying to convince them they were wrong, I saw the nurse play with my IV. Moments later I fell back into black sleep.

When I came to next I saw the silhouette of a tall man staring out the window next to my bed. He must have sensed I had awakened, because he turned toward me, revealing a head of dark chestnut hair, strong features, and tear-filled brown eyes. It was Ross, my longtime lover and best friend. As soon as our eyes met, I started to cry. He held me. We cried together until we were both exhausted.

Still holding me, he said, "I am so sorry about Mary and Bob." His voice cracked and he said in a slightly shakier tone, "I thought I had lost you. I don't think I could have handled that."

This gave way to more crying.

Sounding more in control, he said, "People have been trying to see you since you arrived two days ago. We placed a "do not disturb" on your room and phone. Is there anyone you want to see?"

It didn't take much thought to respond, "No, I don't think I could bear to see anyone except you right now."

Over the next few days, I learned that along with lots of cuts and bruises, I had broken my left clavicle and left radial arm bone, cracked four of my left ribs, bruised my lung, and suffered a concussion. According to Dr. Paul, the trauma, the concussion, and my twin-bond with Mary probably accounted for my certainty that I had seen her in the hospital room with me my first few days there.

Erin stayed with me during the day and Ross stayed at night after he got off work. At least once a visit, each would gently try a new line of reasoning in their quest to convince me Mary had died in the crash. Their efforts were unsuccessful. I steadfastly held onto the knowledge Mary had been by my side through my first few critical days. Eventually, Erin and Ross abandoned the gentle approach, and they brought in newspaper accounts of the crash, which listed Mary and Bob as fatalities. Only after reading all the articles several times did I begin to accept the fact I was the only survivor.

By day three Erin and Ross had me standing and taking walks around my room. The same day, the hospital sent in a social worker, whom I politely declined to speak with. On day five I met the physical therapist who would work with me to regain strength. By day seven I was told I could go home as long as someone stayed with me.

Ross and I didn't live together—we had tried cohabiting several years ago and discovered we were both independent, stubborn, liked things our own way and living together would only end in disaster. Regardless, he took a leave of absence from his job as a ski patroller and made plans to move in until I could take care of myself. I vowed then and there to rehabilitate as quickly as possible for the sake of my independence and our relationship!

Chapter 2

It was snowing as Ross drove up the cul de sac to my home, so it took me a moment to see the get-well banner, ribbons, and notes all over the front of the house. As we pulled in the driveway, I saw the flowers, casseroles, and bottles of wine cluttering the front porch. My driveway had been plowed and the snow shoveled off my decks. I was overwhelmed. Since I first woke up in the hospital, the world had been so small—limited to Ross, Erin, Dr. Paul, the physical therapist, and my grief. I was hit by the veracity of that old cliché, for the rest of the world life still went on.

"A lot of people wanted to be here to welcome you home," Ross said. "I told them that you aren't ready for company yet. But I couldn't stop them from letting you know they care. I hope that's all right."

I couldn't speak. All I could do was nod in appreciation—for Ross and for my friends.

It proved a difficult journey from car to bedroom. Mine is a small two-story home. Like many folks who live in snow country, most of the living areas, including the master bedroom, are upstairs. Ross had to half-carry me up the stairs; every step made me want to scream. For the next few days he had to help me in and out of bed, help bathe me, and prepare meals for me. We left the phone off the hook and avoided listening to the messages on the answering machine, though

Ross did mention more than a few times that the machine was full.

I was sulky and despondent, and spent most of my time either crying or staring off into space. I preferred to keep the house dark and the music off. At some level I knew how difficult it was for Ross, who was walking on eggshells trying not to upset me.

If I hadn't felt so sorry for myself, I might have appreciated the unusual restraint he showed. I don't think I could have tolerated the same sullenness and petulance from him. Usually I am far more tolerant than he is, but that had changed.

After a week I began to be able to fend for myself. While I wasn't ungrateful, I knew my continued irritability and lack of responsiveness was straining our relationship. So I declared myself healed enough to care for myself and sent him back to work and to his own home. Despite my moodiness Ross continued to come over every evening to check in on me, to buy my groceries, and get my mail. He never asked how I was doing or what I did that day. He just listened—often to my depressed silence. Then after a respectable time, he kissed me on the forehead and left.

Gradually my body began to heal. As an avid runner— okay, jogger—I was used to a physical regimen and I knew how important it was to recovery. I weaned myself off the painkillers and the sleep aids Dr. Paul had given me, ate a healthy diet, went to physical therapy three times a week, and religiously completed the home exercises the therapist gave me.

My spirit, however, did not begin to heal. At first I was angry. How could God take them and leave me? Just look at the ledger.

Mary and Bob had been exquisitely aware of their surroundings from the moment of their births, marveling at the opportunities that lay before them. I had been painfully unaware of my environs until I was thirty, always taking things as they came, planning for nothing. Mary was a division level manager in the top high-tech marketing research firm in the Bay Area, and Bob was a hardware and software genius who had survived all of the high-tech downturns and gained a noteworthy reputation as a survivor and innovator. I was a former human resources professional who couldn't stand working in one organization for more than a few months, so I had become a consultant who mediated conflicts and trained people to manage in the organizations I wouldn't work in.

Mary and Bob had been happily—really happily—married for seventeen years. I was twice divorced and couldn't live in the same house for more than a few days with the man I loved.

Mary and Bob contributed much of their free time and about $100,000 a year to a private nonprofit in the Bay Area that helped abused and neglected children. I had never seen $100,000 and didn't even like children.

After anger came guilt. If I hadn't taken on the sexual harassment investigation... If I hadn't so misjudged the volatility of the assignment... If I hadn't run to Mary's to avoid the shit-storm I knew would follow as soon as the results of the investigation were made public... If I hadn't taken refuge in their home... If I hadn't talked them into flying home with me... They would still be alive.

Chapter 3 — A Week Before the Crash

The client was Snowline, a national oil and gas company for which I had conducted some leadership training a few years ago. David Crossley, the company's regional director, asked me to conduct a particularly sensitive sexual harassment investigation. A complaint had been filed alleging sexual harassment in the local office and management wanted someone outside the company to conduct the investigation. I was a human resources consultant, usually dealing with the sticky personnel situations that most managers loathed, and I never took sexual harassment investigation assignments, especially locally. They were usually a "he said, she said" with everyone taking sides. And, in a small community like Mammoth Lakes, they could become quite bitter.

Initially I turned down the assignment, but then David promised more suitable assignments in the future and offered to double my fee. He liked my thoroughness and trusted my confidentiality. I needed the money. I accepted.

Besides, Ray Ratonne, the company's local manager, and the accused, had a reputation for being one of the best employers in the community. He had earned this reputation by offering flexible schedules, job sharing, and childcare options to working single mothers. He had received awards from the local Chamber of Commerce and was regularly lauded in the newspapers for his flexible employee relations practices. I was sure that an investigation would vindicate him.

I couldn't have been more wrong.

My first interview was with the complainant, Molly Burton. She was twenty-six years old, unmarried, with a three-year-old daughter named Ashley. Molly was about 5'7", slim with reddish blonde hair, a heart-shaped face, and delicate features. The teal sweater and jeans she wore hung loosely on her slight frame. They lived with Molly's mother who had a part-time job at Mammoth Hospital. Molly was thrilled when she saw the opening at Snowline Oil & Gas, because she knew of their reputation for accommodating working mothers' schedules.

She was hired as an office assistant. Her duties covered everything from answering phones and filing to making meeting arrangements and running errands. She had first started working for Ray a little more than eighteen months earlier. He set her hours so that she and her mother could coordinate their schedules, making sure Ashley was always with one of them. Molly loved the work. She especially loved the feeling of independence and the chance to earn some money to help with the monthly bills. She liked the people she worked with and particularly liked Ray, whom she believed was a fair and kind manager. She also thought he was quite generous, since he not only gave her the schedule she needed, but also had given her a raise almost every six months since she arrived.

Just after her first year anniversary with Snowline, Kim, the receptionist and a friend of Molly's, abruptly quit her job. She told Molly her husband didn't want her to work anymore. Molly and Kim had worked a later schedule than most of the other employees. Frequently one or both would close the office in the evening. After Kim left, Ray announced that for the time being he would not replace Kim. Revenues were down, and he hoped everyone would pitch in until such time as they could afford to replace the position.

The receptionist's duties were divided up among the office staff; Molly was given the task of closing the office at night. With the new responsibility came another raise. While Molly was sad to see Kim leave, she was thrilled with the increase in pay.

About two weeks after Kim resigned, Ray came into the office just as Molly was preparing to close it up. He was jubilant. He had just signed up a large agricultural company he had been pursuing for months. Molly said his mood had been contagious. So when he pulled out a bottle of champagne and asked if she would share a bit with him, she accepted. They toasted to good fortune, and Ray gave Molly a big hug. Just as she was thinking the hug was going on a little too long, Bill, one of the account managers, came in; Ray let go of Molly and urged Bill to join the celebration.

Over the next weeks Molly noticed that Ray uncharacteristically hung around the office until all the staff left. Sometimes he engaged her in conversation, asking about Ashley or her mother or how she liked her job. Sometimes he stayed in his office. After a while she just became accustomed to his late presence.

Then in late December, during a particularly nasty snowstorm, Ray offered to drive Molly home. He said his car had four-wheel drive, and there was no need for her mother and Ashley to come out in the storm. She accepted his offer and phoned home. On the way to her mother's house, Molly told Ray how grateful she was to have this position. She said that before she had come to work for him, she and her mother were barely making ends meet. Now they were able to keep up with their bills and have a little left over to put into savings.

When Ray pulled his truck up to the curb in front of her house, he took an envelope out of his pocket and said, "Well here is a little more to be happy about. Happy New Year." She looked in the envelope. It was a fifteen-hundred dollar bonus. He told her not to tell anyone else about the bonus because no one else deserved it the way she did. As she was leaving the car, he touched her shoulder in apparent good cheer. As he took his hand away, he accidentally brushed it against her breast. She didn't know what to say or do. She jumped out of the car, waved goodbye and ran for the house. She didn't tell anyone what had happened.

A week later, on a Friday afternoon in early January, when Molly was closing the office, Ray asked to speak with her in his office. As Molly remembered, the conversation began: "Molly, it's time for you to show me just how grateful you are for this position."

Her mouth went dry, she asked, "What do you mean?"

"I want you to call your mother and tell her you will be working late this evening. Then I want you to close up the office and we will go to dinner."

"I can't go to dinner with you. I need to feed Ashley. Besides, it's my night to make dinner," she protested.

Ray answered flatly, "My wife has gone to Reno with the children for the night, and I do not want to eat alone."

Feeling that perhaps she had misinterpreted his demand, she replied, "Well, I suppose you could come home with me and have dinner with my mother and me. I will have to call first."

"You don't understand. I want you to have dinner with me this evening. I am sure there are plenty of other women who would be pleased to do so. If you are not interested, I am sure I can find someone to replace you."

Ray then stood up, took Molly by the shoulders in a vise-like grip, and pressed her roughly to him. When the phone rang unexpectedly, he started and she was able to break away from him and run out of the office. She heard him yell something. She only caught the last part, which sounded like "no one will believe you."

Again, Molly told no one. She was afraid that if she told her mother, she would make Molly quit, and they needed the money. She thought that if she told anyone else, they would think she was making it up.

On Monday morning she was more than a little apprehensive as she arrived at the office. Ray was there, but he ignored her. They worked through the week in a tense, awful silence, broken only by other employees coming in and out of the office, chatting cheerfully, oblivious of the tension. On Friday Ray called her into his office and told her that revenues were off and he was going to have to terminate her. He said he didn't want to damage her prospects for applying for positions with other companies so he would label it a voluntary termination. Then he handed her a week's severance and asked her to remove all her personal items by the end of the day.

Chapter 4

My next interview was with Ray. Interviewing the alleged harasser is always awkward, especially in a small town where everyone knows everyone. And, as I walked into his office, it was clear that Ray indeed knew everyone. The walls of his office were lined with Rotary and Chamber of Commerce plaques, pictures of him with local politicians and business leaders at golfing and charity events, and framed articles from local and regional newspapers about his innovative and family-friendly employment practices.

Introducing myself, I told him I had been hired by the Company's regional director to investigate an allegation of sexual harassment against him. I further explained the process and the need for strict confidentiality. After asking him to explain the reporting relationships and assignments in the office, I began, "Tell me about your relationship with Molly Burton."

He looked comfortable and confident as he leaned back in his chair and replied, "There is really not that much to tell. I hired her a little less than two years ago to be an office assistant. She didn't have any experience, but she seemed bright enough to train. Besides, as you may know, I like to help out young single mothers. My own mother raised my brother and me alone, and I remember how difficult it was for her. It's my way of paying back."

He smiled a little self-consciously at me, and I urged him to continue.

"Molly seemed capable enough at first, but after a while she just didn't seem to have her heart in her work. I watched her moon over the male staff members and soon realized that she was more interested in finding a date than in succeeding at her job. Heck, she even made eyes at me once or twice, though I am married and old enough to be her father.

"Anyway, her performance continued to slide, and eventually I had to let her go. When I terminated her, I told her that she needed to take her work more seriously and keep her personal life out of the office. I also told her that I would classify her termination voluntary so that she wouldn't have to explain her behavior when looking for other employment. That was as much as I could do for her."

As I was leaving Ray's office, he called me back and asked if he would need character references. Gesturing with his arm toward all of the frames on his wall, he said, "I have plenty of people who will vouch for my character."

I next planned to interview Kim, Snowline's former receptionist, who had left abruptly in the summer of the prior year. It took several phone calls and an angry outburst from Kim's husband Mark, before they agreed to meet with me. Mark was not going to permit me to meet alone with Kim. He was a strong union man who believed that management always screwed the employee and that I was there to impugn Kim. When I explained to him that I was an outside consultant brought in to conduct an objective investigation, his only response was, "Who's paying you?"

I met Kim and Mark on a snowy morning in February at their home in Crowley Lake, a small community just fifteen minutes south of Mammoth. It was a comfortable, early 1990s condo, nestled among a grove of aspen. First to greet me when I knocked on the door was a large yellow Labrador named Cindy. As soon as I saw Cindy, some of the tension left my shoulders. How difficult can someone be if one of the family is a Labrador? Right behind Cindy was a tall, slender man, somewhere in his mid-thirties, in a brownish Patagonia sweatshirt and jeans. Cowering behind him was a small, dark-haired woman, twenty-something, in an almost identical outfit.

I had purchased some freshly baked sticky buns (chosen for their inviting aroma) from the Crowley Lake Store and handed them to Mark with a big smile on my face as I introduced myself. He led me into a small living room that was nicely furnished in a sort of cabin-in-the-woods style. Kim offered me some coffee, which I accepted. As she was getting the coffee and placing the sticky buns on a plate, I noticed a silver-framed picture of Mark in a sports jacket and jeans next to Kim in a filmy, ecru summer dress with flowers in her hair and holding a bouquet of wild iris. Nestled between them was a young fair-haired boy of about four or five. The picture appeared to be taken at Crowley Lake Park.

As Kim entered the living room from the kitchen, I asked her about it.

"This is a beautiful picture. Is that your son between you and Mark?"

She gave me a slight, faraway smile, as if remembering the occasion.

"Yes. That's Jeremy. He's five. The picture was taken on our wedding day last June. It was one of the happiest days of my life."

She set her tray down on the coffee table, poured us each a cup of coffee, and offered me a sticky bun. While Cindy looked longingly at the buns, I politely declined. How can you conduct a professional investigation with sticky all over your fingers?

I explained the investigation process and the need for strict confidentiality, and asked Kim to tell me about her time at Snowline working for Ray.

That's when things got a little out of hand.

Mark jumped up, spilling his coffee all over his pants, and screamed, "That bastard! I should just go down and beat the crap out of him."

Almost simultaneously, Kim broke into breath-swallowing sobs, and Cindy took advantage of the commotion to grab a sticky bun and retreat to the next room.

I managed to find some Kleenex and a glass of water for Kim, and talked Mark down a little. Okay, at least I got him to sit down and help me with his wife. I even managed to move the dish of sticky buns out of Cindy's reach.

Several minutes later, when everyone was somewhat subdued, I explained that if Ray had been out of line—these words started to set Mark off again so I changed my phrasing to—if Ray had been abusive, this was their opportunity to be heard.

Kim took a sip of water. The story unfolded.

She gripped Mark's hand. "About six months after I started working for Snowline, after my first raise…"

I interrupted—which I don't usually do when conducting an investigation, especially when everyone is so volatile— "Is it common for new employees to get a raise after six months?"

"No" she replied with a little hint of pride. "Ray said that it was because I had caught on to the job so quickly, I deserved it. He also said not to tell anyone that he gave it to me."

She looked at me expectantly, as if waiting for another question.

"I'm sorry for interrupting your train of thought," I said. "You were saying ... 'after about six months on the job'..."

"Yes. After about six months on the job, Ray started asking me to go down the street to get him a latte. He always told me to get one for myself. Then he would insist that we sit in his office and talk. We usually spoke about me, about Jeremy, and how I liked my job. I thought it was nice that he took such an interest in his employees.

"Then after a while, he started helping me close the office at night if no one else was there to help me. Sometimes he would make me feel uncomfortable..."

She paused and gripped Mark's hand a little tighter.

In almost a whisper, so as not to interrupt, I asked, "Uncomfortable how?"

"Well, like I would be closing the blinds, and he would stand right behind me, almost up against me. When I moved, he would apologize and stretch above me, saying one of the slats at the top of the blind needed straightening. Or I would be reaching up to turn on the burglar alarm—the panel is high, almost above my reach—and he would brush up against me as he activated it himself, and then say something about how clumsy he was, and apologize.

"Things like that were always happening."

She looked at Mark's hand, which was now being so firmly held in Kim's lap, I was surprised he had any circulation left in his hand.

Gently, I asked, "Is this why you left?"

Tears started running down her face. Abruptly Kim looked at Mark and asked him to call their neighbor to let her know that she needed to watch Jeremy just a while longer.

"Tell Maggie the interview is lasting a little longer than I had thought, and we'll come over and get Jeremy when we are through here."

Mark started to object, but Kim gave him a surprisingly sharp look, out of character with the meekness she had displayed so far. So he left the room to make the call.

Then in almost a whisper Kim said, "Just after Mark and I returned from our honeymoon, Ray told me he had volunteered my services to assist in registration and meeting support for the State Association's annual convention that was being held in June Lake the second week of July. He told me I would need to stay at the Double Eagle Lodge where the convention was being held, because meetings would run from early morning until late in the evening. Ray said that a few of the account managers would also be attending the convention and that I might be sharing a room with Ella, one of those account managers. He promised all my expenses would be paid, and he would pay me double overtime for the weekend. He also said that he wouldn't have asked, but it was a big honor to have the convention so close to Mammoth, just twenty miles away, and he knew Mark would take care of Jeremy while I was working.

"Even though I didn't want to leave Mark and Jeremy for an entire weekend, all I could think about was double overtime. It would help pay off some of the expenses from the wedding and honeymoon."

She paused and looked down at her lap for a moment, "I admit I was also looking forward to seeing what the Double Eagle Lodge looked like. I had heard it was fabulous.

"When I arrived, I learned that Ella wasn't able to make the convention so I would have a room of my own. The lodge was beautiful, but I didn't get to see much of it the first day because they kept the volunteers really busy. The second night, right after I called Mark to wish him goodnight and tell him I would be home by noon the next day, I got a call from Ray. He said he had been asked to make a speech in the morning and I needed to come over to his room to listen to his presentation. I tried to beg off, but he insisted.

"When I got to his room, I went to move some papers off the room's only chair and he yelled, 'Don't touch those papers; just sit on the bed.' I also noticed that he had two glasses of wine sitting on the small table next to the chair. When he saw me looking at them, he said, "I poured one for you. It's very pricey wine. Try a taste." I refused and sort of half sat, half leaned against the foot of the bed. I told him I was tired so he needed to do a practice run of his speech and then I would leave."

Catching a movement out of the corner of my eye, I saw Mark had come back into the room. I don't think Kim noticed; she appeared to be lost in thought, blankly staring out the window. He stood quietly at the door, ramrod straight, a picture of pure physical tension.

I urged her on with an almost inaudible, "Yes?" And, simultaneously, I gave Mark a cautioning look.

She continued, her words coming out in a rush: "Ray picked up one of the glasses of wine, sat down on the bed, put his arm around me and told me to loosen up. Then before I could react, he pushed me onto the bed, and grabbed my breast. I shoved him with all my strength and ran out of the room. I called Mark, and he came and picked me up."

"Did you tell anyone?" I asked.

Tears were streaming down Kim's face now. Mark moved back to the couch to hold her, but she gently shrugged him off.

"Mark wanted me to. But Ray knows everyone. He would make sure that I'd never get another job. And, besides, who would believe me over Ray? Mark said he didn't care; he would take care of me. But, I have to work. We need the money."

"So you just quit?" I asked.

"What choice did I have?"

The rest of the investigation confirmed what I had already learned. The pattern was the same. Hire a single mother in her twenties. Build her up with raises and/or bonuses that were just for her. Gradually increase the intimacy of the contacts. Ultimately go for the gold. If the girl didn't like it, whom was she going to complain to. From my investigation I gathered that while Ray was receiving awards and accolades from the community for his innovative practices employing single mothers, he was using company resources to intimidate and entice them into his bed. By the time I was finished, I had four victims—all who now wanted to take their treatment public and legal.

Although I completed my written report on a Tuesday, I waited until that Friday afternoon to meet with Dave Crossley, give him the bad news, and present him with the written report of the investigation. The weekend would give me enough time to travel to Mary and Bob's house and hide out while the shit hit the community fan.

Unbeknownst to me, I had just taken the first step on a journey that would end in Mary and Bob's deaths.

Chapter 5 — After the Crash

While my body continued to heal, my depression continued to grow, becoming something physical, weighing me down, sapping my energy. It was an effort to get out of bed in the morning. My only respite from guilt and sadness were periodic checkups with Dr. Paul, my sessions with the physical therapist, and occasional evening walks with Ross.

Other than Ross and medical personnel, I saw no one. When I first arrived home, I asked Ross to put a note on the front door saying, "For the foreseeable future, I will not answer the door, the mail, or my phone. Thank you for understanding." Since no one knocked on the door, other than an occasional UPS or floral delivery, I gathered my friends were honoring my wishes.

I finally mustered up the energy to listen to my phone messages. They were condolences, worried friends from outside of the area asking how I was doing, a local reporter, a few clients asking me to call when recovered, and a pitch from a salesman who wanted to help me consolidate my debt. I guess not everyone feels bound by the Do Not Call Registry.

Not all the messages were easy to ignore.

"Bitch, you got what you deserved," a woman screamed, then a dial tone. What was that about?

One was from the mortuary asking when I would pick up Mary and Bob's ashes. I had spent so much time not believing they were dead, I never stopped to think about what happened to their bodies. Ross must have arranged the cremations. I would have to ask him.

One from Joan Westin, a Bay Area friend of Mary's whom I had met on a few occasions, wanting to know if I had started to plan a memorial service yet, leaving her number if I wanted any help.

One from Steve, claiming to be Mary's new next-door— or rather down-the-hill—neighbor, saying he would take care of the gardens and watch the house until he heard from me. Odd, if he was Mary's next-door/down-the-hill neighbor, then Pam and John, their longtime friends and neighbors, must have sold their house. I didn't remember Mary telling me Pam had placed her home on the real estate market.

One from a Kevin Anderson, an investigator from the National Transportation Safety Board assigned to investigate the accident, asking me to call at my earliest convenience.

And, two—actually one and a half, since the answering machine had reached capacity in mid-message—were from Nathan Hadley, Mary and Bob's attorney, informing me that I was the executor of their estate and to please call as soon as I was able.

These messages gave me an odd surge of purpose. Continuing to mope around the house all day meant I was letting Mary and Bob down. I had to put their final affairs in order, and I had to do it well. I could go back to bed and feel sorry for myself only after their final tasks were completed.

I phoned the mortuary, apologizing to the woman who answered the phone for the delay in getting back to them, explaining that I had been injured in the same crash that took Mary and Bob. I learned that Ross had indeed made the arrangements for the cremation. I arranged to pick up Mary and Bob's ashes the following Friday. They were in Reno,

Nevada (the closest mortuary from Mammoth with a crematorium), which was three hours north of Mammoth. I realized I better not take my ability to drive injured for granted and to practice driving around town by myself before I attempted to drive all the way to Reno.

Next I phoned Joan, the friend of Mary's who left a message regarding a memorial. She picked up the phone on the second ring. I asked, "Is this Joan Westin?"

I heard a loud gasp.

The woman on the other end of the line tentatively inquired "Mary?"

"No. This is Mary's twin sister Janet. I forgot that we sound alike on the phone. I am really sorry."

There was a brief pause while I imagined Joan was composing herself. "It was a bit of a shock, that's all. You do sound exactly like Mary. I don't recall your voices being so similar, you certainly don't look alike."

"We don't ... er, didn't... Only our voices are similar, not our appearances."

She seemed mollified, then asked in a concerned voice how I was. After giving her more details than I wished regarding my health, I inquired if she thought Carpaccio's, a well-established, upscale Italian restaurant in Menlo Park and Mary's absolute favorite eatery, would let us use the restaurant for an afternoon memorial reception sometime toward the end of March.

"If they haven't in the past, they will now. Let me take care of it." She sounded like a woman who could make things happen.

Just as I hung up the phone, it rang. Without thinking, I picked it up and said hello.

There were a few seconds of silence, then a shrill voice screamed, "You fucking bitch," and hung up.

I was so startled, I just sat there with the phone to my ear, listening to a dial tone. This was the one time I wished I had opted for Caller ID, but my income was sporadic, and I chose to splurge on more pleasurable items. Perhaps Ross could help me figure out what was going on.

While I left a message for Ross on his cell, asking him to come by early enough for a home-cooked meal after work, I absentmindedly played with the Waterford letter opener next to the phone. It gave me pause: Last year on one of my trips to visit Mary, I had discovered it on her desk in the front room. I covetously admired it, hoping she would just tell me to take it, but she ignored my hints. Throughout the visit, I constantly peppered our conversations with how elegant the letter opener was and how nice it would look on *my* desk at home. She continued to ignore me. It was a game we had played since we were children. It usually resulted in being given the desired item, or just taking it when the other wasn't looking. I had lost a lot of clothes to Mary when she used the latter strategy. When I was packing my bags to leave, she kept the letter opener clutched tightly in her hands so I couldn't filch it. I had lost this round, but figured I would quietly lift it during my next visit. When I returned home and was unloading the car, I found it in the side pocket of my travel bag with a blue ribbon around it.

Since I'd promised Ross dinner, I needed to get some food. So a few hours later I mustered up the energy to make my first trip to the grocery store since the accident. In the garage I found out just how difficult this trip was going to be. My left arm was still in a tight sling against my chest, immobilizing my clavicle and protecting my ribs. Getting into the car took five minutes. It took another five minutes to realize with a useless left arm I couldn't close the driver's-side car door and it took another five minutes to exit the car. Next I tried getting up from the passenger side; I could close the car door with my good arm, and scoot awkwardly, in pain, across the console. I ignored the seat belt and made the short drive to the grocery store. Twenty minutes to get out of the driveway. This must be some kind of record.

When I reached the grocery store, I saw several people I knew entering and exiting the store. There is only one supermarket in Mammoth Lakes so it is impossible to shop without running into someone you know—usually several someones. This would be more emotionally than physically challenging. But this was the first step in getting my affairs in order.

It hadn't snowed in several days so I was able to park on the edge of the lot away from most of the foot traffic. This meant that with a little luck no one would notice my labored exit or reentrance from the passenger side of the car and try to help me. Once out of the car I marched, okay, stiffly limped, into the grocery store with my head down and eyes on my list. I attempted to avoid eye contact, knowing that friends would want to chat, and strangers would be frightened by the cuts and bruises that still freckled my face. My anonymity lasted about ninety seconds.

"J, is that you?"

The voice was somewhat familiar.

Is it me? How many people in this town could possibly look this beaten up? Then I remembered that I live in a ski resort town, where cuts, bruises, and broken bones are part of the local color.

It was one of the women who worked Ski Patrol with Ross on the Mountain. Before I could reply, I was surrounded by friends and acquaintances who wanted to know about the accident, inquired about my health, and wanted to help me shop.

I was trying to extricate myself from the well wishers as politely as possible, when Meg, one of my occasional running buddies said, "You sure missed a lot of fireworks around here. The whole town has been up in arms since they learned that Ray over at Snowline was trying to seduce all the single young mothers he was so famous for hiring. One of the newspaper articles said you were the one who conducted the investigation. Is it true?"

Mentally I added onto my to do list: "Call David Crossley and give him hell." No one was supposed to know who conducted the investigation; that was one of the conditions of my taking the assignment.

Before I could come up with something appropriately noncommittal to say, another member of the group chimed in, "I heard the victims are going to sue Ray and the company for millions..."

"Better yet," interrupted a woman I had never seen before. "My neighbor works with one of the victims. She told me the male family members are getting together and are going to beat the crap out of Ray once they find him."

As more shoppers joined in the conversation with the crowd planning Ray's destruction, I quietly moved toward the produce section. No one noticed.

I picked up the makings for a salad and lasagna, and a bottle of Frie Brothers Cabernet. I had to keep my shopping limited to just a few items since I had only one good arm to carry them to the car.

It took me almost an hour to get back to my car, get into it, drive the two miles to my home, and get out of the car with my groceries in hand. I had a strong sense of accomplishment. I had taken the first step.

As I put away the groceries, I found a bar of Godiva chocolate I didn't remember picking up. I smiled. One of Mary's obsessions was a good Cabernet Sauvignon consumed with fine chocolate. She was always slightly disdainful whenever she was at my house if I poured her a glass of Cab without an accompanying piece of fine dark chocolate.

I finished storing the groceries in the refrigerator and pantry, including the chocolate bar that I decided would be a nice treat later. I poured myself a glass of the Cab to celebrate my first small step forward.

Before I could take a sip, my portable phone rang. On the sixth ring I found the phone on my bed. I answered a little tentatively, fearing it might be the shrieker who kept calling me a bitch. It was Ross. He would be a little late for dinner, but said he looked forward to coming.

Back in the kitchen I began making the lasagna. As I reached for my wine, I saw an unwrapped piece of chocolate sitting on the base of the glass. The chocolate brought a feeling of warmth, happiness and familiarity, which spread throughout my being.

I raised my glass skyward and tentatively asked as much as said, "Perhaps you didn't leave me alone after all, Mary?"

Chapter 6

About seven thirty that evening, I greeted Ross at the top of the stairs with a very cold, extra dry Smirnoff martini. Before the accident I would have met him downstairs at the front door, but walking up and down stairs was still a slow and painful journey. The house was fragrant with the smells of lasagna cooking, the upstairs aglow with lamp and candlelight, the fire was burning, and "Sweet Baby James," a classic James Taylor song, was softly playing.

Ross looked truly surprised as he said, "J, a martini I didn't have to make myself? A dinner that wasn't delivered? You are actually smiling! Did something happen?"

I had decided I wouldn't tell him yet that although Mary had died she might not be gone. A former Marine and longtime ski patrolman, Ross was about as left-brained and practical as one can be. If I told him what was happening he might think I was mixing pain pills with alcohol or just having an emotional breakdown. Besides, I needed some time to process this possible new development before trying to explain it to someone else. So I told him about the progress I'd made that day.

"Well, the martini is stirred, not shaken. I'm not up to that yet. But I did manage to go to the grocery store by myself."

Then I related the day's events: beginning with the phone messages, my dawning acceptance of the tasks ahead—taking care of Mary and Bob's final affairs, and ending with my grocery store adventure.

As I nattered on about the day, I finally asked him the question that had been niggling at me. "How did you know Mary and Bob wanted to be cremated?"

He looked a little sad. "Remember when you and Mary went to Paris to run the marathon a few years ago, and Bob flew with you as far as London?"

I nodded, recalling all the misadventures we had in Paris, from taking a cab to the wrong hotel to almost missing the marathon because Mary couldn't find her running shoes.

"Well, Mary sent me instructions in case the flight to Europe crashed. You know what a stickler for detail she was. She wanted to make sure I knew exactly what to do. She indicated that she and Bob wanted to be cremated. Fortunately, I still had the instructions, so I brought them with me when I went to meet with the people at the mortuary. Since Mary and Bob had no family except you, and you were incapacitated, they asked me to sign a waiver, and they performed the cremations."

I had been so lost in my grief I hadn't thought about any of the matters that had to be taken care of. Ross had just stepped up and handled it all. And he never complained or even told me.

I was both grateful and ashamed. "I didn't know…."

Ross gently placed his arm around my right side and said, "You didn't have to. All you needed to do was begin to heal."

We sat for a moment lost in our thoughts. Breaking the mood, I told Ross about the odd phone calls I had received from a strange woman calling me a bitch. We tried to figure out who it could be, but drew a blank.

"I'll call Gary at the MLPD tomorrow and see if there is anything the police can do," he volunteered. "In the meantime, you need caller ID on your phone. May I strongly suggest you call Verizon and have the service added without sounding over-protective?"

Leaning my forehead against his chest, I said, "Right now I like you watching out for me."

"I will remind you that you said so when you are feeling better," he replied with a grin.

For the next hour he entertained me with recent work stories—guests he had helped, accidents at which he had assisted. Ski patrolmen have some of the most bizarre experiences with visiting skiers and boarders, many of which would make good prime time TV.

A little after ten Ross left for his home. I was still sleeping with an awkward assortment of pillows and blankets to keep me from rolling over onto my left side, so a sleepover was out of the question.

I stored the leftover lasagna in Tupperware, placed the dishes in the dishwasher, and went to bed.

Now, hoping Mary might still hear me, I repeated the nightly ritual we had had since childhood, saying, "Good Night, Mary. Don't let the bed bugs bite!"

The next morning I eased myself out of bed, trying as I did every morning not to jar even the smallest part of my body. It was late: nine a.m. Since the accident I had slept until I awakened without benefit of an alarm, given that my unconscious urge to turn over and sleep on my stomach during the night—a definite no-no with a broken clavicle and broken ribs—took a toll on my sleep.

As I walked to the kitchen to make some orange and spice tea, I couldn't resist looking around to see if there were any signs from Mary. I guess I was expecting too much. There was no indication that she had left me any more surprises, but the sky was bright blue and there were no clouds to speak of. It was going to be a beautiful spring day.

The phone rang as I took my first sip of tea. Ross frequently called about this hour to make sure I had made it through the night without hurting myself, so I was slightly taken aback when I heard a professional-sounding woman say, "Good Morning. I hope I am not phoning too early. Is this Janet Westmore?"

"Yes, this is Janet, and no, it's not too early. I have been up for hours," I lied, trying to place the voice.

"My name is Linda Taylor. I am the principal of the elementary school. We've met a few times at school district fundraisers, but I'm not sure if you remember me."

Slowly a picture of an attractive, tall, big-boned, slightly Nordic-looking woman in her mid forties came to mind.

"I believe I do," I said. "What can I do for you?"

A little of the stiffness left her voice. "First, let me say how sorry I was to learn of your accident and the loss of your sister and her husband."

Reflexively I wanted to correct her. Mary had always insisted that we were twins, not sisters.

"Thank you," I replied feeling myself start to close down.

She hurried on: "I don't know if you are taking on any work right now, and I would certainly understand if you aren't. But I have a very unusual situation, and believe you may be uniquely qualified to help me out."

As I was about to tell her that given the circumstances, there was no way I could get my head into a job, she pleaded, "Before you turn me down, if you would just meet with us this afternoon? Or perhaps tomorrow sometime? I am not sure who else could help us."

Before I could stop myself, I queried, "Us?"

"Ian Williams, the police chief, and myself."

That made me pause. What could the police chief and the elementary school principal want with me? All of a sudden I had to know. So I began to rationalize. It's just a meeting. I would politely listen then beg off. God knows I had a legitimate excuse.

Making that informal agreement with myself, I responded, "I can meet you at three this afternoon. I am not making any promises, but I will listen. If I can't help you, perhaps I will be able to recommend someone who can."

She gave a sigh. "Thank you. I will see you at three this afternoon at the elementary school."

The morning flew by. I had decided the night before that when I drove to Reno to pick up Mary and Bob's ashes, I would continue on to their home in Portola Valley. Ross volunteered to go with me, but I declined. The first time I went to the house, I wanted to do it alone. I wasn't physically or emotionally equipped to do anything more than bring their ashes home, spend a night or two, and make sure everything was all right in the house. It would be a relatively short trip. I did need to meet with Mary and Bob's attorney, Nathan Hadley, and the NTSB investigator, Kevin Anderson, who was based in the Bay Area, but I didn't expect either of those meetings to be lengthy. Since I would pick up the ashes on Friday, I scheduled Saturday appointments with the attorney and the investigator, asking each to meet me at the house. As an afterthought, I placed a call to Joan, Mary's friend, and left a message that I would be in town over the weekend and would like to meet with her to discuss the memorial if she had some free time.

I arrived at the school at 2:40 that afternoon. I had not yet mastered getting in and out of the car with any real efficiency so I wanted to give myself ample time. Still, I made it to the principal's office with five minutes to spare. Linda greeted me in the reception area. I recognized her as soon as I saw her. It wasn't so much her height, thick blond hair, or strong Nordic features I remembered, as her presence. She exuded poise and efficiency. It came through in her posture, her precise manner, even her tailored outfit.

She led me into her office, and introduced me to Ian Williams, who stood as I entered, and shook my hand. He was Linda's opposite. Standing about 5'5" with dark curly hair, his stocky build was draped in a shapeless suit. I guessed he was in his mid-fifties. He had a firm handshake and a great smile. I liked him immediately.

We sat at a small conference table on the opposite side of the office from Linda's desk. There were cookies and soft drinks in the center of the table. Judging from the crumbs atop the papers on the table, I guessed that Ian had been eating his share.

He began to say something about the plane accident. This time I was prepared for the subject.

I cut him off as graciously as I could. "Thank you, but it's still so raw that I can't even accept people's condolences yet. Sorry."

After an awkward pause I tried to break the tension. "I am quite curious to know why the chief of police and the school principal are interested in speaking with me."

With that, I took a tablet of paper and pen out of the bag I always carried with me and looked up expectantly.

Ian glanced at Linda, signaling her to begin.

"Just after the beginning of the year, things started appearing in the classrooms," she said.

Things? Appearing? Linda had my attention.

"At first no one gave any notice. As I'm sure you know, schools all across the country have had their budgets slashed while taking on increasing numbers of students. Our school is no exception. We have no budget for extras and very little money for supplies and equipment. So when one of the teachers needed art supplies, and they magically appeared on her desk one morning, she assumed that one of the other teachers had a stash and was anonymously sharing.

"Administrative staff members were having the same experience. One afternoon a staff member announced that we had no more hanging folders, and the next morning two boxes of hanging Pendaflex folders appeared on his desk. Initially, some of the teachers and staff even tried to figure out who had been hoarding all the supplies. There were lots of rumors floating around, but nothing came of them.

"Then the situation escalated. One morning the assistant principal told me we no longer had the capacity to send or receive faxes; the machine had died. The next morning we had an almost new HP fax machine sitting where the old one used to be." Linda glanced at Ian. "This is where Ian comes in."

Ian shook his head. "That same morning, we received a call at the station that an HP fax machine was missing from a local real estate office. When an officer went to investigate, she found no evidence of a break in, and nothing else had been taken. It was, of course, the same machine that turned up in the school. Graciously, the broker, whose office had been burgled, donated the fax machine to the school with very little coaxing, since both his children were students there.

"If it had ended there, it might have been all right, but to date two Dell laptop computers, two HP printers, one Canon printer, one Sharp desk calculator, an air humidifier, an automatic drip coffee maker, and endless supplies have mysteriously appeared in the school and disappeared from local merchants, businesses, and public offices. We have spent hours investigating each scene, including the school. We have found no signs of break in anywhere. We have no suspects, just a lot of angry business people.

"And the 'gifts' just keep on coming. This morning, the school janitor reported he found a case of cleaning supplies in the maintenance closet when he arrived at work." Ian uttered a huge sigh, shrugged his shoulders and looked at the floor.

"This is an incredible story. But how can I possibly help you?" I asked.

Linda responded without hesitation, "When it became obvious that the police were not going to be able to…"

Ian interrupted, clearing his throat with a loud guttural sound, and glared at Linda, cutting off her next words.

She smiled at Ian as if he were one of the students called into her office to explain an indiscretion. "Ian, I know you have done your best. I am at a loss, too. But we can't give up. This has to stop. Some of the business owners in town are beginning to think I condone, maybe even arranged, these thefts."

Ian slightly softened his glare and stuffed a cookie in his mouth.

"Last week," Linda said, "We met with all the teachers, staff, and student representatives from each of the classrooms. Ian and I gave them an update on the situation, assuring everyone that the police would continue their investigation. Then we opened it up to the group for discussion. Our sixth grade teacher, Jeanne Grey, suggested that since no one else can figure out what's happening, we should form a team of teachers, staff, and students to work on it. Jeanne suggested that a team could monitor the comings and goings of the school better than anyone else. Everyone in the room agreed."

I noticed that Ian was giving Linda a very skeptical look. She must have noticed, too, because she quickly added, "I am not saying that I believe such a team can actually solve our little mystery, but it would get everyone involved. And, more importantly, it would demonstrate to the business owners in town that we are doing everything we can."

I finally gave into temptation and snatched one of the cookies Ian had missed, "I am still not sure how this has anything to do with me."

"I'm sorry," Linda said. "I thought it was obvious. I know you have done a lot of group facilitation and mediation around town. We want you to facilitate the team, be its leader. You are local; everyone knows you, at least by reputation; you have no relationship with the school, so you would be viewed as objective; and Ian and his colleagues were impressed with the work you did exposing Ray over at Snowline."

She sat back in her chair, looking relieved and hopeful that she had made her case.

I was intrigued. As a human resources consultant, most of my work involved helping sort out situations when management and staff were at odds, which always involved a lot of teeth-clenching conflict. This could be fun.

Before thinking long enough to talk myself out of it, I cautioned, "I would have to work it around my schedule. There are a lot of matters related to the accident that need the majority of my attention."

Linda smiled broadly and told me they would happily accommodate my time requirements. Ian grabbed the last cookie and said that my participation would lend the process some credibility with the local businesses and the community. We worked out some details, including my fee and a tentative schedule. I agreed to meet with the team once before I left for Reno and Portola Valley.

They walked me to the front steps of the school. Still awkward as I got into my car from the passenger side, they watched me quizzically. I guess I didn't look like someone who could lend credibility to anything. In an effort to look in control, I took my good hand off the steering wheel to wave good-bye and almost hit Ian's police vehicle parked near the exit as I left the lot.

Chapter 7

The next morning felt more like winter than spring. A strong north wind was blowing, and it looked like it could snow at any minute. As soon as I made a few calls, I would go to my physical therapy appointment, and then make a run to the grocery store and post office before any real weather came in. Although I was starting to get used to the extra time my injuries cost me running errands, I was not anxious to learn what additional challenges would be caused by a snowstorm.

My first call was to Nancy, a friend and local computer consultant. Before moving to Mammoth, she had been a high-powered software developer. Now she was an extreme athlete who consulted on the side. If it weren't for Nancy, I would probably still use only a land line, listen to music on a clock radio, and complete all my reports on a typewriter.

When the plane went down, so did all my electronic devices: laptop computer, new Smartphone, and iPod. I needed to replace the laptop and cell phone immediately. The iPod could wait. I asked Nancy to order the electronics for me and told her I needed them yesterday. All she needed was my credit card information. Nancy said she'd order the electronics when we got off the phone and have them delivered to my home. Then she would come over and install all the software I needed as soon as I let her know everything had arrived.

That accomplished, I returned a call to Joan, who had left a message the evening before, saying she wanted to update me on the plans for Mary and Bob's memorial. She answered after the second ring.

"We have the entire restaurant tentatively booked for April 30 at two p.m.," she said. "Since you said afternoon, I thought you would want an open bar with waiters circulating, taking orders, an Italian buffet, so people can help themselves, and a pianist playing some of Mary and Bob's favorite music."

I hope the pianist knows both Mozart and Bob Dylan.

"How does that sound?" Before I could answer, she continued: "I made up a list of some of the people I thought you might want to include. I don't know if you know that besides being friends and running buddies for years, Mary and I served on a couple of nonprofit boards together. There are a lot of people who will want to pay their respects."

I knew that Mary sponsored some charities but, no, I hadn't known she was on any nonprofit boards.

"I also know a good florist near the restaurant who can make up a few tasteful centerpieces."

When she finally paused, I was at a loss for words. Mary was the one who knew how to plan an event. Even when I gave a small dinner party, if more than three guests were involved, I called Mary and she would tell me what to cook, what to buy, how to set the table...

"Oh dear," Joan said. "I always do this. I can be a bit overwhelming to the uninitiated. Someone gives me a little task, and I take over. Please forgive me."

"Please forgive *me,*" I stammered. "I'm at a loss because I would never have thought of all of the details you just described. Planning any kind of get together was Mary's skill, not mine. This sounds like a memorial that would make her proud. And that is all I could ask for."

I thanked Joan, grateful for her help, and arranged to meet with her to finish planning the arrangements on Sunday afternoon while I was in Portola Valley.

The two calls completed, I dressed in sweats for physical therapy and to run my errands. It only took me twelve minutes from my front door to the physical therapy building. Of course, only three of those minutes were actual driving. My travel efforts were improving.

We had a good session. I was exhausted and sore when we finished, and happy that the physical therapist felt I was making progress.

When I arrived at the grocery store a few snowflakes had started falling, so I parked as close to the store as possible. This time I was no longer concerned people would see my awkward ingress and egress from the Subaru. I exited the car, locked it with my remote key, and started toward the entrance.

That's when I heard someone scream, "You fucking bitch. You ruined our lives."

I looked up. I didn't actually see the woman who was screaming. What I saw was a shopping cart she had shoved with all her strength rushing at my left, *injured* side. I froze, uncomprehending. I couldn't make my limbs move to get out of the way. When the cart was only a couple of yards away, and I was beginning to understand that this was going to really hurt, Mary stepped in front of the cart, stopped it, and angrily shoved it back toward the shrieking woman.

MARY?!

In the next instant the woman was on her rear in the parking lot, shouting obscenities, Mary was gone, witnesses came running to see if I had been injured, and I continued to be rooted to the spot.

Mary had appeared out of nowhere. She had protected me. Others had seen her. And, by the way, who was this woman who was still screaming at me?

The next few hours were confusing and chaotic. Two police officers arrived. After speaking with witnesses, one officer arrested the still-shrieking woman and escorted her to the hospital to see if she had been injured in the fall. Still pretty shaken, I was helped to the front passenger seat of my car and given a cup of hot coffee. I waited to be interviewed, while the remaining police officer took the names and numbers of the witnesses.

Sitting there, I recalled how Mary defended me against bullies when we were kids. We were fraternal twins, and I was always the smaller one. Once when we were about four, a bigger kid shoved me out of my place in line for the playground slide. Mary witnessed this affront from the swings. She walked over, pushed the kid out of line, took me by the arm and led me back to my place in line. Then she resumed playing on the swings. I was always safe when Mary was around.

I was jolted back to the here and now when I heard a man who had just given his information to the police officer talking to his companion as he was walking to his car.

Shaking his head, he said, "It was the damnedest thing. This shopping cart is going toward that woman at lightning speed, right toward her broken side," he nodded in my direction, "and she just stands there. Then the cart must have hit a bump or something because a couple of seconds before it hits her, it just reverses direction. Never seen anything like it."

He hadn't seen Mary.

A few minutes later Officer Cole introduced himself to me and asked what happened. He also asked if I saw what the cart hit to make it switch direction. I told him, leaving Mary out of the description, and that I was too startled to notice what made the cart change course. I also told him that I had been getting phone calls at the house, probably from the same woman, and I described the calls to him.

Then I asked, "Who is the woman who attacked me?"

Officer Cole looked a little taken aback. "You didn't recognize her?" he asked. Then he shook his head and almost to himself said, "Of course, you wouldn't. You were in the hospital recovering from the plane crash when she and her husband were in the news."

Small towns... everyone knows everyone's business.

"That was Lynn Ratonne. After the news came out that her husband Ray had been trying to seduce all of those young mothers he employed, he took quite a beating in the press. Lynn kept sending letters to the editor to both newspapers, claiming disgruntled female employees made up the allegations and that her husband was innocent. She claimed that you, as the investigator, were either gullible, incompetent, or part of a conspiracy."

Officer Cole looked slightly embarrassed. "No one took it seriously. In fact, if you ever have a chance to read the back editions of the papers, you will find a lot of folks in town rebutted with letters of their own, talking about your honesty and integrity."

By the time I left the grocery store parking lot, Mammoth was having a full-fledged snowstorm. I left without groceries or mail. All I wanted was to sit in front of my fireplace with a cup of hot tea, listen to Wynton Marsalis play trumpet concertos, and try to process all that had just happened.

Ross found me asleep in a chair in front of a fading fire when he dropped by after work around seven-thirty. I made us both martinis while he rekindled the fire. I told him about

Lynn Ratonne and the shopping cart. He didn't ask questions, he just listened.

I wanted to tell him how Mary saved me, but it just didn't seem to be the right time. When I was finished, he held me. Leaning against him, I felt an odd peace as we listened to the crack and hiss of the logs burning in the fireplace.

A little later we spoke about his day on the Mountain. He told me about an eleven-year-old boy with autism who got separated from his father late in the day, about the subsequent search as the sun was setting, how one of the patrollers found him standing among the trees and shadows, not moving a muscle, standing stock-still, and about the tearful reunion of the frightened young boy and his father.

God bless ski patrollers.

Chapter 8

Two days later while I was preparing to leave for my first meeting with the elementary school team, the doorbell rang. It was Jim from UPS. In Mammoth, a town of about 8,300 residents with stores intended for tourists and not daily living needs, one of the two important people to know is the UPS delivery person. The other works for FedEx.

Jim had a large box marked "fragile—electronics." He volunteered to carry it into my home office, which, fortunately, is downstairs. After he set it on my desk, I saw him out, and quickly called Nancy. Her voicemail picked up. I left a message saying the computer had arrived and asked if she would set it up as soon as possible. I told her I was leaving the next day for a short trip north and reminded her where the spare house key was. Then I left for the elementary school, already beginning to question why I'd taken this assignment when I had so much to do and not a clue about working with children.

Linda and I met in the parking lot. She was returning from a school district meeting. Both of us were bundled up in wool hats, gloves, and mufflers. It wasn't snowing, but it was cloudy and unseasonably cold for March. As she guided me to a small conference room down the hall from her office, she asked me about my encounter with Lynn Ratonne. Ah, small towns!

After I briefly recounted the incident, she told me how lucky I was. "You'd know just how lucky you were if you had ever seen her working out at the Athletic Club. I see her there almost every morning before work. Lynn is not at the gym to chat, she is there to train. She is focused and strong."

Linda changed the subject to the team. "We had so many volunteers that we asked each person to write a brief statement about why he or she wanted to participate. The statements proved quite helpful in making the selections. For instance, the athletic coach said he wanted to participate on the team so he could make a pitch for some new baseball equipment before the thief was arrested. One fourth grader said it had to be his older sister because 'she is always stealing things from me.'

"In the end we chose a team of seven, plus you, of course. All the volunteers will be in our meeting today. There is Jeanne Grey, the sixth grade teacher whose idea this was. The others include the first grade teacher, the office manager who also acts as the school's librarian, one sixth grader, two fifth graders, and the night janitor.

"Both Ian and I will attend this first meeting but won't return unless you invite us. How do you want to start?"

I had been thinking about this all morning. In part it is what caused my second thoughts about taking the assignment. I was used to working with adults, not children. And I really wasn't sure what the team could do about the situation. I knew expectations were low, but I wanted this team to make a difference.

"Well, since you said we would only have an hour for this first meeting, I thought I would introduce myself and then ask you to describe the team's purpose. Next ask Ian to give the team an overview of the situation from his perspective and a description of what the police have done. After that, ask each team member to introduce him or herself and tell us what they can contribute to helping us catch the culprit. If we have time, we can begin brainstorming some strategies for apprehending the... what should we call this person? Thief? Or Robin Hood?"

Linda frowned. "Definitely thief! If the local business people hear us refer to this person as Robin Hood, they will think we are glorifying him."

We walked into the small conference room where everyone was waiting. Predictably, Ian was sitting next to the refreshments, absentmindedly snacking on cookies. With a smile and nod to Ian, Linda went to the front of the room and took charge.

The meeting went as planned, with few questions. There was some spirited group participation when Ian spoke, with everyone trying to second-guess the police investigation. The descriptions of what each could contribute to the team generated the most enthusiasm. I wrote the contributions on poster paper, saying that we would display the sheet at each meeting.

Jeanne (6th grade teacher): "I have great organization skills. And my sister writes for one of the local papers, if we need to get some press."

Trevor and Kelsey (5th graders):"Last year our class won an award from the Town Council for organizing town Clean-Up Day. We're good at getting other kids and adults to pitch in."

Bob (night janitor): "I know every nook and cranny of the school and grounds. And I'm here pretty late into the evening, so I can keep an eye on things after hours."

Lillian (office manager): "I usually know everything that is going on during the school day. In addition, if we decide we need to produce any flyers, I can take care of it."

Nolan (6th grader): "I'm on the football team and a co-captain of the baseball team. I can get everyone on the teams to help out."

Melissa (1st grade teacher): "I like to think out of the box, so I guess I bring creativity."

"We will meet next Thursday," I announced. "Please come prepared to share your ideas on how we might catch the thief. And please, think creatively. This isn't an ordinary criminal. He seems to be imaginative and so should we."

After taking my leave from Linda, Ian, and the team members, I walked out to the car, mentally kicking myself for taking the job. The team members, especially the children, were excited about catching the thief; I thought the process was an exercise in futility. After all, what could this team possibly do that the police couldn't?

I had some errands to run before I left the next day for my trip north. After going to the grocery store, drug store, post office, and the gas station, I treated myself to a large white hot chocolate at the Looney Bean. Nancy walked in as I was leaving, and I asked if she had received my phone message that the laptop and cell had arrived. She said she had, and was planning to work on them this weekend while I was away. I thanked her and hugged her with my good arm, awkwardly clasping my white hot chocolate in my left hand.

When I arrived home, I put on the Beatles *Love* CD and began unloading the car. It took about half an hour to unpack my purchases and put them away, since most everything had to be carried upstairs. "Lucy In The Sky With Diamonds" was playing as I made my way back down the stairs to unpack the computer and cell phone for Nancy and eager to see what she had ordered for me.

The computer and cell were already unpacked, sitting on my desk, the empty boxes stacked neatly in the corner. The computer was on but in hibernation mode. A post-it indicated the password was Oscar. I touched the keyboard, and the laptop came to life. Microsoft Office Outlook, wireless printer connection, Internet access—everything I needed was there. Nancy must have wanted to surprise me, not telling me she had already set up the equipment when I saw her at the Looney Bean. As I dialed her cell to thank her, I couldn't help but wonder how Nancy knew that Bob called his plane Oscar?

She answered on the third ring.

"I can't believe that you had already set up my computer and cell when I saw you today," I chastised. "You had me fooled. I really believed you were going to work on it this weekend. How can I ever thank you? How about drinks at Nevados when I return?"

Several seconds went by before Nancy said, "J, I don't know what you are talking about. I haven't been to your house today. I've been working on a project for the hospital. When I saw you a little while ago, I was just taking a break. I'm back at the hospital now. If your computer is set up, I didn't do it."

It was my turn to be silent. It took me a moment before I could speak.

Then I said almost in a whisper, "No one but you knew that my computer arrived this morning. In fact, I don't even think I told Ross that I asked you to order me a new one." As I said these words, my sense of bewilderment was gradually replaced with a feeling of calm.

Mary wasn't the only one who was still here.

Several more seconds must have passed before I heard Nancy shouting "J. J. Are you there?"

I needed to get off the phone and think.

Mentally scrambling, I tried to sound embarrassed, "I'm sorry, Nancy. Perhaps it was Ross"—even though I knew he couldn't have done it... He didn't even set up his own electronics.

Then I said more certainly, "It must have been Ross. He probably stopped by this morning, saw the boxes and thought he would surprise me. He drops in on me a lot these days. I will still pay you for the job. Please send me a bill."

"J, I can't send you a bill. All I did was order the equipment. You can do me one favor; if Ross didn't set up the electronics, call me. I am interested in knowing who my competition is," she finished with a laugh.

"I will. I will also take you out for drinks when I return from my trip. Thanks for being so understanding, Nancy."

I sat staring at the computer screen ... overjoyed that Mary and Bob were not completely gone from my life, and more than a little puzzled as to why they were still here.

Chapter 9

I left early the next morning. It had snowed lightly the night before, but now the sky was cerulean and the sun bright. It would be a beautiful drive up the eastern side of the Sierra along Highway 395. Even though the trip would be long—three hours to Reno, another five hours to Portola Valley, depending on traffic—I was looking forward to it. So much had happened over the past few weeks that I needed to think about without any interruptions. I brought along all the essentials: a Bob Dylan collection, Mary's favorite; Mozart's piano concertos and symphonies, Bob's favorite; some blueberry Izzes in a cooler; and assorted munchies.

I turned off my cell and put Mozart's 17th piano concerto, "The Starling," in my CD player. I wanted to spend some time with Bob on the eastern side of the Sierra, since he loved its stark beauty the way I did. On the western side, I would be with Mary, who was definitely a western Sierra lover, and as I reached the urban areas, I would spend time with both of them.

As Mozart played, my mind drifted back to Mary's stories of their first encounter.

Mary had met Bob in college on the lawn in front of the library eighteen years ago. She said he just sat down next to her while she was studying for a test, and started talking. Over the years I began to doubt that Mary had told me the whole story since Bob was a man of few words.

A few days later, as she was preparing to go out with Bob for the first time, she told me he was handsome, really smart, and different than anyone she had ever met. From my vantage point Mary had always been a little too trusting, a little too naïve. I mentally vowed to keep tabs on this new relationship.

Bob turned out to be tall, about 6'2", lean and athletic looking, dark brown hair, large warm brown eyes, and big hands—for some reason I remembered his hands. And Mary was right. Bob was like no one I had ever met, and over the years I learned just how multi-faceted he was.

He had his seriously brilliant side that seemed to blend well with his love of toys. As a techie genius, he had a room full of computers, some intact, some dismantled. When the software he and his colleagues wrote exceeded the capacity of existing hardware, he developed new hardware. He was a lover of classical music and had hundreds of classical CDs and the state-of-the-art equipment to play them. He was an amateur astronomer who kept Nikon astronomical binoculars in their third-story bedroom, and a gigantic Celestron telescope in an airtight storage cabinet next to the star-viewing tower he had built on one side of their roof. But his brilliance went beyond his subjects of interest. Bob could explain a complex aspect of any one of these pursuits in language you could understand without talking down to you.

He also had a side that loved speed and adventure. Whether it was skiing, mountain biking, climbing, scuba diving, flying, or driving his 2006 Mosler, if it was fast or dangerous, it was good. He approached it all with passion.

But I liked his soft side best. Early in their relationship I made the mistake of agreeing to go backpacking in the Eastern Sierra with Mary. Bob had left the day before, and Mary had promised to join him at the summit of Banner Peak. Starting at first light, we hiked for hours. As the day progressed, I realized just how much stronger Mary was than I. With increasing frequency I made her stop for breaks, to drink some water, and catch our breath. Eventually, I could go no farther.

"I have to stop," I said, dumped my pack on the ground, and collapsed against a tree. After giving me careful instructions, Mary left me, climbed to the summit, found Bob, and they returned to rescue me. Neither gave any thought to turning around. Nor did they criticize me. Bob just picked up my pack, along with his rope and pick, and carried them until we reached an impossible face of ice that we had to scale to get to the top. Then, with me and my pack in tow, and without complaint, Bob hoisted me to the top on his back. All the way I asked myself, "Why do they do this?" When we got to the top, it all became clear. We were alone, at the top of the world, a silence and beauty so profound I wanted to stay forever.

Bob lived life on his own terms and would take you along if you were willing. He and Mary made the perfect couple...

I was so lost in my thoughts that I had already reached Reno and almost missed the turn for the mortuary. Three hours had passed in the blink of an eye. It took about twenty minutes to sign the necessary papers and take possession of Mary and Bob's ashes. As I carried them out to the car, I realized their ashes combined couldn't weigh much more than ten pounds. It was hard to believe. I wrapped them in a shirt that Mary and I had stolen from one another so many times that I could not remember whose it was originally. Then I put a CD in the player from my Bob Dylan collection and started on the second leg of my journey.

As Dylan's "Watching The River Flow" was playing, I let Mary flood my thoughts. She was about 5'7" but her long legs gave her the illusion of being taller. She had rich, thick brown hair that she wore down, cut just below her square jaw. She had brown eyes full of life that hid nothing. Her build was feminine and athletic. She loved traveling, Dylan—whom she could recite verse for verse, her home, her roses, her Audi TT, and mostly Bob.

Mary approached life with sweet naivety and unstoppable optimism. From the time we were children she was honest to a fault. If you asked her a question, you got the unvarnished truth, with no concern as to how it might be received or what trouble the answer might get her in.

She was also fiercely loyal. If you were her friend, there was nothing she wouldn't do for you. If you were her enemy, you didn't exist. There was no halfway with her.

About the time we turned thirty, Mary went from the most frugal person I knew to one of the most indulgent. I always wondered what caused the transition. For all of our formative years, she would only buy something if it were on sale—and it had to be a great sale. Suddenly, she had an interior decorator, a personal shopper, and a masseuse. She indulged herself, Bob, and me. I remember one afternoon I was sitting in my office working on a particularly time-consuming project when a woman phoned, told me she was calling at Mary's request, and began to interview me. She asked questions like, "What female TV star would you say you are most like" and other ridiculous inquiries like that. I tried to be polite, but it was difficult; I was busy and her questions made no sense. When I phoned Mary later to ask what in the hell was going on, she told me to be patient. Two weeks later I had a brand new wardrobe—complete with jackets, dresses, pants, sweaters, and shoes—that looked custom-made for me. Inside the box a note said, "I told you to be patient. Enjoy. Love, M."

Besides being generous, she was very protective of me. If someone crossed me, they crossed Mary. If she didn't like the way someone treated me, she would call them and ask them to explain themselves; before I met Ross this included boyfriends and dates.

In short, she was the perfect twin.

As I neared Sacramento, Dylan was singing "Maggie's Farm." Now that I was out of the mountains, I saw spring all around me—lots of small waterfalls, flowering dogwoods, daffodils on the sides of the road—not a hint of snow. It was beautiful. Hard to believe there could be two such different seasons within a few hours of one another.

In Davis I stopped to refuel the car and stretch. I had lingered in my memories long enough. I changed the mood with some Billie Holiday. The first song was "Solitude." Now I had to turn my attention to the situation at hand. Why were Mary and Bob still here? There had to be a reason. With only a few supernatural movies like *Sixth Sense* informing me, I knew I was in way over my head. I would have liked to discuss it with someone, but whom? To my knowledge, I was the only one who was being visited, and definitely the only one who saw Mary in the grocery store parking lot.

As I neared the off ramp to Mary and Bob's, I could think of only two reasons: They were here to protect me because I was in danger, or they had some unfinished business not related to me. Either way, I wanted to figure it out so I could help.

Chapter 10

It was six o'clock when I stopped at a small market about five miles from Mary and Bob's house to pick up something for dinner and the next day's breakfast. I had shifted my thoughts to more immediate and practical matters. Had anyone been at the house since the crash? There had been a lot of phone calls those first few weeks, but mired in grief, I hadn't really paid attention.

I had to stop the car at the end of the driveway. Damp eyes were turning to blinding tears; I hadn't realized how difficult coming here was going to be. I knew I couldn't navigate the driveway—which was steep with two switchbacks before arriving at the house—if I didn't gain control of myself. As my vision began to clear, I glimpsed in the lights given off by my headlights hundreds of daffodils peppering the hillside on either side of the driveway. I don't know how long I just sat there looking at the flowers, remembering.

For the last thirteen years Mary had planted a hundred daffodils a year on the hillside. She was partial to the all-yellow daffodils and white daffodils with yellow centers ... I was partial to white daffodils with orange centers. She always planted a few of my favorites so she could put them in a vase in the guest room when I visited in the spring.

After a few moments I was able to get my emotions under control, at least long enough to make it up the driveway. At the top I was amazed to find that the house looked like it always did when I came to see Mary and Bob. Somehow I had imagined it, too, would have changed.

I picked up the ashes and mounted the stone steps to the front door, which was actually in the back of the house, and opened onto the second floor. It was a lovely, still evening with a little chill in the air. I could smell floral scents that I should have been able to identify had my brain been working right. Mary's garden was designed to show off the best of each season.

I opened the front door with the key Mary had given me when she and Bob bought the house and deactivated the alarm. I touched the light panel and lights throughout the house came on. I just stood in the doorway, taking in the sights and smells. Even vacant for these many weeks, I could still feel Mary and Bob's presence. I placed the ashes on Mary's antique desk in the front room. Then I walked through the living room, dining room, guest room, and kitchen, touching furniture, sculptures, and pictures, as if I had never been in there before.

I went downstairs to the office. I'm not sure how long I was lost in the recollections the house provoked when I was abruptly pulled back to the present. Someone was walking around upstairs.

As I cautiously started back up the stairs, I heard a man say, "Hello. Is someone here? I'm armed and have already called the police."

I came face to face with a man holding what looked to be a flare gun. He was forty-something, medium build, balding, soft in the middle, and quite nervous looking.

"Who are you?" he demanded. "What are you doing here? How did you get in?"

He spoke so fast I couldn't respond. Finally, he took a really deep breath and turned a scary shade of red. Was this man going to have a heart attack?

I said in my most calming voice, "I'm Janet Westmore. My twin and her husband own this house. Who the hell are you?"

He stared at me uncertainly for several seconds then said, as he lowered his gun, "You look a little like her, but not like her twin."

"We are fraternal twins, not identical," I barked, trying to sound more in charge of the situation than I was. "But you haven't told me who you are."

He tried to shove the flare gun in his jacket pocket, but the gun was too big. He finally moved it to his left hand, extending his right.

"I'm Mary and Bob's neighbor. I live just down the hill. My name is Steve James. Actually, once I got your number from Mary's office, I left a message for you at your home, telling you I would keep an eye on the house until you were able to make arrangements." He still spoke quickly and appeared anxious.

Ignoring his outstretched hand, I held my ground and asked firmly, "How did you know I was here? And how did you get into the house?"

He broke into a smile, then laughed, and the tension was broken.

"The house has been dark for a long time, Janet. When you turned on what appears to be every light in the house, I suspect everyone in the neighborhood knew someone was here. When I came over to investigate, I found your car in the driveway still running with the lights on, and the front door wide open. By the way, I turned off your car and took the keys—didn't want you making a fast getaway before the police arrived."

Handing me my car keys, Steve apologized for the confusion then extended his hand again, which I shook.

"It broke my heart when I heard about the crash," he said. "They were such good people and good neighbors. Mary especially made me feel welcome from the moment I met her. A couple of weeks before…" he paused and continued softly, "the accident, Bob asked if I wanted to take a ride with him in his plane. I told him no way; no one has ever been able to get me in any plane smaller than a 747, and they never will."

Steve looked up, saw tears in my eyes, "I'm sorry," he said. "That was thoughtless. I should just keep my big mouth shut."

"Don't worry," I said. "I just cry a lot these days. It's all right."

After cancelling the police emergency call, more apologies from Steve, and assurances from me that we would talk before I returned home, he left. I stood by my car and watched as his flashlight swept back and forth down the driveway until he was out of sight. Since my arm was still in a sling, I made a number of trips up and down the stone steps. Once in the house, I reactivated the alarm—I didn't want any more surprises—put my clothes in the guest room and the groceries in the kitchen. I decided to postpone going up to the third floor, which housed the master bedroom and bath, until morning. I was on emotional overload as it was.

I put the groceries away, relieved to see that someone had cleaned out the refrigerator. I made myself a salad, sliced some sourdough bread, poured a glass of Solitude Chardonnay, and ate quietly at the wrought iron and glass table in the kitchen.

As I prepared for bed, I placed the ashes still wrapped in Mary's and my old shirt on a pillow next to me. Leaving most of the second floor lights on in case I woke in the night and didn't know where I was, I went to sleep.

I rose early the next morning, eager to get a start on the day. As I walked into the living area, I took in the magnificent views of the Santa Cruz Mountains. The fog fall that had crept over the mountains earlier was receding, and the morning sun was beginning to fill the sky with a golden light. I dressed in some old running shorts and sweatshirt and went to the kitchen to make some tea. On a sideboard I found stacks of mail, some packages and a couple of handwritten notes. In all the emotion and confusion of the night before, I hadn't noticed any of it.

Before opening the mail and packages or reading the notes, I decided to fortify myself with a short walk. It was going to be a long, stressful day, and some head-clearing exercise was in order. I finished my tea and headed out toward Alpine Road. The air was damp and cool, but with no snow or ice to impair my way. It was revitalizing. The only difficulty I encountered was the walk down the steep driveway. I could hardly wait to get my arm out of the sling so I could regain some balance.

Forty-five minutes later, I headed back up Mary's street. As I passed the house just down the hill from her home, Steve came out and greeted me like an old friend—in a manner I found a little too familiar and ingratiating for comfort. After another apology for last night's confusion, he asked if I would join him and his girlfriend for a glass of wine that evening around six. I knew meeting with him sometime during this trip was inevitable, so I accepted, with the caveat that it would have to be just one glass because I had a lot to do before I left on Monday. Then I continued back to the house to ready myself for the day ahead.

I picked up the ashes and walked up the curved staircase to the only part of the house I had not visited the night before. The top floor housed the master bedroom and bath. Mary and Bob had added on this floor just a few years before. At the top of the stairs was a short hallway with a door on either side. One door led to a large walk-in closet and the other to a spacious bathroom. The hallway opened up into a large bedroom with a solid wall of windows and access to a large deck. The views of the Santa Cruz Mountains covered with redwoods, firs, and oaks from the third floor were even more spectacular than from the second floor living area.

I loved this room. It felt different than every other room in the house. This was the only room that was always cluttered. There were pictures, books, journals, souvenirs, sachets, letters, and writing tablets on every surface. Books and magazines were stacked on the floor next to a large, well-worn, forest-green upholstered chair, and on either side of the bed. There were scarves hanging on a freestanding full-length mirror, hand weights under a bench, and discarded clothes on the bench. Every inch looked and felt like Mary and Bob.

An overwhelming sense of loss began to engulf me. Before I lost myself in the room, I placed the ashes in the middle of the bed and fled back downstairs.

Chapter 11

After showering I went to the sideboard in the kitchen where the mail, packages, and notes were stacked. My first appointment wasn't for another hour so I had some time to sort through it all.

The first note was from Frank, Mary's housecleaner. He said he'd been coming in every Wednesday to dust and make sure nothing had been disturbed. He would continue to do so until I phoned and asked him to stop. He also wanted me to know he had a key to the house and knew the security code. I started to write myself a note to call and thank him, but decided just to call. When I reached his voicemail, I left a message, thanking him, asking him to continue his Wednesday visits, but to send his bill to me.

The second note was from Kate, Mary's assistant from work. Kate had worked with Mary for several years. They had become dear friends, and I knew Mary trusted and loved her.

"Janet, I am leaving you this note, since I'm sure you will be coming to Mary's as soon as you have sufficiently recovered from your own injuries. First, I am so sorry about Mary and Bob. I know you must be devastated. I just want you to know that if there is anything I can do to help, please call me. I'm leaving you some letters and packages that came to the office. Right after the accident, I placed a hold on the mail going to the house and will pick it up for you at your convenience. Just call. All of us at work (especially me) are lost without Mary. My prayers are with you. Call when you need me. Kate."

How could I have been so thoughtless? I was so consumed by my own sorrow, I had completely forgotten about Kate. As I dialed her cell, I tried to remember the last time I'd seen her. It must have been when Mary and I took her to Florio's on lower Fillmore in Pacific Heights to celebrate her birthday. What a hoot. After drinking way too much champagne, we decided to stay in the city instead of trying to drive home. We must have made quite a spectacle, three exceedingly tipsy women walking the five blocks to the Hotel Majestic, checking in with no luggage. The next morning we awoke hung-over and clueless about where we'd left our cars. We ended up paying one of the hotel staff to drive us around the neighborhood until we located them.

Kate answered on the second ring. I apologized for not phoning her sooner. For the next ten minutes we tried to console one another. I mentioned my meetings with Mary's attorney later that morning and the investigator from the National Transportation Safety Board in the afternoon. She told me not to be put off by Nathan, Mary's attorney, whom most people found to be unusually quiet and reserved when they first met him.

"He is really quite nice if you can get past his initial reserve."

Kate also said Nathan and Mary had developed a strong friendship over the last few years, and she and Bob frequently socialized with him.

I told her about the memorial Joan had taken charge of. Kate volunteered to compile a list of Mary's coworkers and professional contacts that should be invited. We ended the conversation by making a date to meet for an early lunch on

Monday at the Playa Grill in the Stanford Shopping Center before I returned to Mammoth.

About an hour later, while I was still going through the mail, there was a knock on the front door. I must have opened the door more quickly than the man standing there expected, because I saw him hastily brush his face with a Kleenex, which he quickly stuffed into his jacket pocket. I liked him immediately. He had tears in his eyes.

As I ushered him into the house, Nathan, who had introduced himself by then, said, "I wasn't sure if there were any goodies in the house so I took the liberty of bringing fresh scones and fruit."

He went directly to the kitchen and set a large recyclable cloth grocery sack on a counter, got out a small platter, and started placing the food on it. It was clear he was a frequent visitor to the house; he seemed much more familiar maneuvering around the kitchen than I was.

As Nathan arranged the fruit and scones on one of Mary's pewter platters, he had his back to me. He appeared to be in his forties, medium height with an athletic build. When he turned around to make a point, I saw he had a strong face, hazel eyes, and a slightly receding hairline. The entire time he was taking food out of the sack, he spoke warmly and nonstop about Mary and Bob. I would have to tell Kate that this man was anything but quiet and reserved.

As he was finishing, I placed some individual-sized bottles of blueberry Izze and Pellegrino on a tray with glasses, ice, small plates, and butter-yellow cloth napkins. I tried to pick up the tray with my good arm, but the tray was too heavy. After placing the food platter on the dining room table, Nathan returned to the kitchen to get the drink tray. I followed him into the dining room.

We sat at Mary's large round glass dining table. Nathan handed me an envelope, "Before we begin discussing the estate, I think you should read this."

The small envelope had a single initial on its front "J." I opened the envelope to find a note in Mary's almost illegible scrawl.

Dear J... One of us had to leave first. If you are reading this, I guess I took the honors. We've been through the sunshine and the shadows from our beginning, and somehow, I always knew I could survive and ultimately thrive because of you. So I have thanked the universe for you daily, my twin, my anchor, my mirror. I just wish I didn't have to leave you.

Since I left this note with Nathan, you two have already met. Over the years I have known him, I have told him a lot about you. You can trust him. I always have, and he has never failed me. He is a great attorney and dear friend. More importantly, he is a twin. He will understand what you are going through and be there to guide you.

Nathan will go over the details. For the most part Bob and I have left you everything, so you should be set financially. I know this is going to be a very difficult time, and the last thing you need to worry about is money.

J, just know that while you may not be able to see me, I will not leave you.

Love, Mary

Nathan sat at the table quietly while I fought for some emotional control. He did not try to calm me or tell me "everything would be all right." After about fifteen minutes, I finally began to regain my composure. As I shifted my attention back to Nathan, I saw in his eyes, which were filled with tears, he did understand. Trust Mary to find an attorney who was a twin!

Nathan told me I had been appointed Executor, and he reviewed the details of the estate. In addition to the house, Nathan guesstimated the rest of the estate was worth in excess of ten million dollars. Mary and Bob had made generous financial gifts to four nonprofits and to Mary's assistant, Kate. They also specified a short list of special belongings to be given to friends. The rest, as Nathan put it, "is yours." I sat there a little stunned, unable to grasp the implications of the inheritance. My face must have reflected my shock.

"You probably need a little time to digest all of this," Nathan said. "We can meet to begin discussing the details the next time you're in town."

He poured a Pellegrino over ice and handed it to me. We spent the next forty-five minutes talking about how Nathan had met Mary and Bob. Just as he was standing up to leave, I asked, "What about the last time you saw Mary? When was that?"

Nathan thought for a moment smiled and said, "We had lunch about a week before the accident. Mary had decided I have been single long enough and wanted to share her ideas about possible matches. I spent the entire lunch telling her I was doing just fine and that a romantic relationship would only complicate my life. I don't think she listened to a word I said. By the next day, she had e-mailed me a list of possible candidates with her assistant, Kate, at the top of the list."

As he walked toward the door, with his briefcase and now empty cloth grocery sack in hand, he stopped, "Now that I think about it, she did ask me one odd question related to her will when I last saw her."

"Which was?" I prompted.

"She asked if I thought she should put a clause in the will delaying the sale of the house for a year. Before I could respond, she said she was just being paranoid, and told me to forget about it. When I pushed to find out what she was concerned about, she laughed and said something about a dream she'd had. Then she changed the subject."

I watched him back his car down the steep driveway, realizing that no part of my life would be the same as it had been before the accident.

Chapter 12

After Nathan left, I went back to sorting through the mail. About thirty minutes into the task, I heard a noise from the street below. Through the window I saw a smallish white sedan slowly making its way up the driveway. At every switchback the driver paused, looking up at the house. I was fairly certain by the car's stops and starts, the driver did not like the driveway.

As I reached the bottom of the stone steps to meet my visitor, a large man emerged from the driver's seat. He was in his late thirties, at least 6'5", 250 lbs., and looked terrified. Sweat was pouring off his face, and his hands were trembling.

"Please tell me you are Janet Westmore. I would hate to think I came up that damn driveway for nothing," he gasped.

I smiled, extended my hand and said, "I'm Janet. You are at the right place."

Relaxing only slightly, he shook my fingers rather than my hand. "Kevin Anderson, National Transportation Safety Board. And that's one hell of a driveway you have there," he said.

Trying to wipe his sweat off my hand on my shirt without his noticing, I led him upstairs for a cold drink and some of Nathan's treats.

He excused himself to freshen up. A few minutes later he returned to the living area, calmer and much more business-like. He apologized for his distress, explaining that the entire time he was coming up the driveway, he couldn't see the ground in front of the car. I offered him a cold drink and a scone, which he accepted.

"I don't ordinarily indulge, but under the circumstances…"

He pulled a small tape recorder from his briefcase, and got down to business. He explained that he was a member of the National Transportation Safety Board team assigned to investigate the plane accident. He briefly reviewed the investigation process, and then asked me some general questions about Bob and Mary. Finally, he asked specific questions about the morning of the accident. I was able to answer almost all of them until it got to the actual plane trip. He asked if I had seen, heard or smelled anything unusual just before the plane went down.

Shaking my head, I said, "One minute we were flying, the next minute I woke up in a hospital."

He gave me his card, and asked me to call if I remembered anything that might assist the investigation. He also said most investigations took a long time, and I shouldn't expect to hear from him for a while. He shut off the tape recorder and stowed it in his briefcase with his notepad and pen. His breathing was becoming more rapid, and he was beginning to sweat again.

Tentatively I offered, "Kevin, I hope I'm not being presumptuous. But would you like me to drive your car back down the driveway for you?"

He rewarded me with his first genuine smile of the afternoon. "Would you?" he asked.

When we reached his car, he held open the driver's door, and he said he would follow me on foot.

As we met at the end of the driveway, he retook possession of his car and said earnestly, "Janet, if you have any questions, I want you to pick up the phone and call."

Kevin took another card out of his pocket, this time writing his cell number on the back, and handed it to me. After giving me a real handshake, he thanked me and drove off.

When I returned to the house, I noticed that it was already five o'clock. I didn't want to arrive late to Steve's because I was planning on leaving early. Before showering, I phoned Joan to tell her I was looking forward to our dinner at Carpaccio's the next evening and would see her at seven o'clock.

As I walked down the driveway to Steve's house, the events of the day began to catch up with me. I felt overwhelmed and disconnected from reality. I needed time to think, time to process everything that had happened. Why had I agreed to go to Steve's this evening? Why did I feel obligated to a man I didn't even know?

He burst out of the door before I could knock, and handed me a glass of red wine.

"I know Mary liked full-bodied Cabernet; I hope you do, too," he said.

I thanked him, accepted the glass, and noticed a tall, slender woman in her mid-thirties with straight blond hair and crystal blue eyes standing just inside the front door. She was striking in white jeans and a blue knit shirt that was the same color as her eyes. Steve followed my gaze.

"Ah, Carole, there you are. Janet, this is the love of my life, Carole Nelson. I'm hoping to convince her to be my bride someday soon. Carole," he said taking her hand, "this is Mary's twin sister, Janet."

The last time I was in this house, it was owned by Pam and John, dear and longtime neighbors of Mary and Bob. Their house always looked like a work in progress, which made it feel warm and homey. The centerpiece of the house had been a large French country kitchen that I envied. I never saw it when it wasn't cluttered with cookbooks, food, wine, flowers, and people. So I was a little startled when I walked into a minimally furnished great room, starkly decorated in black and white with a few red accent pieces. My surprise must have been evident.

Fortunately, Steve interpreted my reaction as delight, saying, "I know. It's a big improvement, isn't it? Lucky for me, Carole is an interior designer. Didn't she do a magnificent job?"

I just nodded.

Steve continued, "I knew I wanted to take out a few of the interior walls and get rid of the grandmother décor, but when Carole saw the place, she told me to leave it in her hands. And, voila!"

Having recovered from my shock-induced muteness, I complimented her on her creativity and sense of balance. Then I took a big sip of a remarkably good Cabernet.

I was surprised that the next two hours flew by. Neither Carole nor I did much talking. Steve entertained us with stories from his childhood and of his various business projects. Apparently, his parents had died when he was quite young, leaving him a very wealthy orphan. He was raised by an aunt and uncle in San Francisco who had a penchant for travel and parties and loved taking him along with them. After graduating from Stanford University, he had occupied himself with a series of "investment-focused partnerships," which he claimed were enjoyable and sometimes profitable.

Glancing at my watch and seeing it was after eight, I thanked them both for a lovely evening and began making my way toward the front door. Steve insisted on walking me home, and grabbed a flashlight and jacket. He continued to amuse me with anecdotes, this time about the remodel of the house. When we reached the top of the driveway, he told me that if I needed anything just to phone him. Then he gave me a quick kiss on the cheek and left. As I watched him vanish down the driveway I felt oddly violated by the kiss. I did my best to shrug off my misgiving and walked up the steps into the house.

I went to bed immediately, exhausted both by my injuries and the demands of the day. As soon as my head hit the pillow, I fell into a deep, dreamless sleep; so deep that it felt like I blinked and seven hours had passed.

Reluctant to leave the warmth of the bed, I burrowed farther beneath the covers and contemplated my next several hours. The next time I came here, it would probably be to start disassembling Mary and Bob's home, so I had left the day unscheduled to spend some time in their surroundings. I had until this evening when I would meet Joan for an early dinner.

Not bothering to change out of the t-shirt I slept in, I made a cup of orange tea and went up to the master bedroom. I knew Mary would frown at my sitting on her bed while drinking tea, so I sat in the large upholstered chair next to the window. I draped the blue and green afghan sitting on the back of the chair over my shoulders. Mary and I had purchased the afghan on a weekend trip to Santa Barbara. Actually, after bickering about who found it first, I had bought it and took it home. Then after one of Mary's visits, I realized it was missing. I guessed the afghan had now come full circle.

I sat there for a couple of hours, reliving memories. My cell phone ringing downstairs jolted me back to the present. When I leaped out of the chair to run downstairs to answer the phone, I spilled what was left of the tea all over myself. I guess Mary was right about not sitting on the bed, drinking tea. Predictably, the cell stopped ringing by the time I found it. I must have really been spacing out because it indicated that I had received four voice messages in the last hour and a half.

The first was from Ross, checking to see how I was doing. He said he loved me and not to bother calling back, knowing I had enough on my mind already. He was so dear.

Next was Nathan, letting me know that he was sending some documents to my home in Mammoth and to call when I received them so he could review them with me.

The third message was from a rather flustered Linda. Apparently, things had escalated at the school. She had gone to her office late Saturday to catch up on some paperwork and found two new camcorders on her desk—still in their boxes. Next to the desk were three cases of copier paper and a case of Coke with two cans missing. When she phoned Ian to tell him about the new "merchandise," he was sitting in his office being yelled at by the owner of the camcorders. And the owner was a retiree, not a merchant. Linda said she was rescheduling Thursday's meeting to Tuesday at eleven a.m. and hoped that would work for me. She also said she would like to see me at ten a.m. before the team meeting so she, Ian, and I could discuss the situation.

Who could be doing this? Why did no one ever see anything suspicious? Didn't whoever was doing this know that all the items would have to be returned? Was someone just making a statement? If it weren't causing so much friction between the school and the community, it would be a smile.

The last phone call was from Steve thanking me for spending time with Carole and him the night before and reiterating his offer of assistance if I needed anything.

Mulling over the messages, I went back upstairs to clean up the spilled tea and return the afghan to its home on the back of the chair. I opened the bedstand drawer on Mary's side of the bed and began to go through its contents. Among the clutter of papers and mementos I discovered a bundle of notes and cards I had sent to Mary commemorating various occasions over the last several years. Resigning myself to an emotional meltdown, I took the bundle and returned to the upholstered chair to read and cry.

Chapter 13

I walked into Carpaccio's at exactly seven. As usual, the upscale restaurant felt inviting with its smells of Italian cuisine and sounds of people enjoying each other's company. Joan was already there, sitting at a table in the front of the restaurant next to the window. As I walked to her table, I was struck by the realization that I had never been in this restaurant without Mary.

Joan greeted me warmly and called the waiter over. In a clipped tone she told the waiter she would like an oaky, buttery chardonnay and to please be sure the wine was not sweet or fruity. I smiled at the waiter in an effort to offset Joan's brusque manner and ordered an extra dry Absolut martini up with two olives. As soon as he left to get our drinks, Joan instructed that we should be prepared to order when the waiter returned so we wouldn't have any more interruptions. Then without another word she picked up her menu and studied it.

Since I already knew what I wanted, I had a moment to consider Joan. I had met her only a few times, most recently at a holiday dinner party Mary and Bob gave last November. She was petite, attractive, sixty-something, wealthy, intelligent, and connected. Her black hair was pulled back in a chignon and she wore a black pants suit with a shimmery silver silk scarf around her neck. She and Mary had met years ago at a wine tasting dinner in Napa Valley, and kept in touch. Soon after they met, Joan had asked Mary to be on a wine auction committee with her for one of her charities, and they quickly became good friends. I remember Mary telling me she liked Joan because she was pithy, honest to a fault, driven, a perfectionist, and she had a big heart.

The waiter returned with our drinks, and Joan immediately took a sip of her wine. She smiled approvingly, nodded at the waiter, and said, "Perfect. Thank you."

The waiter told us about the specials, we placed our dinner orders, and he left. Joan held up her glass and offered a toast to Mary and Bob. There was a moment or two of silence as we made our own private toasts, then we drank.

Joan slowly appraised me as she took another sip of wine. "How are you, J? You look pretty fragile."

Reluctantly, I updated her on my injuries, stressing that the arm sling was now more protective than therapeutic, and that by the memorial service I would be back to normal. That led us to a discussion of the service. It was clear that Joan was on familiar ground when it came to planning any event. She was on top of every detail, many that I would never have thought of.

I told her Mary's assistant, Kate Richards, was compiling a list of business associates who should be included, and asked if they had ever met.

"Kate!" Joan exclaimed. "Of course I know Kate. I introduced Kate to Mary. Kate grew up across the street from us. Her mother, Dorothy, still lives there, though I am afraid her mother is not doing very well. She has metastasized breast cancer and is losing the fight.

"Kate has arranged for round-the-clock hospice care so her mother can stay in her own home. A few months ago when it was evident that Dorothy was failing, Kate moved back home. It's been a difficult time for her, and then when the plane crashed, well...."

I was astonished. Kate never said anything when we spoke. She was not only taking care of her mother and of Mary's affairs, she was also dealing with the emotional impact of both.

"I am having lunch with Kate tomorrow on my way out of town," I said. "Do you think there is something I can do to help her?"

Joan's expression tightened. "I wouldn't even let on that you know about her mother's condition. She is a very private person. If she wants you to know, she will tell you."

Our dinners arrived and we worked out the final particulars for the memorial as we ate. Just as we were ordering two decaf cappuccinos, Mary's former neighbors, Pam and John Hathaway, entered the restaurant and headed toward the bar. Rising to greet them, I couldn't help thinking how much they looked like Mr. and Mrs. Santa Claus. They seemed delighted to see me and accepted my invitation to have their cocktails with Joan and me. Hugs were exchanged all around. They expressed their sadness about Mary and Bob.

I asked them why they sold their house.

"One morning I'm walking down the driveway to get the newspaper, and this gentleman walks up to me and asks if he can have a moment of my time," John said. "I was a little apprehensive at first. He clearly didn't live in the neighborhood; I think I know just about everyone after thirty years of living there. But he seemed friendly enough. He introduced himself as Steve James and said he was interested in buying my house. I told him it wasn't for sale. Then he asked if it was for sale for $500,000 over a reasonable asking price. Well, an extra $500,000—that's an amount you can't ignore.

"So I told him I would have to discuss it with Pam, and I would get back to him. He gave me his business card. It had his home and cell numbers on the back. He told me to call as soon as we came to a decision. As he turned to leave, I asked him if he didn't want to see the inside of the house before he made an offer like that. He said, 'No. It is the perfect location.' I was so blown away, I walked back into the house without remembering to pick up the newspaper."

Pam chimed in: "We had been talking for years about moving to Marin County to be closer to our grandchildren. We saw the offer as a sign that it was time to do it! It was hard leaving the neighborhood, though."

Then she looked at her hands folded in her lap and said, "Especially Mary and Robert." I had forgotten that Pam always called Bob by his formal name. She brightened and said, "But it is so nice to live near the kids. We have dinner together every Sunday night like we used to do in my family when I was growing up. And the grandchildren are always over. Never knew babysitting could be such a pleasure."

For the next half hour we looked at pictures of and listened to stories about Pam and John's grandchildren. I had never been much of a "kid person," but Pam and John were so genuinely thrilled by every little antic of their grandchildren that it was easy to get caught up in their joy.

As Joan and I stood to leave, Pam said, "By the way, J, did you know that Steve asked Mary and Robert if he could buy their home before he asked us?"

"No," I responded, sitting back down in my chair. "Mary never said anything, and when I was at Steve's last night, he didn't say anything."

Pam started putting all her pictures back into her purse, and said, "I didn't know either until our farewell party. John and I decided to have a party a few nights before we moved to

say goodbye to the neighbors and introduce Steve to them. I
noticed that Mary and Robert already seemed to know Steve
when we were introducing him to everyone. So I asked Mary
about it. She told me that Steve had asked them a couple of
times if they would sell their house to him, but that they had
told Steve they would never sell."

Pam smiled at John, then looked back at me. "John and I
have often wondered how many other houses in the
neighborhood Steve tried to buy before he came to our
house—though we were happy we were the last."

There was another round of hugs as we all said goodbye.
Pam gave me their new phone number and address and
promised to come to the memorial. Joan and I walked out of
the restaurant together. At her car, I thanked her for taking
care of the memorial arrangements. She waved me off, saying
she had a knack for planning events, and she knew I already
had enough on my plate.

It was still early when I returned to the house. I changed
into a pair of Mary's sweats, pulled on some socks and a light
jacket, and poured myself a glass of Cabernet. I went out onto
the small deck off the guest bedroom. Sitting on the single
weathered Adirondack chair, which took up almost the entire
deck, I felt lonely and a strong sense of disappointment. It was
my last night at the house, and Mary and Bob had not given
any indication they were here. I had been sure they would
make an appearance or at least leave a sign of some sort. After
all, I was in their home. Did this mean they had left?

I must have fallen asleep almost immediately. When I
opened my eyes, I saw the sky was changing from gray to a
light bluish pink. I had spent the entire night in the chair. My
full glass of wine was sitting on the deck next to my chair.
After a few moments I rose to go back into the house. That's

when I realized that I was wrapped in the blue and green afghan that I had left on the back of Mary's chair in her bedroom. A sense of relief washed over me. Mary hadn't left me... yet....

Chapter 14

Despite the fact that I would be back in a few weeks, it was hard to leave Mary's house. I felt connected to Mary and Bob while I was in their home. But I had a busy week ahead of me in Mammoth. I had an appointment on Wednesday with Dr. Paul, who, I was hoping, would tell me that I didn't have to use the sling anymore, as well as take off a few uncomfortable bandages that made showering a challenge. There were also tomorrow's meetings, first with Linda and Ian, and then with the team. Besides, I missed Ross, my home, and the mountains, in precisely that order.

After packing the car, activating the security system, and locking the house, I got into my Subaru, gently placing the blue and green afghan on the passenger seat next to me. I put the car in reverse and eased it down the steep driveway. Just as I reached the end, I saw Steve in front of his house. It appeared that he was just finishing a conversation with his gardener. When he saw me, he started toward the car. I opened the driver's side window and told him that I was going back to Mammoth, but would return in a few weeks.

Almost as an afterthought I said, "I ran into Pam and John at Carpaccio's last night."

His smile widened and he asked how they were.

"They love living near their grandchildren. I don't think they spoke of much else," I responded. "They did say that you asked Mary and Bob if they would sell their house to you before you made Pam and John an offer," I said, watching his face for any reaction.

His expression darkened slightly. "Oh... I didn't know they knew." He paused then added, "When I made the offer I wanted them to think their house was the only one I was interested in."

Relaxing a little, he said, "Actually, I made offers to several of their neighbors before I spoke with them. I hope they don't find out their house was about sixth on my list of prospective homes."

I assured him I would keep his secret, then said goodbye and drove off. As I made my way down Alpine, I turned on the radio to hear Elton John singing "Someone Saved My Life Tonight," and headed toward the Stanford Shopping Mall to meet Kate.

We met in the parking lot. We greeted each other like old friends and walked into Max's Opera Café. The bistro was crowded and noisy, but we managed to get a table in the back, away from the bar. As we followed the hostess to our table, I noticed a few business types glance admiringly at Kate. And who wouldn't? She was tall, lithe, and had the statuesque posture of a model. Her thick short-cropped hair gave way to perfect features. She wore black pants, a cream silk blouse, a hip length red jacket, and had a black and cream scarf fashionably wrapped around her long neck. She was the essence of a lady.

After we ordered, Kate took a large envelope out of her purse and handed it to me. "Here are the names and addresses of the people I think Mary would want at the memorial. I dropped a copy off with Joan this morning," she said.

When Kate mentioned Joan, I broke eye contact with her. Kate didn't miss the gesture. "Joan told me this morning that you had dinner together last night and she told you about my mother," Kate said softly.

"I am so sorry, Kate," I blurted. The patrons in the next booth looked over to see what I was apologizing about. I lowered my voice and asked, "Is there anything I can do?" Then I shook my head and said, "That's a stupid thing to say. I know there isn't. But you have to worry about your mother and her care, while you are still working. Then I thoughtlessly ask you to help with Mary's memorial."

Kate took my right hand and said evenly, "J, don't worry about it. Mother has been ill for a long time. We have all the help we need, and we have established a routine that works for both of us. Besides, my work is a good distraction from the daily realities of her illness."

She gave my hand a little squeeze, saying, "I'm worried about *you*—trying to recuperate from the plane accident and coping with the loss of Mary and Bob."

We fell into an easy silence for a few moments, and then I asked, "Has Nathan told you about Mary and Bob's will?"

She said he hadn't, so I told her that Mary and Bob had made a bequest to her in the will. As I explained the details of the gift, there were tears in her eyes. She was genuinely touched to be remembered.

Lunch came and our conversation turned to becoming better acquainted. I told her what it was like to live in Mammoth, and she told me about growing up in the Bay Area. The more we chatted, the greater my sense was that we, too, would become friends. The only disagreement we had was over the bill. Not having the decorum of a lady, I won. I paid the bill while she insisted that it would be her turn next time." Then we got into our cars, waved and drove off in different directions. My direction was home.

Six and a half hours later I pulled into my driveway next to Ross's Honda Pilot. I scooted to the passenger side, and opened the car door. I took a moment to breathe in the fresh, cold mountain air. It felt good to be back in Mammoth. Leaving all but the afghan and my purse in the car, I made my way up the front steps. Ross opened the door just as I reached it. Before I could say anything, he wrapped his arms around me and kissed me. He carried me up the stairs to my bedroom and properly welcomed me home. All the while not a word was spoken.

Later, as we emerged from the bedroom, I saw that the fire was lit, yellow roses in my favorite vase sat on the coffee table, and the dining room table was set for two.

"Ross, this is wonderful."

"Ah, but there is more. Come with me."

I followed him into the kitchen, where herb meatloaf—the only indoor-cooked entrée Ross knew how to prepare, and my favorite—was cooking in the oven. There were potatoes waiting to be mashed, and the makings of a salad were spread across the counter.

Then he opened up the freezer, took out two martinis, handed one to me and said, "I missed you, J. Welcome home."

We drank our martinis while Ross made the salad, and he caught me up on what he had been doing. Over dinner I told him about Steve and what he had done to the Hathaways' house, about Nathan and the will, the NTSB investigator and his fear of the driveway, Joan's plans for the memorial, and my lunch with Kate. I talked so much and so fast that I was surprised to discover I had consumed two helpings of the meatloaf and potatoes. I barely gave Ross a chance to ask a question.

After dinner I hugged the blue and green afghan around my shoulders to give me the fortitude I needed to initiate the discussion I had planned for the evening, and we sat in front of the fire with glasses of Cabernet. I had decided this afternoon on my trip home that it was time to tell Ross about Mary and Bob. He was my best friend and I knew he would be as excited as I was. I was a little anxious because Ross tended to believe in the concrete not the esoteric. But I knew Ross. He would get it.

I began tentatively. "Remember when I was in the hospital, and I kept seeing Mary?"

Although I phrased it as a question, I didn't pause or give Ross a chance to respond. I continued, "And we thought that it was part of the shock of the accident and of losing Mary and Bob? Well, they really were there! In fact, they still are here."

I told him about the Godiva chocolate that had mysteriously appeared in my shopping cart and again next to my glass of wine, how Mary had stopped the shopping cart when Lynn Ratonne had hurled it at me, how I came home to find my computer unpacked and set up, and finally about waking to find the afghan wrapped tightly around me after falling asleep in the deck chair. When I looked up to see his reaction, I was shocked to see that Ross's smile had changed from warm and affectionate to a face filled with dismay and concern.

After a prolonged and awkward silence, he said in a low, slow cadence, "J, Mary and Bob are *dead*. Mary isn't mysteriously leaving you pieces of chocolate and Bob didn't magically appear to set up your new computer. There are logical explanations for all of these incidents. You need help, J. I think you need to see a grief counselor or a professional therapist."

I was stunned. I was so sure that Ross would get it, I hadn't prepared myself for this response. All I could comprehend was that the only person who mattered in my life didn't believe me. As I began to formulate a rebuttal, I realized I was too hurt and disappointed to try to convince him that Mary and Bob were really here and helping me. I couldn't look at him. I couldn't think. I just sat there staring at the fire. Ross didn't believe me. How could my homecoming start so beautifully and end so badly? I gazed at him mutely, at a loss, then returned my focus to the fire.

I'm not sure how long I just stared into the fire, lost in thoughts of sorrow, disbelief, and bewilderment. When I checked back into the present, Ross had left. It appeared to be about an hour since I had shared my secret. The fire had died. I stood up from the chair to go to bed. I found a note on my pillow. It read:

"J, I guess I said the wrong thing. But I had to be honest. Please think about talking with a professional about these 'apparitions.' I love you. If you need me, just call and I will come. R"

I didn't know whether I felt abandoned or betrayed.

Chapter 15

I slept fitfully, finally falling into a deep sleep about three. When I awoke at dawn, I reflexively stretched out my hand, searching for Ross, and then remembered the events of the evening before. I couldn't believe Ross thought I was hallucinating—that to cope with my loss my subconscious had made up my visits from Mary and Bob. But he must believe it because he wanted me to see a therapist! There was no way we could continue our relationship if he thought I was crazy. First I lost Mary and Bob, now I was losing Ross. I tried to push the conflict out of my mind, and rose to prepare myself for the day ahead. Perhaps he just needed some time. Ross and I would eventually work everything out. We always had before.

But the morning had more obstacles in store for me. The first surprise came when I glanced out the window expecting to see a bright sunny day. It was snowing, hard. A quick trip to the kitchen to prepare tea ended in another disappointment; no more orange and spice tea in the house. Settling for some water, I listened to the messages on my answering machine and heard a message from Linda. She said Ian had a schedule conflict. He could only spare us an hour today, so she was canceling our pre-meeting with him and rescheduling the team meeting from ten a.m. to eight a.m. It was now 7:15 a.m. This day just kept getting better and better.

I hurried into the bathroom and jumped into the shower. As I toweled off, I looked into the mirror to find red and swollen eyes looking back at me. I looked like I had been awake for days.

I walked into the conference room at 8:05—the last one to arrive. Students and staff were milling around, sharing stories about their weekend activities. Noticing my entrance, everyone moved to take a seat at the table. Frances Mills, the long-term, now unpaid school secretary, strolled in with some papers for Linda to sign.

Students, teachers, and staff all loved Fran. Two years ago when the school district was forced to cut all of the school budgets, they had eliminated funding for her position. On her last Friday, the PTA, school, and community came together to give her a retirement party, honoring her thirty-two years of service to the school. The following Monday, Fran showed up to work at her usual time. When Linda asked the spry sixty-four year-old why she wasn't out enjoying her retirement, she announced, "This is what I enjoy." And, she hasn't missed a day of work since.

I went to the front of the room to begin the meeting as Fran was leaving. When she reached the door, she turned and said halfheartedly to no one in particular, "I hope you don't catch this guy before he replaces my office chair. It's way too soft for this old back of mine." Then in a flash she was gone.

After welcoming everybody back, I turned the meeting over to Ian for a report of the most recent incident. Between bites of a blueberry scone, he told everyone about the camcorders, copier paper, and case of Coke that had arrived over the weekend. He also told the group about the very angry senior citizen who owned the camcorders. Everyone agreed the situation was escalating. We brainstormed strategies, and settled on establishing a number of "look outs" that would require participation by some community members as well as those on the team. Assignments were made and the meeting was dismissed.

When I left the school, it was still snowing. It was one of those wet and slushy early spring snowstorms with a lot of wind. Driving was slow and treacherous. My cell phone rang twice while I was driving, but I kept my attention on the road. I stopped at the grocery store and the post office before making my way home. In keeping with the rest of the morning, my street had not yet been plowed. It took several tries to make it up the hill through the thick snow to the end of the cul de sac and my garage.

Once I arrived home, I saw that the missed calls plus two others were from Ross. I wasn't ready to speak with him yet; I needed some time to think. So I turned off my cell, unplugged the house phone, and turned on the Beatles' *Love* CD to almost full volume. I spent the rest of the day doing chores around the house, steadfastly avoiding any thoughts of Ross. Warmed by a dinner of Campbell's chicken noodle soup, cheddar cheese, and rye crisps, I went to sleep early, praying there would be no surprises the next day.

My prayers must have fallen on deaf ears because at 6:45 the next morning while I was preparing my tea, Linda called to say that Fran's wish had been granted. There was a brand new office chair at her desk—with a bow on it! I told Linda I would come over within the hour.

I arrived forty-five minutes later. I saw Fran just outside Linda's office, looking delighted with her new chair. I entered the office to find a frustrated-looking Linda and an angry Ian—who, for the first time since I had met him, wasn't eating. It was Ian's new office chair that had been filched for Fran. Before I could say a word, Ian started ranting. How was he going to explain that his chair had been stolen out of the police station? And how was he going to take the chair back from Fran?

I, on the other hand, felt better than I had in thirty-six hours and said so. Linda and Ian both looked at me as if I were nuts.

Before either spoke, I said, "Now we have narrowed down our list of suspects to seven, plus, of course, the two of you."

As realization dawned, anger and frustration faded. Linda and Ian began to share in my excitement. We began to discuss our next steps, Ian said, "Linda, can someone get us something to eat? I'm starving."

Linda and I exchanged smiles, and she went to the cafeteria in search of sustenance for Ian.

When she returned with oatmeal cookies and individual sized cartons of orange juice, we went to work. Once we settled on a plan, we decided to call a team meeting for Friday morning. That would give us three days to make all the necessary arrangements.

The next three days were busy.

I met Ross for a late lunch Tuesday afternoon. I began our lunch by saying that while I could intellectually understand his skepticism about Mary and Bob, it hurt my feelings that he thought I was either making up or hallucinating the visits. Then I told him I needed some time to think without any pressure. I could tell by his mannerisms he was still very concerned and having difficulty holding back suggestions of therapists or counselors I might see. In the end we agreed that we both loved one another deeply and a week or two apart shouldn't hurt us.

On Wednesday morning I met with Dr. Paul. He said he was pleased with the progress I had made. He asked me how my physical therapy sessions were going, and after listening to my report, recommended I stay with them for at least six more weeks, although I could quit using the sling. Which, unbeknownst to him, I had quit wearing by the time I returned from Mary's. We scheduled another appointment in April, and he moved on to his next patient.

On the way out I ran into Erin, the R.N. who had taken such good care of me. I was delighted to see her—I hadn't seen her since my hospital stay. I had been so consumed in my own physical and emotional pain at the time that I really hadn't seen her—though I had greatly depended on her. Now I realized she was beautiful. In her mid-thirties, she had rich brown hair and eyes, almost perfect features, and a lissome, feminine build. We spent a few minutes catching up on each other's lives.

On Wednesday afternoon, Joan phoned. She sounded unusually soft and subdued. "J, Kate's mother died last night. I thought you would want to know."

A blackness that you experience when you have recently lost someone very close to you threatened to overwhelm me.

I must have gasped or made some other unintelligible sound, because Joan said in her familiar take-charge tone, "J? Are you there? J, it was a blessing for Dorothy, she was in a lot of pain. And she and Kate have been preparing for this day for a long time."

"I know," I said weakly. "I'm not sure why I am reacting so poorly. I didn't even know her." Then I paused and said anxiously, interrupting Joan who had begun to speak, "How is *Kate*?"

She assured me Kate was fine. "She is staying at my house for the next few days. I will take care of her and help with the arrangements, though she and Dorothy seem to have taken care of most everything a few months ago."

She gave me the information for Dorothy's funeral service, and I asked her to let me know if there were anything I could do. She added that she and Kate had sent out all the invitations to Mary and Bob's memorial on Monday.

Wednesday evening Steve phoned. "Did you know we had a big rainstorm in Portola Valley on Monday night?"

The question seemed to come out of nowhere. I hesitated, "No. But I'm not surprised. We had a fair-sized snowstorm here Tuesday."

"Well, it washed away some of my shrubs and flowers on the west side of the house. So I took a walk around your house...." I didn't hear the rest of his statement. It wasn't "my" house. It was Mary and Bob's house...

When I tuned back in he was saying, "I hope that's all right with you?!"

"I'm sorry, Steve. I must have become distracted. You hope what's all right with me?"

He jumped in, "No problemo! I was just saying that this morning I had my gardener replace the shrubs and flowers you lost when he replaced mine. Hope that's okay."

"Sure. Thank you. Be sure to send me the bill"

"They're on me," he said. "What are neighbors for? When do you will be returning to Portola Valley?"

"I will probably be back a week from Friday, the day before the memorial service."

"Have you given any thought yet about what you want to do with the house?" As he asked the question, I realized that I hadn't given it much thought.

"Probably sell it," I responded.

There was a brief pause and he said, "If you do decide to sell it, please let me know before you list it. I would like to make the first offer."

"You already have a lovely new house."

"Ah. But yours is much nicer."

My "conversation quotient" had reached its limit for the day, so I unplugged the phone and went to the kitchen to make dinner. I poured a glass of Solitude Chardonnay and began preparing angel hair pasta with tomatoes, basil, and garlic. As I chopped up the fresh ingredients, my head was cluttered with thoughts of Ross, Kate, and the neighbor who wanted to buy Mary's house.

Chapter 16

Friday morning as I dressed for our scheduled special team meeting at the school, there was a knock on my front door. I threw on my navy and green plaid flannel robe and rushed downstairs. I was surprised to find Erin at my front door—after all, it was seven thirty in the morning.

Before I could think of anything to say, she handed me a business card and said, "J, I am sorry to disturb you so early in the morning, but I wanted to drop this off for you on my way to work."

I froze. It was a business card for the hospital's social worker, Lisa Jeffers, who specialized in grief counseling. Now I really was at a loss for words.

Erin looked alarmed as she registered the mixture of pique and confusion on my face. Taking a step backward, she tentatively said, "I saw Ross at the hospital when he was checking on one of the injured skiers he took off the hill yesterday afternoon." Ross was behind this? I was really upset now. "I told him I had seen you earlier in the day, and asked if you were recovering from your loss as well as you were healing physically. He said that you were still … uhhh … seeing Mary. I … I thought … well, Lisa is really good… maybe you would want to talk with her." While Erin spoke, she stared at her shoes. When she finished, she looked up, and

I could see the hint of tears in her eyes. She ended by almost whispering, "I just wanted to help. I'm sorry."

What a jerk I was. She was just trying to help. She had no way of knowing that Mary and Bob really were still around. And if Ross didn't believe me, Erin certainly wasn't going to.

"No. I'm sorry. I wish I could explain, but it's all really complicated. I do appreciate that you are trying to help me." I held up the business card and gave her what I hoped looked like a smile saying, "Thank you."

She smiled back cautiously. "Well, I guess I better get to work."

As she turned to go, I lightly touched her arm, "I really am sorry for my reaction, Erin. Mark it up to a bad morning."

With a quick nod, she walked down the front steps, got into her Subaru and took off. It wasn't until I watched her drive down the street that I realized how cold I had become while I was standing on the front porch in an old robe and bare feet. I closed the door and turned up the heat.

I was furious with Ross. When we spoke on Tuesday, I thought we had agreed to disagree. I also naively thought that taking a little time off from one another included not sending someone else to continue the argument or make their own case. Maybe our relationship had finally found a challenge it couldn't overcome. I hoped not. I would phone him tonight after he came home from work. For now I needed to let go of all these feelings. This was no time to be emotional. Linda, Ian, and I had a job to do, and if we were lucky, our job would be over by this time Saturday.

Two hours before the emergency team meeting scheduled to be held at the school, Linda, Ian, and I met at the Looney Bean, one of my favorite Mammoth Lakes coffee houses, to finalize our plan of action. I was the first to arrive. I ordered a sinfully wonderful white hot chocolate with a touch of whipped cream and secured the table in the corner farthest from the front door so we would have some privacy. Linda arrived next. She ordered a small Chai tea and joined me. We were comparing notes from our assignments when a college-age barista came over to the table with a large vanilla latte and a plate stacked with several scones.

As we moved our notes to give her some room for the drink and food, she said, "Ian called to order ahead; he said he was running a little late." She gave a little giggle, "Actually, we encourage him to call ahead since his orders are usually large. He's one of our best customers!" Linda and I eyed the tray of scones, shook our heads, and returned to our conversation.

As the barista went back to her station behind the counter to wait on a customer, Ian walked in. He was looking happier than I had seen him in a while.

He tossed his forest green fleece parka on one of the two empty chairs and fell into the other one, saying, "Ahhh. My breakfast is here." Grabbing his first scone—blueberry—he asked, "Did everyone do their homework?"

We both nodded, and I said, "Let's start with each of us sharing who we think is the most likely suspect and why. Then we can concentrate on the mechanics of the sting." Linda and Ian agreed, and I indicated that Linda should go first.

"Well," Linda said. "I've given this a lot of thought over the last few days, and I think it is Melissa, our first grade teacher. This is her second year at the school. Before her new husband convinced her to move to Mammoth, she taught at a private girls' academy in the East Bay. I can't tell you how many times she came into my office during her first year complaining about all the materials and tools she couldn't buy because there was no budget for them. She was as reliable as the sun." Glancing out the window to discover it was snowing again, she amended, "More reliable."

Ian chimed in, "Could be. Doesn't Melissa's husband have an office and house cleaning business here in town? That would give both of them access to a lot of properties."

Ian went on. "My money is on your night janitor, Bob. He has access to the entire school anytime he wants it, and he has been a very vocal proponent of increasing taxes to supplement the schools' budgets. But, more importantly," he said, lowering his voice "I did a background on him, and he was arrested twice when he was in his early twenties for petty theft." Ian snatched a second scone—lemon poppy seed this time—and gave us a self-satisfying grin.

"Oh, Ian," I admonished. "Whoever is doing this is not stealing for personal gain. Besides, Bob must be in his mid-fifties now. And lots of people in town supported the tax increase—including me."

Squelching a chuckle, Linda asked, "Well, who do you think is our culprit, J?"

"The only team member who caught my interest is Jeanne, the sixth grade teacher," I said. "It's been a long time since her husband Hank died. Since his death the school, the students, even the community, have become her whole life. It seems whenever I see her at the market or the post office, she is putting up posters, asking the community to support yet another fundraiser she has organized to assist her class in a field trip or other unfunded endeavor." Feeling ashamed, I added, "Frankly, when I'm short on cash, I do my best to avoid her."

The discussion continued. All three of us were surprised and a bit dismayed that we had all targeted a different candidate. Since we had only a short time left before we had to go to the school for the team meeting, and understanding we were not going to agree on a suspect, we planned the team meeting agenda, and sketched out Friday's sting.

"I spoke with Fran yesterday and she knows exactly what to do in our meeting today," Ian pouted. "And she's keeping my office chair as compensation."

As we stood to leave, the Barista asked Ian if he wanted a bag for his scones. He thanked her and said he would only need a small bag—there was only one left.

The team meeting began promptly at eleven. Linda opened, "Aside from the fact that our situation is escalating, I called this emergency meeting because we have a new bureaucratic wrinkle. I received a call from the superintendent of the school district yesterday. She told me that unless we have 'resolved this situation', as she phrased it, by a week from Friday, she will send in an investigator from the school district."

Melissa, the first grade teacher, raised her hand, and asked, "How did she find out about it? The newspapers?"

Linda said, "Not really. I think she was vaguely aware of it through the media but hadn't paid much attention to it. No. It was the retired gentleman from whom the camcorders were stolen. He made her aware of the problem. Apparently, he has threatened to call his congressman and his senator if there is not an immediate resolution to the, and I quote, 'larcenous behavior taking place in our school.'"

There were some indignant murmurs from the teachers and students.

After giving everyone a moment to settle down, Linda announced, "So we have decided to set up a sting to flush out the culprit, and it is scheduled for tonight."

The room became electric with anticipation.

Ian outlined the plan. He explained that in a few hours the local sporting goods store was expecting a big shipment of spring sports equipment, including baseballs, bats, mitts, face masks, and other protective gear. Ian had already arranged for the owner of the store to leave the shipment in unopened boxes on the dock behind the store overnight.

"All the team has to do is to start a rumor that our baseball equipment is really old and in desperate need of replacement," he announced.

Trevor, one of the fifth graders, said just loud enough for everyone to hear, "That won't take much imagination. Our equipment is very old."

As some of the other students started to share their opinions of the age of the school's baseball equipment, Ian raised his hands to quiet everyone. He continued, "I will have police officers at the store, watching the boxes tonight. Since the boxes will only be accessible tonight, whoever has been stealing items for the school should make an appearance. Then we can clear up this situation once and for all."

Everyone started speaking at once: students wanting to be there when "it all went down," teachers wanting to know about the back-up plan if the culprits didn't show, and, someone asking if we really wanted to put an end to the stream of equipment and supplies coming into the school. While Ian attempted to respond to the questions and I tried to restore some semblance of order, Fran walked in with letters for Linda to sign.

Fran said to her, just loudly enough for the people sitting near Linda to hear, "Did you tell them? Is that what this fuss is all about?"

"Tell us what?" Jeanne, who was sitting next to Linda, asked.

Fran looked uncomfortably at Linda and leaned closer and whispered in her ear, "Sorry. I guess you decided not to." Now Fran and Linda had everyone's attention.

With an uncharacteristically sharp look at Fran and a heavy sigh, Linda announced to the curious group: "The owners of the new golf course in Crowley Lake have had to renege on their offer to pay for the new sprinkler system for the ball field."

A collective groan rang through the room.

Linda raised her hands to quiet everyone, "If you remember, they offered to order and pay for a new system for the school at the same time they ordered theirs, but the price they were quoted a year ago when they placed the order has increased by fifty percent. Now they can't afford to pay for ours."

"You mean we won't be able to use our ball field again, this year? Using the high school's ball field doesn't work. They are always practicing. They never let us on," whined Nolan, the sixth grader. And, once again, verbal chaos erupted.

Just as I shouted to Ian loud enough so he could hear me over the bedlam, "Are those pipes and valves and stuff sitting in the parking lot of the new golf course what everyone is upset about?" Linda raised her hands to silence the group. The sudden quiet made my question sound like I had blared it through a megaphone. All eyes turned and stared.

Before Ian could respond, Linda, exerting her authority, said, "I will try to find other funding to replace the ball field sprinkler system. Now, let's get back to the issue at hand. We have a sting to plan. Does everyone know what they are supposed to do?"

The group, some anxiously, some reluctantly, focused the discussion back on what to say as they spread the rumor about the new baseball equipment at the sporting goods store.

Wrapping up, Ian stood, attempted to look stern, and told all present, "I want to make it clear to everyone that your only job in our little operation is to start the rumor. I do not want to see anyone tonight when we are staking out the sporting goods store. You are civilians; you could be placing yourselves in danger. Leave tonight in the hands of police professionals. You will know the outcome soon enough."

As everyone got up to leave, Linda, Ian, and I remained seated. We all heard Trevor, one of the fifth graders, saying, "What good is a lot of new baseball equipment if we don't have our own ball field?" He and Kelsey were out the door before we could hear her response. We looked at one another and smiled.

Chapter 17

It was almost five o'clock by the time we completed the last-minute details for the evening's activities. I assumed I would find a note or voicemail from Ross when I got home, but I didn't. Instead of contemplating what that did or didn't mean, I readied myself for the night ahead.

One of my assigned tasks was to bring sandwiches and beverages for the three of us since we anticipated a long evening of waiting. This would have been easy, but Ian was one of the three so I made four smoked turkey sandwiches on whole wheat, four roast beef on sourdough, and four avocado, alfalfa sprouts, and tomato on sweet French bread. I packed them in a cooler with diet Cokes, blueberry Izzes, and bottled water. As an afterthought, I threw in my secret stash of Oreos.

I put on a charcoal gray turtleneck, black jeans, heavy Smart-Wool black socks, with a dark pair of running shoes. After toting the cooler downstairs, I donned a dark baseball cap, a heavy Eddie Bauer black ski jacket, a black flannel scarf and black gloves. It was 6:15 p.m.; I was supposed to meet Linda and Ian in the library parking lot at six thirty. That was when it hit me: I was a group facilitator, a human resources consultant. What in the world was I doing going on a stake out? Granted, how "bad" could someone be who stole from businesses to give to a school. But still.... Whoever was doing this was breaking the law. He would probably be angry when we caught him and even angrier when we stopped him.

Feeling my blood pressure rise, I told myself I was being stupid. Ian would never permit Linda and me to accompany him if he thought we would be in any danger. I packed the car and left for the library parking lot.

When I arrived at the library, Linda and Ian were waiting for me in Ian's SUV. Ian approached my car even before I had turned off the engine. As soon as I rolled down the window, he asked if I had remembered the food. Did he think of nothing else? I assured him I had, pointing to the cooler on the passenger seat next to me. He walked around to the passenger side, opened the door and took out the cooler, while I was exiting the car.

As we walked over to his vehicle, he turned and looked at me, and started laughing, laughing hard. Failing to understand what could be so funny, I just stared at him, secretly praying that he wouldn't laugh so hard he would drop the cooler. I had spent a lot of time making the sandwiches.

As we reached his car, he finally calmed down so I could ask, "What's so funny?"

"You," he chided. "You have seen too many cop shows on TV. I am surprised that you didn't black out your face."

To my utter humiliation, I had thought that Ian might have something to black out our faces! I could feel heat spread up my neck to my cheeks. As I was trying to think of some clever retort, I saw that Linda, who was also laughing, had on a white long-sleeved tee shirt, a pair of jeans and a red Patagonia jacket.

"Well..." I stammered defensively, "I thought we needed to make ourselves..." I trailed off, trying to think of a less humiliating response. Then attempting to assume a more assertive posture and project a little attitude, I said forcefully, "These were the only clean clothes I had in the house."

Ian helped me into the backseat of his car, treating me almost as gently as he did the cooler that he placed on the seat next to me.

He climbed into the driver's seat and said, "I have two men in a car outside the sporting goods shop. They will stay there until something happens or I call them off. On my way to meet you, I stopped by to review the plan with them." With a smile he said, "I saw two of the teachers, Jeanne and Melissa, across the street in a car, trying to look invisible. From what I could see, Janet, they were dressed just like you—all in black."

Linda broke in before I could respond to Ian's jab. "Well, if they are there to watch the sting, then our only remaining suspects are Bob, the night janitor, who called in sick this evening, and Lillian. And she was still at the office working on payroll when I left late this afternoon. Lillian takes her job as office manager quite seriously."

We drove ten miles south on Highway 395 to reach Crowley Lake. There was a full moon that permitted us to appreciate the vistas as we traveled down the highway. Linda and I couldn't help but comment on how a twelve hundred foot decrease in elevation could so quickly change the landscape from winter to spring.

As we arrived at the Crowley Lake Golf Course, I could only see snow on the highest peaks. Pulling into the parking lot, Ian pointed out another police car with two officers parked between two large loaders. Had Ian not indicated the other car's position, I would have never seen it among the idle construction equipment. As we passed them, he gave the officers a wave. Then he drove to the opposite side of the parking lot, backing in next to a large storage shed. The two cars were facing each other; almost equidistant between the cars were an orderly pile of PVC pipe and a large assortment of valves and sprinkler heads.

Ian turned off the headlights of his SUV and went over to check in with the two officers in the other car. I pulled two sandwiches and two bottles of water out of the cooler and handed them to him for his officers.

He paused. "How many sandwiches did you bring?"

With a don't-worry-you-will-have-enough-to-eat sigh, I responded, "Plenty."

He departed with the sandwiches and water. "I'll be right back."

Time crawled. We had exhausted all attempts at conversation by ten o'clock. By eleven Linda and I were taking turns dozing. Remarkably, Ian was alert and focused, even though he had already consumed four of the sandwiches and half of the Oreos. The only interruptions to the quiet occurred when Ian checked in with his officers at the sporting goods store or his officers across the parking lot. At 11:15 p.m., I heard him say quietly into his radio, "I see some movement." There was an affirmative response from the other officers. Then we heard a loud crash. Linda and I were alert now. Both Ian and the officers on the other side of the parking lot turned on their headlights, which shone directly onto the sprinkler equipment.

The light startled two bear cubs playfully pushing the pipes with their paws. After a moment the cubs' mother must have made some gesture or noise that her cubs understood because, as if on cue, they turned and followed her back into the trees. While Ian grumbled, I started to take deep regular breaths to slow my heartbeat down. Linda was doing the same thing.

As we settled down, the quiet returned. And so did the boredom.

About midnight, Ian said, "I think we should give it one more hour. If nothing happens by then, we should call it a night. The car thermometer indicates twenty-six degrees Fahrenheit and it's dropping."

The next hour passed even more slowly because the silence was now mixed with frustration. At 12:50 a.m., as we were resigning ourselves to a wasted evening and a failed strategy, we saw two vehicles in the distance driving up the road toward the golf course. As they came closer we could see that the vehicles were pickup trucks. When they pulled cautiously into the parking lot, I could feel the adrenaline pump through my body. I was awake. Linda was awake. Ian was talking quietly into his radio. The trucks stopped next to the pile of pipes. I heard Ian saying, "Not yet. Let's see what they do."

As we watched, people started pouring out of the truck beds, but the drivers remained in the trucks. Both Linda and I strained to see what was happening. It must have been the lack of light coupled with fatigue, but these people looked short, really short. Having been cautioned by Ian not to speak, even whisper, I kept my observation to myself.

Soon it was clear from the noise being made, the pipes were being lifted and put into the trucks. Ian said softly into his radio, "Now," and the headlights from both police vehicles were turned on. The two trucks and the fifteen or so people holding pipes, valves and sprinkler heads made a strange tableau. There were a few moments of eerie silence as everyone in the parking lot froze.

"Oh, my Lord. That's my fifth grade class," Linda gasped.

The next few hours were chaos. The culprits were indeed fourteen of the seventeen members of the fifth grade class led by Trevor and Kelsey. The drivers of the trucks were Kelsey and Trevor's older brothers—sixteen and seventeen years of age respectively. Initially, the police officers hadn't known what to do with all of the ten-and eleven-year-olds and the two teenagers. Linda suggested to Ian that the children all be taken back to the school auditorium, where parents could be called and decisions made on what to do next. Ian and one of the police officers drove the trucks to the school with the teenagers and some of the fifth graders. The remaining children were taken to the school in Ian's car, which Linda was driving, and in the second police car.

Trevor and Kelsey were in our car with three other fifth graders. As Trevor climbed into the car, I looked at him, still not believing what my eyes were telling me, "Why?" I asked.

Trevor gave me a goofy smile saying, "No one else wants to help the school so we decided we could take care of it ourselves."

Kelsey got into the car right behind Trevor, and gave him a jab in the ribs. "Be quiet," she shushed. On the drive back to the school I could only hear breathing and an occasional nervous giggle.

Linda phoned Bob, the night janitor, at home as soon as we reached the highway and she could pick up a cell signal. She asked him to go to the school and open the auditorium. Initially he protested, complaining that she woke him up and that he hadn't gone to work because he had been ill all evening. Ignoring his complaints, Linda briefly explained the circumstances. As soon as he understood, Bob assured Linda the auditorium would be open in fifteen minutes.

It was after two a.m. by the time we arrived at the school auditorium. Once Ian had all the children's names and home phone numbers, Linda and I began to phone their parents. The next few hours were consumed by dozens of angry parents, fourteen unrepentant fifth graders, two apprehensive teenagers, and lots of confused police officers. Because of the hour and the uniqueness of the situation, Ian decided to briefly speak with the parents of each child as he or she was released to their custody. He wanted the parents' assurance that their children would receive strict supervision while he came up with a proper course of action.

Trevor, Kelsey, their brothers, and parents were the last to leave the auditorium. Ian was still conferring with the other police officers as Linda and I looked at the big round clock on the wall and realized it was almost five a.m. Exhausted, we were both still wired. I was about to ask if she knew of anyplace that was open at this hour where we could get a cup of coffee and decompress, when Ryan, Trevor's father, returned to the auditorium.

Before I could ask him if he forgot something, he said, "Ms. Taylor? Ms. Westmore? Could I have a moment of your time?" Almost too tired to speak, both of us just nodded. "I know it's late—or I guess early—but we were wondering if you would come over to our café." Trevor's father owned Le Coquetier Café, which was one of the best coffee shops in town.

Before either Linda or I could respond, he continued, "Trevor and Kelsey are going to explain themselves. And, after all you have been through, we thought it only right that you should hear their story firsthand. Besides, my wife Sue is already preparing breakfast for all of us."

With the promise of hearing why and how the fifth grade class pulled off this string of escapades, as well as a good breakfast, Linda and I grabbed our coats and followed Ryan out of the auditorium.

Chapter 18

We asked Ryan if he would drive by the library on the way to the Café so we could pick up our cars. After he dropped us off, we went to our own cars without a word; it was apparent that we were both anxious to get some closure on the night and the ordeal. I followed Linda to the Café.

The "closed sign" was still on the door of Le Coquetier Café, but the door was unlocked. My mouth started watering the moment we entered the restaurant. The aromas of a coffee shop breakfast switched my priorities from curiosity to hunger. As I looked around for the source of the smells, I saw a petite, round, dark-haired woman in her late thirties working at a grill behind the counter.

"I'm so glad you came!" she exclaimed. "Do you mind locking the door behind you? We don't want any early customers to stumble their way into our little gathering."

Linda locked the door and took me over to meet the small, industrious woman who turned out to be Sue, Trevor's mother. Once introductions were made, Sue sent me to the back room with a cup of coffee in hand, while Linda stayed to help her serve breakfast.

In the back room a large table was set for ten. Seven were already seated, all deeply engrossed in conversation. As I walked in, Trevor stood and introduced me to his brother, Justin; Kelsey's parents, John and Julie; and Kelsey's brother,

Matt. In the course of the introductions, I learned that Trevor and Kelsey's families had been next-door neighbors and best friends since before the two of them were born.

When Trevor felt comfortable that I knew who everyone was, he took me to an empty chair at the table next to Kelsey, who stared worriedly at her lap. Then Trevor returned to his place at the table next to his father. Moments later Sue and Linda entered the room with trays of scrambled eggs, bacon, sausage, corned beef hash, fried potatoes, cups of fruit, and English muffins. Once the food was served, everyone fell silent as they devoured the food.

After about thirty minutes when most of the food had disappeared and we were starting to relax, Ryan looked at Trevor and said loudly enough to end individual conversations at the table, "Start at the beginning, and do NOT leave anything out."

I wasn't surprised when Trevor stood up to speak so everyone could hear him; I *was* surprised that he looked neither nervous nor apprehensive. He actually looked as if he were excited to share his story with everyone. This was in direct contrast to Kelsey, who looked as if she were going to be ill.

Trevor began. "Do you remember last fall when the Town Council gave us…" looking at me he said, "the fifth grade class…" then returning his attention to the full group, continued, "the award for organizing the most successful Town Clean Up Day Mammoth had ever had?"

People at the table nodded. Ryan gave Trevor a what-does-this-have-to-do-with-anything look and urged him to go on.

"Well, while we were waiting for our turn on the Town Council agenda, the council members were talking about trying to get voters to raise taxes to help pay for things at the school: things like computers, sports programs, and even raises for teachers. And people from the audience kept going up to the microphone and telling the Council that they didn't have kids so why should they have to pay extra for the school. Do you know what I'm talking about?"

As we all nodded, I started to understand.... As I glanced at Linda, I saw she did too. It was happening all over the country. States were slashing their budgets, including their school budgets. School districts, faced with increasing student populations and decreasing resources, were trying to find other sources of public funding to continue their programs. And this scenario had played out just a few months ago in Mammoth. Those citizens in favor of raising taxes argued that programs were being cut, children were being given inferior equipment, teachers were forgoing, once again, any kind of raise—which was exacerbating turnover, and class sizes were too large. Those against raising taxes for our schools argued that the economy was declining; many residents were struggling to make ends meet; our visitors/tourists numbers were down, impacting local businesses. Basically, it was a good cause but no one had the extra money to help. Despite the hour and the long night, the energy in the room was growing.

"So we figured if we could organize a clean-up day for the town, we should be able to do something to help our school—even if no one else wanted to," Trevor continued.

Kelsey left her chair and went to stand beside Trevor. She no longer looked worried; she looked proud. He turned, lightly touched her on the arm and smiled, "So Kelsey and I sent a note around to all of the kids in class to meet with us at the park one Saturday. Everyone came except for a couple of the kids. And they have to help with their families' businesses after school and on the weekends; so that was okay."

As Trevor spoke, the genius of the plan was revealed. The fifth graders figured since they couldn't get money for the school, they would get whatever supplies and equipment the school needed. During their first meeting they realized that almost anything the school needed, one of their parents or relatives had at home or in their businesses. And they didn't consider taking something from a parent or relative stealing. They had even developed a phone tree so if a student heard that the school needed a new fax machine, he would call the people on his list, who would call the people on their list, until someone was found who had access to a fax machine. Then the student with access to the fax machine would just take it at the first available opportunity and bring it to school with him. They also realized that because they weren't yet teenagers, no one ever paid much attention to them. So they could go in and out of the businesses and stores their families worked in without being noticed. Once in a store, they could locate the items they needed and leave a window unlocked for later pick-up.

As Trevor finished his presentation, I heard Linda say under her breath, "Brilliant. Simply brilliant." All of the adults in the room were awestruck.

Ryan broke the spell, saying to Trevor and Kelsey, "And just how did you convince your brothers to go along with your plan?"

Kelsey's brother Matt stood up before Trevor or Kelsey could respond and said indignantly, "They didn't have to convince us. We saw what was happening to the school and we didn't think it was fair. Justin and I even heard that the school might have to fire the football and baseball coaches because there was no money to pay them." Realizing he was shouting, he sat down, but not before Justin defiantly said, "Yeah!"

It was apparent that it was time for the two families to be alone. The four parents were already posturing themselves to have a stern discussion with Trevor, Kelsey, Matt, and Justin. I knew it would be difficult because it was also apparent by the hint of tears in their eyes that Ryan, Sue, John, and Julie were immensely proud of their children. I motioned to Linda, and we gathered our coats and purses, mouthed thank you to Sue and started to quietly leave.

As we reached the door, Trevor asked tentatively, "Ms. Taylor, what do you think the police are going to do?"

Linda turned and shook her head. "I'm not sure, Trevor. I can't condone what you did. But I have to tell you, after your story gets out, I am sure happy I am not in Police Chief Williams' shoes."

It was almost eight a.m. when I finally arrived home. I couldn't remember the last time I was this exhausted. I turned off both the landline and my cell phone, kicked off my shoes, stripped down to my panties, and got into bed. Sometime during the early afternoon, I briefly awoke to sounds of laughter and conversation coming from the house next door. The house was a second home owned by a couple from Phoenix. It sounded like they and their friends were returning to the house after a morning of spring skiing. I fumbled in the bedstand drawer, found some ear plugs, pulled the covers over my head, and returned to blissful, dreamless sleep.

It was dark when I finally climbed out of bed. The house was cold so I put on a pair of my heaviest sweats and furry UGG slippers and went to the kitchen to make some hot chocolate. As the milk was heating, I checked voice mail. There were calls from Steve, Joan, Dave Crossley, and a few from Ian, all of which could wait until tomorrow or Monday to be returned. There were no calls from Ross.

I finished making my hot chocolate, built a fire, grabbed the remote and sat in my favorite oversized wingback chair to watch a movie on TV. It was a mindless pleasure I hadn't availed myself of in a long time. Scrolling through the guide, I found only two old movies that interested me: *Meet Joe Black* with Brad Pitt and Anthony Hopkins and *De-Lovely*—the story of Cole Porter—with Kevin Kline and Ashley Judd. I selected *De-Lovely*. I wrapped myself in Mary's afghan, nestled into the chair, and turned on the movie.

About five minutes into the movie, the channel suddenly changed to *How It's Made* on the Discovery Channel. The narrator was explaining how small single-engine aircraft are constructed. Realizing I must have unconsciously hit the remote and changed the channel, I punched the "last" button on the remote. Nothing happened. So I punched in the numbers for the Channel that *De-Lovely* was on, and still nothing happened. I turned off the TV and turned it back on— it was still on *How It's Made*. Irritated now, I untangled myself from the afghan and climbed out of the chair, almost spilling my hot chocolate in the process. I went downstairs to the guest room where the other TV in the house was located. I turned on the TV to find the *How It's Made* narrator explaining the benefits of turbochargers used in some single-engine planes. No matter how many times I tried to change the channel, the program remained the same.

I went back up to the living room and called Julia, my only full-time neighbor. From the noise in the background, it sounded like I was interrupting a dinner party. I apologized profusely and asked if she would mind turning on her TV and telling me what program was on. There was a long pause on the other end of the line; then Julia asked if I was all right. I assured her I was fine. I was just having problems with my TV. She told me to wait a moment and put down the phone.

After a couple of minutes she returned to the phone and told me a basketball game was on. I asked her if she could change the channel. She let out a long sigh and asked me to wait again. As she put the phone down, I could hear her mumble something to her guests, and the laughter that followed. I didn't care. When she returned, she told me she could change the channel to any program she wanted and "was there anything else?" In the middle of my second apology, I heard the dial tone.

By then my hot chocolate was cold, the fire was dying, and the *How It's Made* narrator was wrapping up his presentation with comments about the safety of the single-engine plane. "According to the U.S. Air Safety Foundation, when an engine failure leads to an incident—that is, some damage or injuries—it has a ten percent chance of causing fatalities in a single-engine aircraft, but a fifty percent chance in a twin. This higher percentage of fatalities in a twin is likely because they are designed for higher speed and higher performance, generally compromising low speed handling while increasing stall speed." As the narrator concluded his remarks, the TV abruptly returned to *De-Lovely*.

The rest of the night I fretted over my stupidity. How obtuse could one person be? I should have learned by now that when something "unusual" happened, it was Mary and Bob sending me a message. What were they trying to tell me about the plane? Was there some construction flaw that needed to be uncovered? Is that why the plane went down? Why they died? Or was it something else? As always, my first inclination was to call Ross and see what he thought. But then I remembered—he thought I was crazy. If he thought I was still having "visits," he would probably send a psychiatrist over, instead of a nurse. No. This was something I was going to have to figure out on my own.

I logged onto the Internet, typing in "Discovery Channel>How It's Made." I went through all of the listed video clips but couldn't find one on single-engine aircraft. Then I typed in "single-engine aircraft" into the search engine. While I learned a lot about planes—and read a lot more that I didn't understand—nothing jumped out at me. Periodically, in between searches, I asked Mary and Bob out loud to be a little clearer ... be more precise ... if they were sending me a message. But I was met with silence. Feeling like Ross could be right—I might be crazy—I gave up around two-thirty and went to bed. My sleep was troubled. My dreams were a collage of Mary, Bob, Ross, planes falling from the sky, small rooms with no doorknobs, and an utter feeling of helplessness.

Chapter 19

The next week was intense. By Monday morning the local TV news station had broken the story about the fifth graders and their "unorthodox efforts to help their school." Locals squared off against one another, either believing the children had the hearts of community heroes or little hoodlums. On Wednesday, just as the story hit the state newspapers, Linda phoned and asked if I wanted to sit in on a meeting with Ian, the District Attorney, the heads of the Chamber of Commerce, Tourism and Recreation, the PTA, and her.

"I know this is no longer something you are officially involved in, but we could really use your objectivity. Will you come?" I agreed to be at their one o'clock meeting.

I had about two hours before leaving for the meeting. That would give me just enough time to shower and change both my clothes and my frame of mind. I had spent the last few days trying to figure out what Mary and Bob had been trying to tell me with the documentary on single-engine planes.

After an exhaustive Internet search over the weekend, I had decided to start the week employing a more direct strategy of talking to people on the phone. On Monday I phoned the Discovery Channel and spoke with a gracious and seemingly informed woman from their *How It's Made* team. When I asked if the segment on single-engine planes was trying to expose some flaw in the construction of those planes, she said no and explained that the show simply reviewed how a single-engine plane is made. I kept pushing, telling her that there must have been more to the story. About the time I started raising my voice, trying to get her to hear what I was asking, her demeanor changed and she started to speak to me as if I were a child. When I bellowed that I had recently been in a single-engine airplane crash and I knew there was a message about it in the story, she hung up. I couldn't blame her. I was out of control, but I couldn't stop myself.

After the humiliating phone call to the Discovery Channel, I spent some more time on the Internet narrowing my search to the track record of the Cessna Turbo Skylane. I couldn't find anything.

Next I phoned Kevin Anderson, the investigator from the National Transportation Safety Board, whom I had met at Mary's house. When I couldn't reach him at his office, I tried the cell number on the back of his card. I asked if his investigation had uncovered something wrong with the plane. He said no but it was far too early in the investigation process to know anything substantive. Then he queried, "Why do you ask?" I told him not to worry; I just had been having some bad dreams. He assured me that nightmares were common after a crash, and told me to take care. He concluded by saying he would let me know if he learned anything, but not to expect a call in the near future.

As a last resort, I phoned Bob's airplane mechanic, George. I had never met him, but I knew he and Bob had known one another for a long time—they shared a passion for small aircraft and fast cars.

He answered on the first ring, barking, "This is George. Speak."

Before I could think twice about having made the call, I said hello. I must have been talking quite softly, because he said, "Speak up. I can't hear you."

More forcefully I said, "Hello. George, my name is Janet Westmore. We have never met. You were friends with my twin sister Mary, and brother-in-law Bob. And I believe you were Bob's airplane mechanic." Tears started to fill my eyes. I suddenly became mute with grief.

After an awkward pause, George said in a rush as if he were trying to fill up the empty air, "God. You sound just like Mary. Has anyone ever told you that? Of course they have… J. May I call you 'J'? That's what Mary and Bob always called you. They said you didn't like being called Janet. Sorry. I'm … I'm just not sure what to say. Nothing has been the same around here since … since the accident. I'm really sorry, J, really sorry." George's voice had softened noticeably.

We spoke about Mary and Bob for a few minutes. "I figured you would be calling sooner or later. It's about the Mosler, right?"

"The Mosler," I responded tentatively, not understanding. "Oh, you mean Bob's car? No. That's not why I'm calling, but *what about* the Mosler?"

A little taken aback, George answered, "Well, it's here. Here in the hangar. I figured you were looking for it. Since Bob's hangar lease is paid through the end of the year, and I read that you were hurt in the accident, I just thought I would keep it here until you phoned." I had spent an entire weekend at Mary's house, and I hadn't given a thought to where either of the cars was. I was going to have to add the disposition of the cars to my list of things to discuss with Nathan when I next met with him.

Not wanting to get sidetracked discussing the Mosler, I suggested, "If the hangar lease has been paid through the end of the year, then I suppose we should just leave the Mosler there for the time being—if it's no trouble."

I heard George let out a little sigh. "Actually, that's great. I like having the car here. It's like having a bit of Bob around. I don't know if Bob ever told you, but I have not only been his airplane mechanic, I have done the work on all his sports cars."

"Good," I said. "That's settled. Actually, what I was calling about is the plane. George, do you know any mechanical reason the plane could have gone down?"

I could hear George stiffen and his voice grow cold. "That plane was in top shape. I would never have let it go up otherwise."

"Oh, no, George," I almost shouted. "I didn't mean to imply that I thought the plane wasn't in top mechanical shape. I'm sorry. What I am asking is—well, have other planes the same make and model as Bob's crashed due to flawed design or recalled parts or something like that?"

The edge left George's voice and was replaced by concern. "J, I have been on the Internet ever since the crash, looking for an answer to the same question. It's a good plane. I can't find any evidence to the contrary. The accident still doesn't make sense to me. Bob was one of the most obsessively careful pilots I've ever flown with. And the plane was in excellent condition. There is no reason it should have crashed."

We both fell quiet, faced with a conundrum we couldn't solve.

"Thank you, George. I'll call when I know what I am going to do with the Mosler." I gave him my cell number and started to ring off when I thought to ask, "We are having a memorial service..."

"I know. I'll be there. Kate made sure I was sent an invitation. I hope that's okay with you."

Grateful and making a mental note to call Kate to see how she was doing, I said, "I'm so glad she did. I look forward to meeting you in person."

The meeting was being held in the conference room of the newly built Mammoth library. As I entered the room, I recognized the President of the PTA standing with Ian in quiet conversation next to a table of refreshments. Where else would one expect to find Ian! The Director of Tourism and Recreation was speaking in low tones with the President of the Chamber of Commerce, and Linda, accompanied by a member of the unified school district, was trying to mediate an animated discussion between the district attorney and Trevor's father Ryan. The latter, I was sure, was not an invited guest. Linda caught my eye, giving me the universal look for "help me." As I walked over, my suspicions were confirmed when I heard Linda say gently, "Ryan, you really have to leave now. We need to start the meeting."

Just as Ryan started to object, I reached the group, nodded at Linda, then took Ryan by the arm and said, "Do you have a minute?" leading him out of the conference room and into the library's entryway.

He protested that he had every right to be in the meeting, since they would be talking about his sons. I explained to him why this wasn't a meeting for the parents, and after some discussion he begrudgingly departed for his car. I didn't return to the room until I saw him drive out of the parking lot.

The meeting was difficult. Trevor, Kelsey, and their parents had held their own news conference with the local TV and newspapers on Sunday, basically telling the same story that they had shared with Linda and me Saturday morning at the Café. Ian had been particularly angered by their breach of protocol with the media, thinking he had made it clear to each of the families not to speak with the press until matters could be resolved. Now, not only had the state media picked up on the story, but rumors were also floating around that the national media, including morning news shows and daytime talk shows, had contacted many of the fifth graders for interviews.

Locally there were already three schools of thought: Either the kids should be treated like heroes; publicly punished for breaking the law; or quietly and privately disciplined. The participants in this meeting were not immune to the debate. The representatives from the Chamber of Commerce and Tourism and Recreation thought no punitive action should be taken against the children since they hadn't hurt anyone and the children were becoming national folk heroes, giving the town some sorely needed publicity. Ian and the DA wanted the children prosecuted, believing they had deliberately broken the law, and the two men were currently researching what charges could be filed. Apparently, they had reached a bit of a legal obstacle when all of the "victims" dropped their charges. The PTA and the school district thought that the children should be disciplined within the context of the school and their families.

Linda explained to all that the purpose of this meeting was to develop and obtain general consensus of the meeting's participants on a recommendation, detailing what action should be taken, for the presiding Superior Court judge—who happened to be up for reelection this year.

After three hours of squabbling, the group finally reached consensus. They would recommend:

1. The Court should *informally* meet with the children—with no formal charges being filed—to ensure that the children understood the gravity of their actions.
2. The children should be given a yet-to-be-determined amount of community service hours to be performed over the summer. The community service hours should be with the school, the police department, or the victimized businesses.
3. Each child should write an essay explaining why what they did was wrong. These essays should be reviewed by a panel chosen from those at the meeting to ensure that the writing of the essays was taken seriously.
4. All requests for interviews by the media or press should be directed to Linda for response.
5. One of the approved essays would be sent as an official response to requests from the media for interviews.
6. No child or his or her family may give an interview to the media.
7. And, finally, once the recommendation is approved by the Court, it would be published in the local newspaper with the signatures of all in the room.

It was a grueling meeting, at times acrimonious, but as we walked out of the library conference room, it was apparent that all thought we had come to a fair and equitable recommendation.

Linda walked me to my car and said, "I think we would still be in there arguing if you hadn't come, J. Thanks."

As I drove off, I felt like this was one evening I had truly earned a martini.

Chapter 20

As I drove the short distance from the library to my house, I decided to call Kate to see how she was doing. When Mary and I lost *our* mother, we had each other to share our grief. Kate was alone. She was an only child, and had no partner with whom she could share her sorrow.

Rummaging in my downstairs home office to find Kate's number, I was startled when the phone rang. It was Ian. He got right to the point.

"I just wanted to call and say thanks, J. At first I didn't understand why Linda wanted to bring you in, but you did a good job for us."

I was flattered that he would call. "That means a lot coming from you. Thanks, Ian." As I waited to see if he had anything more to say, I heard what sounded like a bite from an apple.

"Just wanted you to know," he said with his mouth full. Had this man ever gone for more than twenty minutes without eating?

I found Kate's cell number and punched it into my portable phone. It rang while I walked upstairs.

She answered breathlessly, "Hello. This is Kate."

"Hi, Kate, this is J. Did I catch you at a bad time?"

"No, not at all. I was going through my mother's desk, trying to see what needed to be saved and what should be tossed. I figured I had to start somewhere."

"Are you still staying at Joan's?"

"No. Joan had to go out of town to attend a conference so I moved back to Mother's this morning. You know, J, I grew up in this house, and I never realized how big it was until this morning…" she trailed off with a soft sigh.

"Kate, are you all right?"

"I will manage. I'm just a little lonely, I guess. But thank you for asking." We both fell silent for a moment.

"Would you like some company? I just finished my last assignment up here, and I have no more distractions to keep me from feeling sorry for myself. How about if I drive out tomorrow and help you with your mother's things? We could keep each other company."

There was another pause in the conversation. Perhaps I had gone too far. After all, I really didn't even know Kate. Our only real bonds were Mary and loss.

"I'm sorry. You probably want to be alone. I guess it was a pretty dumb idea…"

"You would do that for me?" said an emotional Kate. "You don't really know me, but you are willing to drive here from Mammoth and help me? I can't believe it. Please come. You would be saving my sanity."

"I will leave tomorrow morning. When we finish packing your mother's belongings, I will go to Mary and Bob's and sort through theirs."

That's when Kate said, "And, if you would let me, I will help you!"

"Great," I exclaimed. "Neither of us will have to go through memories alone. First, we can stay at your mother's house, and then at Mary and Bob's. See you tomorrow evening."

Just as I placed the phone back into its charger, it rang. Thinking that it might be Ross I answered in my sanest, cheeriest voice. "Hello?"

"Steve here," was the reply from Mary's neighbor. "I thought I would check in and see when you are coming back to Portola Valley and invite you to have dinner with Carole and me."

I was about to tell Steve that I would be arriving in his general vicinity tomorrow but decided to hold back. I was going there to help Kate, not have dinner with this neighbor. Besides, I expected that he would want to know if I had made the decision to sell the house, and I wasn't ready to consider it yet. "I'll probably drive to Mary's the day before the memorial, that's in a little more than a week. Then I'll stay for a while after."

"Great," Steve said, sounding a little deflated. "Plan on having dinner with us the night you arrive. I found this great new restaurant...."

I interrupted, "I'd love to have dinner with you and Carole while I'm at Mary's, but not that first night. I am never quite sure what time I will arrive—especially with the volatile spring weather on both sides of the Sierra. We can schedule a date after I arrive." I quickly added, "Thanks for all of your concern, Steve. I will see you at the memorial," and hung up before he could respond. He seemed nice; so why did all of his apparent thoughtfulness and attention make me so uptight?

I sat down at the dining room table and stared out the window without seeing. So much had happened in the span of a few months. My life didn't feel like my life anymore. Mary and Bob had perished in a plane crash, parts of my body had been broken, one of the most respected employers in the region was found guilty of sexual harassment and had a wife who wanted to kill me, the town's fifth grade class planned and executed a scheme of robbing from businesses to give to the school, Mary and Bob were trying to send me a message I was too dense to understand, and Ross and I were estranged because he thought I needed psychiatric care. I was overwhelmed. It was time to get some help.

I went to my computer, and emailed my friends Denise and Karen. On the subject line I typed, Book Club — 6:30. Then I went into my bedroom to change.

Several years ago, when we all three had live-in boyfriends or husbands, Denise, Karen, and I had come up with this code. "Book Club" meant "Help! I need a night out," "6:30" indicated the time, and the place was always the Restaurant at Convict Lake. Denise and I lived in Mammoth; Karen lived in Swall Meadows, about thirty miles south of Mammoth; and the Convict Lake Restaurant was about halfway between the two communities. Any of us could invoke the code for any reason, and all three of us would show up. No excuses. No questions. Over the years the code had been used sparingly, but always for good reason. Tonight I needed my friends. I needed to tell people who cared that I no longer recognized my life.

I arrived exactly at six thirty and was led to a table in the back of the restaurant where Denise, Karen, and an Absolut martini with two olives were waiting for me. As I sat down, no one said a word. I held up the martini, Denise raised her Lemon Drop, and Karen her Cosmopolitan. We had a silent toast, and I began. I started with my first memories at the hospital and didn't stop until I told them about my last conversation with Steve. I left nothing out. As I talked, more drinks arrived and dinner was served, all without ordering. Denise and Karen had taken care of our orders before I arrived. Throughout my monologue, my friends sat with rapt attention. The only sounds they made were an occasional "Oh" or "Hmmm." Nothing else.

When I finally finished, they asked a few questions. Karen asked, "What can we do for you?"

"Help me think it through."

And they did. We gave no attention to the sexual harassment assignment and only a little to the fifth graders' school caper. Mainly we focused on Mary and Bob, and of course, Ross. They never questioned whether the visits were real—though they admitted their husbands would probably not believe them if they claimed to have visits from lost loved ones. They focused most of their attention on *why* Mary and Bob were still here. It was after eleven when Mike, the owner of the restaurant, told us he needed to close up. As I walked out with my friends, I felt blessed, immensely stronger, and better prepared to face whatever the next several weeks had in store for me. I treasured these ladies. We gave each other hugs and assurances that we would always be here for one another.

I arrived home at the stroke of midnight. As I marched up the stairs to my bedroom, I realized I had consumed way too much alcohol. I went to brush my teeth, wishing Mary was here. Whenever we imbibed more than we should have, she gave me a mysterious concoction of vitamins and aspirin and make me take them with a glass of sparkling water. She always swore that if I took them, I wouldn't have a hangover. And she was *always* right. Although I had asked her many times, Mary refused to give me the hangover recipe, saying she liked to have me depend on her. This night I was painfully aware I should have insisted.

Resigned to a night of fitful sleep and a morning headache, I turned off the bathroom light and climbed into bed. On a small tray on the bedstand were a glass, a bottle of Perrier, and a concoction of vitamins and aspirin. I smiled, took the pills, drank all the water, and went to sleep feeling loved.

Chapter 21

Mary's concoction worked once again. I awoke early the next morning alert and ready to drive to Kate's—without any hint of a hangover. It didn't take much time to pack. The only essential outfit I needed for the trip was the clothes I would wear to Mary and Bob's memorial. I chose a beautiful Tahari suit dress and scarf in shades of forest green and dark gold with complementary Via Spiga heels. Mary's personal shopper found the outfit for me a month before Mary died. It was supposed to impress my high-end clients, but now it was fated to have its inaugural showing at an event to commemorate Mary and Bob's lives. The rest of the clothes I packed were predominantly sweats, jeans, pants, turtlenecks, and running clothes in all of my favorite shades—black, bone, brown, and grey. I knew that if an unexpected occasion came up and I needed a more sophisticated or colorful outfit, I could wear something of Mary's.

The trip was beautiful. Once again, I was awestruck by the grandeur of the Eastern Sierra and the contrasting lushness of the western side of the mountains. Mary and I always argued which was more spectacular.

When I was less than an hour away from Kate's mother's home, my cell rang. I didn't recognize the number but it was a 650 area code, the same as Kate's, so I answered. I was surprised to hear George's voice.

"J?" he asked hesitantly. "This is George ... Bob's mechanic." Not stopping to see if I recognized him he continued, "Where are you?"

Responding without questioning—unusual for me—I said, "George? I'm on the 80, just heading into San Francisco. Why? Is something wrong?"

"Well, sort of," he said. "You haven't arrived at Kate's yet?" Before I could answer his voice took on a more serious tenor, "I just left Kate's. I have been taking care of her mother's cars for years, and Kate asked me if I could sell them for her. So I went to her home to pick one of them up." He paused and somehow I knew he was trying to find the right words to explain himself. After a moment he tentatively continued, "She ... she said you are on your way to her house to help her sort through her mother's things. I know you are in the middle of your own grief..." He paused.

"Don't worry about me. I'm all right. What's wrong?"

In a rush he responded, "I'm worried about Kate."

George went on to tell me that when he arrived, he found Kate going through her mother's desk drawers crying. He said she was disheveled—which was particularly unusual for her, and looked like she hadn't been eating.

"When I asked if she wanted me to help her, she said that you were on your way. J, I hope it's all right that I called. I've known Kate and her mother since Kate was a teenager. She has always been so composed—such a lady—but I'm afraid that she is losing it. I thought you needed to know what was happening before you arrived."

I thanked George, told him that I thought I might have an idea for helping Kate, and that I would call in the next few days and let him know how things were going. George was almost effusive in his thanks. Before arriving at Kate's, I needed to make a few extra stops.

Fortunately I had left Mammoth early so I arrived at the Pacific Heights address Kate had given me only half an hour later than promised. I stopped my car in front of a tall wrought iron gate at the end of the driveway of a beautiful, old Edwardian mansion. While I had expected a *nice* neighborhood, I wasn't prepared for what I found. My San Francisco experience had been limited to shopping in Union Square and working with clients south of Market. My Pacific Heights experience had been the Hotel Majestic, a hundred-year-old boutique hotel where Laura Ashley meets Old San Francisco. But I had never seen a neighborhood in the City quite like this one. The homes were large, old and elegant. In a city with the population density of San Francisco, I guess I thought any homes this size must house multiple family units.

I pushed the intercom button and the gate immediately opened. Kate greeted me and motioned for me to park in the garage next to her silver Audi TT. As I climbed out of the car, I got my first good look at Kate. Clad in dark rose-colored sweat pants and a white long-sleeved tee shirt, her tall beautiful frame looked like it had shrunk. She was quite pale, had dark circles under her eyes, and her thick, short hair appeared to be hand combed. She looked like she hadn't slept in days. For a few moments neither of us could think of anything to say.

Kate broke the awkward silence, "I know. I look terrible. But you, J, you look wonderful. I am so happy you came." She put her arms around me and started to cry. I silently held her. We stood that way for a minute or two. Her body started to tense as her tears subsided.

She pulled away, and said in a small, defeated voice, "I'm sorry. I just can't seem to quit crying." Drying her eyes on the back of her sleeve, she said, "Let's get your things and bring them into the house."

"My clothes can wait," I said pulling out five grocery bags from Mollie Stone's Market. "But these can't. Where's the kitchen?" Then we entered one of the most striking foyers I had ever seen, resplendent with at least three dozen long-stemmed white and peach roses in a crystal vase on a beautiful table in the center of the foyer. As I followed Kate through the entry and into a maze of halls, I caught glimpses of a library, a formal parlor, and what looked like a ballroom. Despite the fact that they were only quick glances, each room looked feminine and elegant with a wonderful mixture of antiques and contemporary furniture. I could hardly wait to get a tour of the house.

Finally arriving in a reasonably sized kitchen, I told Kate to sit down at the large oak table and I would show her what I brought. As she protested that there was plenty of food in the house, I unpacked the first three bags, placing before Kate two bottles of 2002 Merryvale Profile red wine and containers of Maryland-style mini crab cakes, Thai peanut chicken satay skewers, Spanakopita (a heavenly mixture of spinach and feta cheese wrapped in phyllo dough), Caesar salad, vegetable lasagna for two, and an assortment of brownies and cookies—all chocolate.

"What are we going to do with all of this?" Kate asked incredulously.

"Eat it," I promptly responded. "Then you are going to give me a tour of the house!"

And despite Kate's initial objections, I opened the wine and containers while she got plates and forks. We started with a toast to Kate's mother Dorothy, and to Mary and Bob. While we ate I told Kate stories about Mary from our childhood. As I did, she visibly began to relax and color started to return to her cheeks. Pretty soon she started telling me stories from her own childhood. I learned that this house was originally built in the

1880s and had been in Kate's family for three generations. Her mother had restored and redecorated it soon after Kate left for college. She had considered the renovation her life's second greatest achievement after her daughter.

When we had consumed our fill, we closed the containers and placed them in the refrigerator. That's when I asked why such a big house had a normal-sized kitchen. She laughed and told me that this was really the family kitchen. She would show me the real kitchen when she gave me the tour.

"What's in the other bags?"

"Breakfast."

As we walked with our refilled glasses of wine toward the foyer where Kate thought a proper tour should begin, she said wistfully, "I'm going to miss this house."

Not understanding, I asked, "I thought it was yours? You aren't going to sell it, are you?"

"Not sell it exactly," she said slowly. "When mother was diagnosed the second time with breast cancer, she asked me if I would mind her donating the house upon her death to the Susan G. Komen for the Cure organization. They are one of the leading foundations in breast cancer treatment research and education. It was a wonderful idea. Then about three weeks before she died..." Kate said, staring off into space, her voice becoming hoarse, "She asked if I was having any second thoughts about bequeathing the house. I assured her I had not changed my mind." Unconsciously assuming her normal upright posture and looking directly into my eyes until she held my gaze, she added proudly, "And, J, I do think it is a noble way to honor a noble lady."

Overwhelmed by both women's commitment, I returned her gaze and said, "I do, too." We stood there a moment, our eyes and thoughts locked, then without a word, simultaneously turned to continue our journey to the foyer.

Kate guided me through the parlor, the library, the ballroom—an actual ballroom with three magnificent chandeliers—six bedrooms, four full bathrooms, three half baths, a greenhouse full of orchids, a formal dining room, the real kitchen, and rooms I don't even have names for. As she showed me the garden at the rear of the house, she pointed to a separate house near the four-car garage, which was larger than my home in Mammoth, and explained that it held the butler's and maid's quarters.

Throughout the tour Kate seemed nostalgic, proud, wistful, and like she was saying goodbye to a beloved childhood friend. When I asked if she were really ready to part with this magnificent home, she said, "It's time for me to strike out on my own." Slowly turning to look directly at me she asked, "Do you know what I mean?"

"Yes," I responded softly. "I'm sad to say I know exactly what you mean."

Chapter 22

Early the next morning I awoke eager to get us organized. I went out to my car—which also serves as my mobile office—and collected some organizing provisions off the floor in front of the passenger seat. Returning to the family kitchen with Post-its, marker pens, and poster paper, I found Kate arranging the breakfast I had brought with me the night before on a beautiful Wedgwood platter. The food looked sumptuous—sliced smoked salmon, bagels, cream cheese, red onion, capers, and melon—a perfect meal to prepare us for the day ahead. However, when Kate saw me armed with all my supplies, she looked overwhelmed and ready to retreat back to her bed.

The night before, over our second bottle of wine, Kate admitted she was anxious to complete the packing process and turn the property over to the Foundation. Voicing her fear that the task was too daunting and could never be finished, she confided, "Every time I pick something up, it brings back a flood of memories. J, I will never finish. I have been working on my mother's desk for three days and have barely made a dent. And, I promised the Komen Foundation officer that I would vacate the house by the middle of next month."

"Here's what we are going to do," I announced cheerfully, as I poured myself a glass of freshly squeezed grapefruit juice. "This morning we are going to write room summaries and post them on the door of each room; this afternoon we will tag furniture. That should get us started!" I explained that room summaries—a concept I had made up that morning while brushing my teeth, although I didn't tell Kate—were brief descriptions of what we thought would be in the room, with notations for what should be saved, remain, given away, or sent to Goodwill.

"Tagging furniture with these colored Post-its follows the same concept," I told Kate. "Blue means you want to keep the piece; yellow you want to give it to someone; pink means that we will leave it for the Foundation, and white means you haven't made up your mind yet."

Whether it was my enthusiasm or the fact that at least we had a plan, Kate perked up. Over the next few days we were able to assign, pack, or gift most of the contents of the house, with the exception of Kate's mother's room. We decided we would leave Dorothy's room for last since it was sure to have the most emotional landmines.

On the second day I phoned George to let him know how Kate was doing. He seemed relieved to know that she was all right and asked if there was anything he could do for us. I told him I couldn't think of anything, but would call if something came up.

As I was finishing my call, Kate entered the room and asked, "Was that George you were speaking to?" I told her it was. She smiled. "He's such a dear. You know for years I have thought he had a crush on my mother. When she became ill, he was over here almost every day, asking what he could do for her." She looked out the window of the library where we had been working and said softly, "Her death was very difficult for him."

"You asked George to sell your mother's cars for you?"

She gave a soft chortle, "Is that what he told you?" Without waiting for a response she continued. "Actually, I tried to give him the cars, but he wouldn't take them. If mother had owned a Mosler like Bob's, he would have accepted, but a Cadillac and a Range Rover were of no interest to him." Shaking her head, she smiled to herself and we went back to work.

Kate and I worked easily together. Ignoring conventional time, we worked until we got tired or hungry. It was as if we had known each other for years. As we labored side by side, we occasionally paused in our activities when Kate wanted to tell me the story of a particular object or piece of furniture or I had a question about something I had found. Sometimes we worked in silence with some music playing on Dorothy's stereo; other times we chatted about ourselves, Dorothy, or Mary and Bob.

Packing a box with historical novels, I lamented, "I wish I had met your mother, Kate. Being in her home, listening to stories about her, I get a sense of her. But, it's not like knowing her."

"I wish you had too. She always had a special fondness for Mary. I think she would have felt the same about you."

The stories and the rhythm of our work were comforting—helping us both cope with our emotions as well as the size of the task.

At breakfast on the fifth morning we were unusually subdued. Our daily chatter became "Good Morning" and "Please pass the salt." It was time to tackle Dorothy's room, and it seemed both of us were mentally preparing ourselves for an emotionally difficult day. Suddenly the front doorbell rang, startling both of us out of our reveries.

As Kate went to answer the door, I realized that for the past five days there had been no visitors, no deliveries, and no interruptions of any sort. We had been living in our own universe apart from the world outside. I also realized that I was a little resentful of whoever was breaking the spell.

A much more energetic and cheery Kate returned moments later followed by Nathan. Before I could comment about her change of mood, she poured Nathan a cup of coffee.

"J, isn't this lovely? Nathan stopped by to see how I was doing."

Nathan sat down at the kitchen table, looking slightly abashed, put cream and two sugar cubes into his coffee and took a sip. Giving me a feeble smile he said, "I didn't know you were here, J. I just thought I would stop by and make sure Kate was all right." He straightened, looking surer of himself, and said, "But I am glad you are. In my car I have some papers for your signature I was going to send you today. If you don't mind, I'll go and get them so I can review them with you." He rose from his chair and left the room with, "I'll be right back."

As soon as the door was shut, I turned to Kate and whispered, "You *like* him?"

Turning crimson, she looked down at her feet, saw her pink bunny slippers and whisper-shouted, "I've got to change. I'll be right back." Then she rushed off.

Twenty minutes later while Nathan was finishing up his explanation of the status of Mary and Bob's estate, a new Kate returned. Gone were the sweats and slippers of the last five days. She was now sporting a Joan Vass long sleeved top that was the same color as her hazel eyes, cream-colored cropped pants and sandals. Her hair was combed, and she had on a touch of make-up. She was beautiful. When Nathan looked up and saw her, his mouth actually hung open for a moment. As quickly as I could, I took my leave, murmuring something about needing to make some calls, but I don't think either of them noticed my departure.

As I made my way up the stairs to the guest suite, I reflected once again on how much I missed talking to Ross. Every evening before I went to bed, I checked the voice mail on my cell—every evening I was disappointed. Should I call him? What would I say? How could we continue to be together if he thought grief was making me crazy, making me hallucinate? As much as I loved him, I wasn't going to go to a therapist just to make him happy. It was the same logic loop I went through every evening—always ending with the realization that if he didn't believe me, we couldn't go forward together, and I didn't know if I could make that journey without him. Feeling conflicted and alone, I lay down on my bed, pulled a rose and sage colored quilt over myself, and drifted to sleep.

Kate gently shook me awake about an hour and a half later. Even though I was still half asleep, I could sense a new energy in her that hadn't been there a few hours ago when we were having breakfast.

"Why didn't you tell me you liked Nathan?"

Color rose in her cheeks as she turned her face away from me, saying softly, "I never told anyone. Nathan has never treated me like anything but Mary's assistant, so there was no point."

Getting up from the bed and folding the quilt, I said, "Well, that's changed. When you returned to the kitchen after going upstairs to put on more presentable clothes, his mouth actually fell open!" I paused and watched her color grow into an even deeper shade of red. "What did the two of you talk about after I left?"

At his request she had given him a tour of the house, and they ended up spending most of their time in the greenhouse, talking about the orchids. "I told him how mother and I used to spend hours with the orchids. I assumed he would look at those plants that are blooming and be ready to move on. Most people do. J, as he walked around and looked at the plants, I could hear him naming them under his breath 'ah, a zygopetalum', 'very nice, some militinopsis'—and most of the plants he identified weren't blooming. It seems that his twin brother used to raise orchids commercially. We spent most of our time in the greenhouse talking about the plants and his twin until we were interrupted by a phone call from the Komen Foundation."

Kate took a deep, long breath before she continued. As she blew out the air she said a little nervously, "I know I have asked a great deal of you over the past several days, but…"

She took another deep breath then blurted out in a rush, "I need to attend a press conference and formal reception at the Foundation tomorrow evening. Apparently the Board of Directors will be meeting, and they thought it would be the perfect time to publicly announce mother's bequest." She paused then said in a much more hushed tone, "I told them you would be coming with me…." Thinking she had finished her announcement I started to protest and almost didn't hear her say "… and Nathan."

In an effort to assuage my concerns about being a third wheel, Kate explained that *she* hadn't invited Nathan. Apparently he performed occasional legal work for the Foundation, and he was already planning on attending the reception. When the third wheel argument didn't work, I told her that I had nothing to wear to a formal reception.

"Nothing to wear?" she exclaimed. "Mary has an entire closet of beautiful clothes that should fit you. Let's drive over to her house and pick out an outfit."

Though I tried to demur, she finally secured my agreement by simply stating, "J, I think it would be good for us to venture out for an evening and see what the rest of the world is doing. Don't you?"

Chapter 23

K ate and I spent the rest of the day sorting and packing Dorothy's belongings in her bedroom suite. I'm not sure whether it was Nathan's visit, the anticipation of going out the next evening, or something more spiritual, but the undertaking felt more like a celebration than a chore. We carefully wrapped each picture in tissue paper, while Kate told me the stories behind the plethora of photographs that were displayed on almost every surface of the bedroom and sitting room.

"I'd forgotten about this one," Kate said as she handed me a picture of a young couple dressed in 1930s evening clothes—both holding martini glasses, he also holding a small toy dog—both laughing at the camera. Oddly, they were standing amid a group of runners and hippies on Market Street in San Francisco.

"Who...?"

Before I could get the sentence out of my mouth, Kate said, "Mother and Dad when they were dating. They decided to dress up like Nick and Nora Charles from the *Thin Man* films, and run the Bay To Breakers footrace. Mother said they carried the martini glasses and Asta, the toy dog, for the entire race."

"Bay To Breakers?"

"It's a footrace started in the early 1900s that starts downtown near the Bay and ends near Ocean Beach—that's why they call it Bay To Breakers. Lots of people dress up for it. From what I understand it is more party than race." With a wistful sigh, Kate added, "Mother said that was the day she knew her relationship with Dad was the real thing." She gently wrapped the picture with tissue paper and placed it with others in a moving box.

We tried on fine jewelry, and read old letters to each other. We found a book of e e cummings' poetry Kate's father had given to her mother with a heart-touching inscription on the inside cover and a faded rose pressed among the pages, lamenting the current absence of romance in our lives.

We discovered a cache of 1950s-vintage dresses, hats, shoes, and purses in the back of one of the closets and decided to try some of them on. As I am a little on the petite side—the dresses did nothing for me, but on Kate, they looked stunning. I was elated when I found the dress, high heels, and hat Dorothy had worn in a photograph on the bedstand taken with Kate's father. After a little coaxing Kate tried on the outfit. We were both startled to realize that she looked exactly like the picture of her mother.

It was eight p.m. when we finished. Neither of us felt tired, but we were hungry. As we left the room to get a glass of wine and make some dinner, I saw that most of Dorothy's belongings were packed in boxes Kate had marked "deliver to Kate's house." I smiled to myself. I still had most of my mother's personal belongings in boxes at home. And, what I didn't have, I was sure I would find at Mary's.

The house was quiet when I arose the next morning. As I made my way downstairs to the kitchen in a blue fleece robe and slippers that I had borrowed from Kate, the stillness in the house led me to the conclusion that I was the first out of bed. I prepared some coffee for Kate and tea for me. Deciding to surprise her with a breakfast of waffles, berries, and fresh-squeezed orange juice, I began looking through the kitchen cabinets for the needed ingredients and utensils. In the cupboard just over the coffee maker, I discovered a small TV. I turned it on and searched for a local news program.

Flipping through stations, I heard one of the personalities from the *Today Show* announce, "And when we return, you will meet California school principal, Linda Taylor, and two of her fifth grade students who risked incarceration to offset the school's budget woes and triggered a nationwide campaign to increase public school funding."

I was stunned. I thought there was a no-interview mandate—especially with the children. And what did the announcer mean by a nationwide campaign? While the commercials aired, I ran upstairs toward Kate's bedroom. She was just opening her bedroom door when I reached the hall.

"Kate, come with me. There is something you must see. Hurry, I don't want to miss it." Then I ran back downstairs so I wouldn't miss the beginning of the interview.

Sure enough, as the Today Show reappeared on the screen, Linda, Kelsey, and Trevor were sitting on a couch across from the show's anchor, Matt Lauer. Linda looked nervous, Kelsey looked like she was going to be sick, and Trevor looked like it was his birthday.

Kate walked in dressed in an identical fleece robe—only moss green—and her bunny slippers. I pointed to the TV and turned up the volume.

Lauer commenced the segment with a brief chronology—beginning with supplies and equipment appearing in the school as they disappeared from community businesses and stores, to flummoxed police chief, to alarmed community, to the sting. He explained how the police expected to find real criminals when they executed the sting, and instead discovered "the entire fifth grade class of the local public school—with the assistance of two older siblings—were their culprits."

"*This* is the assignment you were working on before you came here?" Kate asked in a whisper.

I nodded as Lauer said, "Since this unusual case of community activism hit the airways, there have been hundreds of copycats across the country. Most recently a group of seventh graders in Florida stole a bus from a retirement community because their school bus had broken down."

As Lauer continued, Kate and I looked at each other, shocked. How could something done by a fifth grade class in Mammoth Lakes, California, a small mountain town of about 8,300 people—initiate a nationwide crime spree by prepubescent children?

Lauer concluded his introduction of the situation, and turned to Linda. "Ms. Taylor, we understand there was a general consensus by your local authorities, the school district, and community leaders that no interviews would be given to the media. Why have you changed your mind?"

Linda unconsciously moved to the front of her chair and brushed an invisible strand of hair from her face as she said, "These are unusual children. In my twelve years as a public school principal, I have never had a fifth-grade class like this one. They not only grasped the impact of the school's budget deficit, but they also wanted to do something about it. Unfortunately, while their intentions were good, their choices about the best way to help were not. We, by that I mean the police chief, the superintendent of the school district, and our local community leaders, felt that permitting them to be interviewed by the media would send the wrong message. We would be, in essence, rewarding poor judgment." Linda went on to explain the correctional plan we had developed just a week earlier.

As she finished, Matt Lauer cut in and addressed the children, "So, Trevor and Kelsey, I understand that while you are not supposed to be interviewed, you have something to read to us."

Kelsey unconsciously moved closer to Trevor on the couch. Dressed in a simple chocolate skirt and beige turtleneck, looking frightened but determined, Kelsey nodded at Trevor. They both stood up. Trevor took a piece of yellow-lined paper out of his pocket and unfolded it. By the creases in the paper, it had been folded and unfolded several times.

In a pair of khaki chinos, a white button-down shirt, and a navy cotton long sleeve sweater, he smiled at the anchor and said in a loud, clear, confident voice: "By now everyone knows what we did. We are sorry for taking things from people in town for our school. We know that stealing for whatever reason is wrong. And we want to tell all of the kids across the country not to steal—not even if you think it is the only way to get stuff for your school."

He took a deep breath, looking at Kelsey for encouragement. She smiled at him, then Trevor returned his gaze to the anchor and continued: "But we also want to say to the all of the adults in the country... even if you don't have kids, you were once a kid, weren't you? And you probably went to public school. So why do you keep voting against helping schools? Don't you care? We aren't asking for fancy things. We just want grass for our baseball field, supplies for our art class, and money to pay Mrs. Mills, the school secretary who has to work for free. We promise not to steal anymore. And... we hope you will promise to help us have the things in our school many of you had when you were growing up."

With that, Trevor and Kelsey sat down. On a program where people usually spoke over one another, there was an unusual moment of silence. It appeared that Lauer was struggling to find an appropriate response to Trevor's speech. Then he noticed, as we all did, the tears in Linda's eyes.

Sounding a little abrupt after the silence, he asked, "Ms. Taylor, did you help Trevor and Kelsey write their speech?"

Looking at the children rather than Lauer, Linda shook her head and said in an uneven voice, "No, I didn't. In fact, this wasn't the statement we agreed they would read." Raising an eyebrow, she smiled at the children, then turned to the anchor and said affirmatively, "This one was better."

Chapter 24

As we ate our waffles and bacon, I told Kate about the fifth graders' Robin Hood approach to offsetting the school's budget problems from my perspective. Then she did the dishes while I turned on my laptop and Googled some news bureaus for stories about the copycats. I was surprised to find twenty-seven similar incidents listed.

Next to the Mammoth Lakes story, the most hits came for the seventh graders in Florida mentioned by the *Today Show*. As Kate continued to tidy the kitchen I read the story to her. Apparently at a Florida school, the bus the school used for transporting sports teams to their games broke down the day before the seventh grade soccer team was supposed to play in the district semifinals. So the team captain and four of the players went looking for alternate transportation. What they found was a thirty-six-passenger bus idling at the curb in front of a senior community center—the driver had gone into the main building to collect his passengers. The kids got into the bus, together they figured out how to drive it, and motored to the school parking lot where they locked and left it. Then they left a note with the keys on the coach's desk that read, "Heard you needed to borrow a bus for Saturday's soccer semifinals." Now I understood why Linda, Trevor, and Kelsey had appeared on a national morning show. It was clear things had gotten out of hand.

Just as I started to read a story to Kate about two Montana siblings, seven and eight years of age respectively, who emptied their father's wallet of cash and "donated" it to the principal of their school, the phone rang. Kate answered, sounding, to one who knew her, a little annoyed at the intrusion.

"Good morning," she said and paused to listen for the response. The transformation was immediate. She lifted her head, combed her hand through her hair and said, "Nathan... no, you're not interrupting anything. J and I just finished breakfast." Whatever Nathan was saying made Kate smile. She responded, "Six thirty is perfect. We'll be ready."

"Nathan was calling to confirm what time he'll pick us up for the reception this evening. Isn't that thoughtful?" Noticing my reaction, Kate cut me off before I could beg off. "You promised you would come with me this evening, J. I need you there for moral support. Please."

"Well, if I am going, we better both shower and get dressed now. We need to go to Mary's and see if she has something I can wear this evening. Otherwise, it's jeans and a turtleneck."

When we drove by Steve's house, I was happy to see his Range Rover was not in its usual spot in his driveway. I had told him that I wouldn't be leaving Mammoth until next week, and I didn't want to explain myself. Besides, his constant attentiveness made me edgy.

As I turned into Mary's driveway and put my car into a lower gear for the trek up the hill, Kate made a little noise of alarm. Immediately halting the car, I asked what was wrong. Kate explained that she never drove up Mary's driveway; it was too steep. She said she would get out of the car and walk up. Stifling a laugh, I told her that I would park the car on the street and we could walk up together.

Cresting the top of the second switchback, we paused to catch our breath. I was just about to chide Kate for her refusal to traverse the driveway in the car, when I saw a man and a woman standing just above us next to the house engrossed in conversation. Kate and I looked at one another and she pulled out her cell phone as I progressed towards the couple. Neither had noticed us. It appeared that he was making notes on a small handheld computer as she gave him instructions.

"Excuse me," I said a little too loudly for the mid-morning quiet. "May I ask what you are doing?"

They looked up in unison, startled out of their concentration. "I beg your pardon?" the woman said, sounding a little annoyed by the interruption.

Now that I was close to her, I realized she looked vaguely familiar, but I couldn't place her. It was difficult to tell how old she was, possibly fifty—whatever her age, she was striking. She towered over the man she was with; I judged her to be about 5'11". She was attired in black pants, a soft pink cashmere turtleneck, a charcoal suede jacket, and running shoes.

She must have noticed my gaze pause at her feet because she said dismissively, "I keep these shoes in my car for walking sites. Now, if you will excuse us, we have work to do and only a short time to do it." She turned her back to me saying something to her companion, and he made another note on his computer.

Kate joined me, holding her cell up for me to see that it indicated no signal. With indignation replacing curiosity, I said in a more authoritative voice, "This is my home and you are trespassing. You need to leave or I will be forced to call the police." As I completed my pronouncement, the woman turned back around to address me, looking confused and more tentative than before.

As she queried, "Your house?" Kate asked in surprise, "Gwendolyn?"

With a hint of relief in her voice, the woman said, "Kate? Kate, what are you doing here?" Then glancing back at me she suggested, "Perhaps you can introduce us so we can clear up this confusion."

A little bemused herself, Kate said, "Gwendolyn, this is Janet Westmore. She just inherited this house from her twin sister and husband. J, this is Gwendolyn Parker, one of California's more notable architects."

"I thought you looked familiar," I said shaking her hand.

Gwendolyn introduced her companion, Bill Reese, an engineer in her architectural firm. Anxious to learn what an architect and an engineer were doing walking around Mary's property taking notes, I took out the keys to the house, and we adjourned to the comfort of Mary's living room.

"Perhaps I should begin." Gwendolyn said. I nodded, still wary, and she continued. "It's really quite simple. I was engaged to draft a plan to remodel and expand this property. My client told me that the owners had passed away, and he was purchasing the property from the estate. He was quite adamant that the plans be drawn up as quickly as possible because he was anxious to begin work—he said something about a wedding. We came here today to get a feel for the property, its assets and its challenges."

I was dumbfounded.

For a moment I couldn't speak. When I finally found my voice I asked, "Who is your client?"

Gwendolyn looked at Bill who scrolled through his computer then looked up and said, "Steve James. It appears from his home address that he lives close by."

Now I truly was speechless. When I recovered I said weakly, "Steve told me he wanted to make an offer when I put it on the market, and he's phoned a few times asking if I have decided to sell. But that's as far as it's gone."

Kate, who had been quiet through this entire exchange, said hopefully, "Maybe he just wanted to get everything in order so if you did say yes, he could move quickly."

Gwendolyn perked up. "Kate's probably right. It would make sense from my end; he seems like a man in a hurry. He even offered to double my fee if I could expedite the plans."

I could feel some of the tension leave my body. That must be it. It would fit with Steve's aggressive, confident nature.

"You are probably right. I don't know what I was thinking." After a pause I added, "I'll have to chide Steve when I see him at the memorial for jumping the gun."

Gwendolyn asked if she and Bill could tour the house interior, and I told them to stay as long as they wished. About half an hour later Gwendolyn came upstairs to the master bedroom where Kate and I had spread out some of Mary's formal wear, and told us she and Bill were leaving.

As we walked them to the door I asked, "When did Steve contact you for this project?" Gwendolyn's eyebrows rose in question. "If I am going to tease him about assuming that the house would be his, I should have as much information as I can," I said with a smile.

Gwendolyn looked at Bill, who pulled his computer out of its case. After a moment he said, "The initial request was logged in on January 30 at 10:15 a.m." Both Kate and I froze.

Oblivious to our reaction, Gwendolyn and Bill said goodbye and made their way down the stone steps to their car.

The plane had crashed just after noon on January 30.

Chapter 25

Kate took me by the arm and guided me into the living room to sit down. Steve had called Gwendolyn's firm at 10:15 in the morning on January 30, approximately two hours before the plane went down. This changed everything. He knew the plane would crash. He knew the house would be for sale. Pam Hathaway had told me Steve had first offered to buy Mary and Bob's house before making Pam and her husband a similar offer, but Mary and Bob had refused to sell.

Did Steve kill Mary and Bob for their house?

That made no sense. No one would kill someone so he could buy their house. But he must have. There was no other explanation. How did he do it? The NTSB investigator had given me very little information, but he had said the agency was fairly certain it was an accident. How did you prove something like this? Was this why Steve was always calling me and was always around when I was at Mary's? My mind was spinning. I had so many questions and no clue as to how I would find the answers.

Kate touched my shoulder and handed me a small bottle of water. I took a sip trying to regain my grip on reality. As the noise in my head started to subside, I realized Kate was speaking.

I shook my head and said, "I'm sorry. What did you say?"

"I phoned Nathan," Kate said. She had gone very pale, and I noticed her voice was as shaky as mine. She continued, "I hope you don't mind, but I thought we needed someone to help us think this through. I told him about Gwendolyn's assignment and the time of Steve's first contact with her firm. Nathan will be here in about twenty minutes."

We just sat there. Both of us stared off into space, trying to make sense of what we had learned from Gwendolyn. We were tugged back to the present when we heard a car coming up the driveway. Kate rose to get the door for Nathan. He entered, sat in one of the leather wingback chairs. Kate took a seat on the couch next to me.

"J, why don't you start at the beginning. Tell me everything you know about Steve."

I am not sure how long I spoke. Nathan just listened, taking occasional notes on his laptop. The first time I had heard Steve's name was when he left me a phone message while I was recovering from the accident, introducing himself as a neighbor of Mary and Bob's and telling me that he would watch the house and gardens for me. I told him about my first visit to Mary's after the crash, when he thought I was an intruder. I included my evening with him and his fiancée Carole, his regular phone calls to me in Mammoth, and his request to be notified if I decided to sell the house so he could make the first offer. I described Kate's and my unexpected encounter with Gwendolyn and her engineer, and what we learned about the timing of Steve's request to the architect. Then I told him about my initial impressions of Steve, how they had gradually improved—mostly because of his solicitousness—but also of feelings that he was too attentive.

Concluding my story, I placed my hands in my lap, looked at Nathan and said, "What do you think?"

Nathan set his computer on the side table, leaned forward in the leather chair and said, "I know you want answers, and you want them now. But we are going to have to move slowly. If what we think is true—that Steve knew about the plane crash before it happened, maybe even caused it—you could be in a great deal of danger."

He paused. "We need to buy some time so that we can get some more information. If you believe you can pull it off, I think you should go ahead with your original plan to tease Steve the next time he calls about jumping the gun and hiring an architect—since Gwendolyn or her engineer will most likely mention something to him about your unplanned encounter. Do you think you can do that—convincingly?"

Nathan was right. If we were right about Steve, most likely I was in danger—especially since I refused to sell him the house. But how was I going to be convincingly civil to Steve when it appeared he might have had something to do with Mary and Bob's deaths?

Interpreting my silence as fear, Nathan looked at Kate for approval. "You can continue to stay at Kate's. You will be safe there. In the meantime, we'll change the locks and security code for this house. I could arrange for a bodyguard if that would make you more comfortable."

I gave Nathan and Kate a weak smile, "I would like to stay at Kate's, at least for a little while more. And, I agree that we should change the locks and security code on this house, since I am not sure how many people Mary and Bob shared the code with. However, I think a bodyguard would be conspicuous and tip Steve off."

But that wasn't what was worrying me. I was just wondering if I were capable of having a casual conversation with someone I thought might have caused Mary and Bob's deaths.

Looking out the front window past Mary's early spring garden to Steve's house, I said in a more confident voice, "But I will keep my cool and do what needs to be done. No matter how long it takes, we are going to find out what really happened." After a pause I added almost to myself, "And, if he had *anything* to do with the crash...."

Putting her arm around me, Kate whispered, "Me, too."

We spent the next few hours sketching out a plan of action. While the plan took shape, my anger hardened into resolve. As difficult as it was, Nathan convinced me that nothing was going to happen quickly. My frustration, however, was tempered by the knowledge that Kate and Nathan would see the plan through with me—whatever it turned out to be—to the bitter end.

I would remain at Kate's until Mary and Bob's memorial. Kate and I would then move over to Mary's house. In the meantime, Nathan would have the locks and security code changed. He would also have his lead investigator conduct a thorough background check on Steve and look into what progress had been made by the NTSB accident investigation team. I was to let Nathan know if Steve phoned and to keep notes on any conversations. I was not to agree to meet with Steve unless absolutely necessary. And, in that event, I was to arrange for the meeting to be in a public setting, bring Kate with me, and let Nathan know ahead of time. By the time we were through developing our plan, we were on our way to becoming a formidable team of three.

It was about three in the afternoon when we finished. I went out on the front deck, saw that Steve's driveway was still empty, and suggested we should leave before he returned home. As Nathan placed his computer in its case, he offered to follow us back to Kate's. I smiled for the first time in a few hours and told him it would be nice if he followed us out to the 101 freeway; we would be fine from there.

As Kate and Nathan stepped out the front door, I went to the security panel to arm the system, but Kate ran back into the house saying, "I forgot something." A moment later she returned with Mary's Tahari silk and wool black suit in one hand and a pair of very high black leather heels in the other, saying over her shoulder as she ran out the door, "I will loan you some pearls and earrings."

I had forgotten about the press conference and the reception at the Komen Foundation. Knowing how important the announcement was to Kate, I tried to stifle a groan. Fortunately, she was occupied, navigating the stone steps and couldn't see my face as she said, "You will look stunning this evening."

The press conference and reception were a success. More than 300 people attended, most whose pictures regularly adorned local and state newspapers. I stood next to Nathan during the presentation. While we waited for Kate to speak, he pointed out the dignitaries and celebrities in the crowd. When Kate took the microphone, a respectful silence fell over the room. Even the noisy and frequently annoying press was quiet. Kate painted a picture of her mother, her mother's battle with breast cancer, and decision to fight back by bequeathing her Pacific Heights home, which had been in her family for three generations, to the Susan G. Komen Foundation.

By the end of the presentation, there were few dry eyes in the room. As Kate left the podium, our eyes locked. In that brief look I tried to communicate how proud I knew Dorothy must be of her. I actually think she received my telepathic message because she suddenly smiled and nodded, only moments before she was surrounded by a throng of emotional well wishers. My heart warmed as I saw that Nathan was among them.

It was past ten p.m. when Nathan pulled into Kate's driveway in his black Acura Coupe. As he started to say good night, Kate insisted that he come into the house for a glass of champagne. She told us she had promised her mother that on the day the house was given to the Foundation, she would open the bottle of Louis Roederer Cristal Champagne Dorothy had set aside for this occasion, and drink a toast to Kate's ancestors who had, for so many years, lived in this gracious and formidable house.

Kate led us into the greenhouse, stopping on the way to get the bottle of champagne that she must have placed in the wine cooler before we left for the reception. Since I had arrived at Kate's, the only time I had been in the greenhouse was on my first day when she gave me the grand tour of the house. As we entered Kate switched on some low lights that reflected off the leaves of the plants, giving the room an, albeit refined, jungle feeling. Adding to the effect was the warm, moist air. It was eerily beautiful.

Kate handed the champagne to Nathan to open then walked over to a side table where three crystal flutes on a silver tray were covered by a large cloth napkin. She gave us each a glass.

Nathan poured the wine, we held up our glasses and Kate, looking around, reminisced. "Mother spent most of her time here in those last few months." Pointing to a wicker chair in the corner, she continued, "She sat in this chair reliving my father's patient mentoring on the care of orchids. Orchids were his passion. After he passed away they became my mother's. She felt closest to him here. About a week before she died, I came in to check on her. She must not have heard me because she was having an animated discussion with my father, earnestly explaining why she felt so strongly about bequeathing the estate." Kate's voice faltered and she seemed a little shaky. Nathan took her free hand to steady her.

"I know I have said this before, but I wish I had known her," I said.

Kate nodded, "I wish you had known her too." We all extended our flutes for a silent toast.

After the toast I excused myself, claiming that it had been a long and emotional day. As I made my way back to the guest suite, my thoughts returned to the encounter with Steve's architect at Mary's house. I could feel the warmth of Kate's toast to her mother's generosity drain out of me, replaced by a cold, fierce anger. I had assumed the plane crash had been a tragic accident. Now it appeared that I might have been wrong. I made one more toast—actually, more of a promise— to Mary and Bob. I held my half-full glass and swore I would find out what really happened.

Chapter 26

There was activity in the kitchen when I walked downstairs the next morning to get a cup of tea. Half expecting Nathan to be sitting at the table drinking coffee with Kate, I was surprised to find the kitchen table cleared except for two legal-sized tablets, pencils, my laptop, and some white-board marking pens.

When I gave her a questioning look, Kate energetically replied, "I figured you wouldn't be content to just wait around until Nathan's investigator was finished, so I thought we could do a little research of our own." She handed me a cup of orange and spice tea as she left the room. "I'll be right back. I just have to get something out of mother's office."

Kate returned moments later pushing a five by eight foot white-board on wheels and positioned it next to the table. I gave her my second quizzical look of the morning, and she responded, "My mother kept this in the back of her office closet. She used it when she planned large dinner parties. She preferred it to modern technology." Kate smiled to herself, lost momentarily in a memory, then picked up her mug, filled it with coffee and sat down at the table. As I refreshed my tea, she continued, "I thought we could use it to keep track of everything we are doing and what we learn."

I joined her at the kitchen table and thought to ask before we started our planning, "What about your job? When do you have to return to work?"

That's when Kate really surprised me. "My job? Oh, I quit."

"You what"? I snapped, choking on my tea and spraying it on the front of my sweatshirt. "I thought you loved your work?"

Kate looked down at her coffee mug on the table and said softly, "I loved it when I worked for Mary. It's not the same anymore. And..." she colored slightly, "As you probably guessed, I have enough money so I don't *have* to work." She straightened her back, as I was learning she always did before making a declaration, and said indignantly, "Besides, WE have to find out what really happened to Mary and Bob. Don't WE?" The tone and fierceness of her voice warmed my heart almost as much as her words. I had barely known Kate before the crash. Now we were like sisters.

Relenting, I smiled, "Yes, WE do."

Over the next couple of hours Kate and I made plans. Nathan had already said he was going to have his investigator perform a thorough background check on Steve, and he was going to speak to the lead NTSB investigator assigned to look into the crash. So Kate and I focused our attention elsewhere. I thought that Carole, Steve's fiancée, might know something or at least be able to give us some insights to Steve. I told Kate she was an interior designer. Then I briefed her about my evening with Steve and Carole; how she had redecorated Steve's house, transforming it from warm, country French decor to large, open rooms, minimally decorated in black and white.

I ended my description of the evening, "Carole seemed quiet and aloof. Somehow I didn't get the sense that she feels as strongly about Steve as he does about her."

Since Carole knew me, we decided Kate would schedule an appointment with her to discuss redecorating her home. I

Googled Carole Nelson and there she was: Contrasts in Interior Design for the New Millennium, Carole Nelson—Designer.

Kate grabbed the portable phone off the wall and punched in Carole's number. She told the receptionist her name and asked to speak with Carole Nelson. When asked the purpose of the call, she explained that she required some emergency decorating in her Pacific Heights home, and that Ms. Nelson had come highly recommended. Within five minutes she had scheduled an appointment to meet with Carole at her studio at three in the afternoon. Kate placed the phone back in its cradle, looking triumphant.

"What will you be doing this afternoon while I'm meeting with Carole?" Kate asked.

I told her that I wanted to meet with George, Bob's mechanic. "If something happened to the plane," I reasoned, "Then maybe George saw something or noticed something that seemed of little importance at the time—like seeing a stranger near Bob's plane, or someone asking questions about Bob's schedule." I phoned George, reached his voicemail, and left a message asking if I could meet with him in the afternoon.

While Kate and I were discussing strategies for her meeting with Carole, my cell rang. Thinking it was George, I answered, "That was quick. How are you, George?"

After an awkward moment I heard Steve say, "J? This is Steve James."

I froze. I wanted to scream, *"Did you kill Mary and Bob?"* But, fortunately, even those words were stuck in my throat. Kate became aware of my distress.

Steve shouted into the phone, "J! J? Are you there? Is something wrong?"

Kate began to shake me, mouthing, "What's wrong? Who is it?" When I had regained some control over my motor skills, I thrust the phone at her and soundlessly whispered "Steve."

Kate closed her eyes tightly, as if summoning a great strength, and said in a remarkably clear and calm voice "Hello." She opened her eyes, looked at me, and said, "He must have disconnected."

Relief and shame engulfed me. Without looking directly at Kate, I moaned, "I just wasn't ready to talk to him. I had no time to prepare."

She pushed the phone in my direction and said sternly, "Well, you better prepare quickly because he is probably going to call back."

As I took the phone, it chirped.

I pushed my thumbnail deeply into my thigh in hopes the pain would help me focus. I pressed the call button. "Hello?"

Steve said, "J? Is something wrong? Couldn't you hear me? I just called."

"Oh, hi, Steve," I said in a relatively steady voice. "Was that you? I'm sorry. I'm driving and I dropped the phone when I was answering it." As I glanced at Kate, I could see her shoulders relax a little, but she was still alert and focused.

"No problemo. I just called to ask when you came into town. I haven't seen any lights at the house."

How did Steve know I was in town? Had he already spoken with Gwendolyn, his architect? Before I could over think the question, I responded as lightly as I could, "A few days ago. I'm staying with friends in the City. How did you know I was in town?"

Kate raised an eyebrow as I listened to Steve respond, "Well, your picture in the Chronicle, of course. Haven't you seen this morning's newspaper?"

I scribbled on a sheet of paper and shoved it at Kate. "I haven't seen the morning newspaper yet. I got a late start this morning."

"It's a great picture, J. I'm just a little disappointed you didn't call and let me know you were in town. You do remember you promised to have dinner with Carole and me, don't you?"

I assured Steve I remembered his invitation, saying that it would have to wait until after the memorial. "Between the memorial in two days and the estate, there is just no extra time," I said, instantly regretting the reference to the estate.

"Well, okay," he said, "I won't let my feelings be hurt this time. We'll get together after the memorial. And don't forget, when you are ready to put the house on the market, I want to make the first offer."

With his last words I could feel my blood pressure skyrocket. I hit disconnect and ended the call. Being civil to Steve might just be the hardest thing I would ever have to do in my life.

Kate returned a moment later with the Chronicle. Sure enough, there was a picture of Kate, Nathan, and me smiling and talking, next to a headline that read, "Prominent Pacific Heights Resident Bequeaths Family Estate to Susan G. Komen Foundation for the Cure." Steve was wrong. It was a lousy picture of me.

Kate and I spent the next few hours discussing meeting strategies.

We reasoned that if Steve had seen our picture in the Chronicle, we should assume Carole had, too. We decided that if Carole asked who referred Kate, she would tell her that I did. She would explain that we are acquaintances through Mary and we ran into one another at the reception last night, and when Kate complained to me about an interior design problem, I had recommended Carole. Since aside from knowing her occupation, our only information about Carole came from my brief encounter with her, Kate would have to look for an opening in the conversation to start talking about boyfriends.

When I fretted that Kate's meeting with Carole might just be a big waste of time, Kate responded with a confident grin, "You underestimate me, J. By the time we end our meeting, Carole is going to be my new best friend."

"Kate, I think you are fooling yourself. You wear your feelings all over your face. You won't be able to fool Carole. If you insist on going through with the meeting, try and speak as little as possible, and pick up anything you can."

Taking my advice as a challenge, she straightened her back and declared, "One hundred dollars says that I come home with more information than you do."

"You're on." And we turned our attention to my meeting with George.

"Kate, you know George much better than I do. Should I tell him what we know or should I confine our discussion to a few specific questions?"

She stood up from her chair, went to the refrigerator and started pulling out the makings of a chef's salad. I could see that she was considering my question with renewed intensity. "The problem is that while George was around a great deal, especially after my mother fell ill, I really don't know him well. My mother knew George best, and I know she confided a lot in him during her final days. I think if she were here, she would advise telling him everything."

"Then I will do that," I said.

Kate finished making our salad, and I logged onto the Internet and Googled Steve. About twenty-five of the 269 results were articles concerning local and state events that he had attended. I ignored these since I knew Nathan's investigator would be looking into Steve's background; I looked for an article with an accompanying picture of him. There were only three pictures, and only one in which you could make out his features. This would have to do for now; I sent it to Kate's printer for a copy.

Chapter 27

It was two in the afternoon when I reached the small airport where George worked and Bob had kept his plane. Earlier, when George returned my call, he said he would be working on an aircraft in Hangar 6B all afternoon and just to come find him when I arrived. He had been more than a little curious about the nature of my visit, but I had put him off, saying I would explain everything when I saw him.

I drove into the airport entrance and parked in the visitor lot. It took me several minutes to find the correct hangar. Whoever had numbered the hangars must have valued whimsy over numerical order! When I finally found Hangar 6B, the door was open and the lights were on. As I walked into the hangar I saw a man stooped over a workbench, looking at a manual and muttering to himself. He looked small, wiry, and hard as nails. When he finally noticed me standing tentatively just inside the hangar door, I saw his face transform from frustration to pleasure.

Before I could ask if he was George, he exclaimed, "You may not look like twins, but there *is* a strong family resemblance."

He grabbed a rag and walked toward me. I went to shake his hand, but he stepped forward and hugged me. Making a mental note to check the back of my jacket for grease stains when I returned to Kate's, I hugged him back.

We walked outside into the crisp spring air and settled on a bench in the sun between two hangars. Not knowing what amenities might be available at the airport, I had come prepared. I pulled two bottled iced coffees out of my bag and offered him one. He looked pleased with my choice of beverage, twisted off the top, and downed half the bottle in one long swallow.

"So, what's this all about, J? What can I do for you?"

On my drive to the airport I had debated with myself on how much I should tell George despite his close relationship with Kate's mother. Since I didn't know him, I had decided I would just ask him if he had ever seen Steve at the airport. But George's warm reception and concerned manner changed my mind.

I spent the next twenty-five minutes filling him in, beginning with my first meeting with Steve, to running into Steve's architect Gwendolyn, to our last phone call. I told him my attorney was having his investigator conduct a background check on Steve, and he would also be speaking with the lead investigator for the NTSB team assigned to the crash. I even told him that Kate was meeting with Steve's girlfriend as we spoke. He gave me his full attention, not making a sound, while I told my story.

When I was finished he shook his head, "I knew something wasn't right. That plane couldn't have been in better shape, and Bob was one of the best pilots I know. How can I help?"

I pulled the grainy Internet photo of Steve out of my purse. "The problem is we not only have to figure out *what* happened, but then we have to *prove* it." Handing the picture to George I asked, "Have you ever seen this man around here?"

George pulled a pair of glasses out of his pocket and putting them on said, "Damn. These aren't my reading glasses." Then he handed me back the photo, stood up and patted himself down. "God damn it," he swore more seriously this time, and went back into Hangar 6B. Looking triumphant, he reappeared with a second set of glasses. When I gave him a puzzled expression he said, "One pair is for working, one pair is for reading. It's hell getting old." Then he took the photo from me and studied it.

He held the picture tightly in his hand, examined it closely while I sat quietly and watched him. We remained this way for several moments. Occasionally George closed his eyes and rubbed the bridge of his nose with his first two fingers.

After what seemed an eternity he said, "About three or four months ago I was in the hangar working on Bob's car. Bob had left that morning for a meeting in San Diego and asked me to take a look at the Mosler because it was running a little rough. This guy came into the hangar looking for Bob. I told him Bob wouldn't be back until the next day. I remember him because he hung around for a little while and we talked planes. He said that he was in the market for a four-seat single-engine plane and that he had been hoping to take a look at Bob's Cessna Turbo Skylane."

George paused, and looked at the picture again. His voice became guttural as if his throat were constricting as he murmured, "He wanted to know all about the Skylane from a mechanic's perspective. He was particularly interested in what kind of maintenance schedule Bob's plane required." As he looked up at me I saw a tear glisten from the corner of his eye as he held up the picture and croaked, "I… I can't be certain, but this looks a lot like the guy."

"Can you remember anything else he said?" I asked softly. He just shook his head.

"Did he tell you his name?" I persisted.

"J, if he did, I don't remember it. He was just another pilot asking questions about a plane," responded George in a tone of frustration and regret.

"How about the date, do you remember *when* he stopped by the hangar?" I continued to prod.

"Not the date. But it *was* the first week of January. I remember because when Bob returned the next day from his trip he was complaining about people who left their Christmas lights up on their houses after New Year's." George gave a slight smile. "For some reason people leaving their outside Christmas lights on their houses after the New Year really pissed Bob off. I told him to at least give people a full week to take down their decorations."

We spoke for another hour. I spent most of that time trying to calm George down. He was full of self-recrimination, remorse, and anger. I finally convinced him that if he were going to help Kate and me find out what really happened, he needed to set his personal feelings aside for the time being.

As I prepared to leave he said, "I wish I could get a look at him in person. Then we would know for sure if it's the same guy."

"You will be at the memorial the day after tomorrow at Carpaccio's, won't you?"

"Definitely," he replied.

"Well Steve should be there, too." Halfway through my reply I knew we had another problem.

With tightly clenched fists George half yelled half growled, "If I see the bastard, I will *make* him tell me what he did."

185

It took almost another hour to convince George that we couldn't let Steve know we were on to him until we knew if he caused the accident, how he did it, and we could prove it.

By the time I pulled into Kate's driveway it was after six. Before I could turn off the engine she bolted out of the house toward my car, her face flushed and excited. "I thought you would never return, J. I have so much to tell you."

"And *I* have a lot to tell you!"

Before she could launch into her story I told her I thought we should call Nathan and ask him to come over. "What I have to tell you, Nathan needs to hear."

She looked momentarily disappointed at having her news postponed even for a moment. She acquiesced more quickly than I expected—most likely because of the prospect of another chance to see Nathan. "Good idea. Nathan should hear what I learned from Carole, too. I'll go call him."

Walking into the kitchen, I smiled when I saw five twenty-dollar bills fanned out on the dining room table. I opened my purse, found my wallet, and left five more twenties next to Kate's.

I found a cocktail shaker, the Jack Daniels, sweet vermouth, Peychaud's bitters, and some cherries with stems, and placed them on the counter. I generally preferred a vodka martini, but Manhattans were Nathan and Kate's cocktail of choice. By the time I heard Kate say into the phone, "Great. We'll see you in 20 minutes," I had also brought out some sharp cheddar, McIntosh apples, and whole grain crackers.

The next twenty minutes—well, twenty-four minutes to be precise—were agonizing. Both Kate and I were anxious to tell each other what we each had learned.

When I asked Kate if she would like her Manhattan while we waited, she admonished me, "Don't you think we should wait for Nathan? He said he would come right over."

I briefly demurred, then grabbed a few slices of apple and cheese, and sat down, resigned to waiting. When we heard Nathan pull into the driveway, I assembled the Manhattans while Kate went to greet him.

As they walked into the kitchen, I handed one of the drinks to Nathan and one to Kate, "We have a lot to talk about. Let's get started."

Chapter 28

By prior agreement Kate went first. The excitement she had exuded when she greeted my car a half hour earlier reemerged. "My first forty-five minutes at Carole's Design Studio were unexciting. When I arrived I was ushered into a small, windowless stark white room where there was a diminutive glass conference table with four backless ergonomically correct black chairs, white carpet, and nothing on the walls. In fact, the studio's décor makes most minimalists look like pack rats. Carole's office was next to the meeting room, because I could hear almost every word she spoke on the phone. From the obsequious way she responded to her caller, I suspect she was chatting with one of her wealthier and more demanding clients. After about twenty minutes—which seemed interminable—partly because of those damn chairs, and partly because I was starting to get nervous and over-think my meeting strategy, she joined me."

Kate took a sip of her cocktail and continued with a sigh. "After Carole introduced herself, she barely looked at me. She opened her MacBook and started asking me questions—mostly about the property I was interested in decorating. She didn't even look up when I responded to her questions. It wasn't until she asked who referred me—and I told her you, J—that she started to pay attention to me. She wanted to know how well I knew you and if we were close friends. I told her that I had met you through Mary, which seemed to interest her even more.

"She started studying me, which was a little unnerving after being ignored. She said I looked familiar. Before I could think of some sort of a response, she asked if I was related to the Richards, the ones who had donated their Pacific Heights estate to the Komen Foundation. Then, answering her own question, Carole announced she saw my picture on the front page of this morning's Chronicle. That's when she started to fall all over herself trying to make me more comfortable. The first thing she did was move us into her office, where she had *real* chairs with cushions and chair-backs, and a window. Next she called her assistant in, ordering her to get us some cappuccino and biscuits—making a show of chiding her for not doing so as soon as I arrived."

While Kate was telling her story, she stared into her cocktail glass as if she could see the afternoon's meeting in its amber liquid. When she looked up at me, I frowned a little impatiently and twirled my index finger, signaling her to get to the point.

"Be patient. I'm coming to the point," she cried. Unlike me, Nathan looked like Kate could take all the time she wanted.

"When we went into Carole's office, I thought I needed to change tactics. I decided to mimic her snobbery and narcissism while treating her like a confidante." With a self-congratulatory grin she went on, "I told her I had lied when I said that the property in need of design help was mine. I confided that my boyfriend wanted me to move in with him, and I couldn't stand his colors, his furniture, his art—any of the interior. I needed to find out if the house-situation was salvageable before I gave him my answer. Carole said she completely understood; then disclosed that a few months ago she had to totally redesign and redecorate her boyfriend's home. Carole recounted how her boyfriend purchased the house and 'wasn't going to do a thing.' She said it looked like an old folks home."

Glancing up at me, Kate said incredulously, "Can you believe she thought the Hathaways' charming country French home looked like an old folks home?" Again I twirled my index finger.

With a slight smirk Kate ignored my impatience. "Then she told me her boyfriend was purchasing Mary and Bob's house—actually she said it was *in escrow*—and that she would be in charge of the interior renovation. Carole was really excited when she told me she wanted to make it the showpiece for her business."

"In escrow!?" I was stunned. Nathan and I exchanged looks.

Before I could ask Kate how she responded to Carole's statement, she furrowed her brow. "I tried to sound matter-of-fact when I told Carole she must be mistaken. I said when I saw you last night at the Komen presentation, you confided that you didn't know whether you were going to put Mary's house on the market or keep it.

"Carole went ballistic! She didn't try to come up with an excuse or apologize. She just abruptly ushered me out of her office, telling me we would have to continue our discussion another time. She handed me off to her assistant and told her to schedule another appointment for me early next week. Before I could say goodbye, she was back in her office with her door closed. As I was leaving I could hear muffled shouts coming from her office."

Kate sat back in her chair looking proud and a little exhausted. I pushed the two stacks of twenty-dollar bills towards Kate. We sat silently, sipping our Manhattans, contemplating this new information. Why would Steve tell Carole the house was already in escrow?

Nathan was the first to speak. Looking at me with some concern he said, "I suspect you are going to start getting a great deal more pressure from Steve to sell Mary's house. We need to consider how you should respond to his calls."

As if on cue, my cell rang. I looked at the number, saw it was Steve, held it up so Kate and Nathan could see, and turned the cell phone off.

"Perhaps I should tell you about my meeting with George *before* we start discussing how to handle Steve."

Then I told them about George's exchange with someone who looked a lot like Steve, focusing on the topic of their conversation—Bob's airplane, and the timing of the conversation—three weeks before the crash. I also related that the picture I had showed George was Internet-fuzzy so we had decided he would give us a firmer response after he saw Steve at the memorial.

Before I surrendered their attention I said uncertainly, "Something about what George said has been bothering me all afternoon. When I first met Steve, you remember, the night he followed me into Mary's house thinking I was a burglar. Well, once we cleared up the confusion, and he was offering his condolences, I am almost positive he told me he would never fly in a plane smaller than a 747. So why would someone who doesn't like small planes be interested in purchasing a single-engine, four-seat Cessna?"

Shaking his head, Nathan rose from his chair, "It appears it is going to be a long evening and I am starved. Before we continue this discussion, how about if I order us some food? Osaka will deliver and they have great sushi."

Simultaneously Kate said, "I love sushi," as I said, "I hate sushi."

Nathan assured me that Osaka had lots of delectable cooked entrees, and pulled up their menu on his laptop. He and Kate wanted Suimono soup—something with mushrooms and seaweed—and a deluxe sushi platter to share. I asked for some Miso soup and a medium rare New York steak. As Nathan ordered the dinners and Kate set the table, I made us another round of Manhattans.

When dinner arrived all three of us discovered how hungry we were. Because it is awkward and inefficient to take notes while eating, we decided to reserve our serious discussion for after dinner. This, however, didn't stop us from trying to make sense out of what we had learned from Carole and George.

When there was no food left either on our plates or in the delivery bags, Nathan cleared the table while Kate and I pulled in the white marker board. For lack of knowledge of any investigative techniques we decided to list "what we knew" and "what we needed to find out."

Under what we knew the three of us listed:

1. Steve made an unsolicited offer to buy Mary and Bob's house, which they adamantly refused.
2. Although Steve purchased the house next door, he still is anxious to buy Mary's house.
3. Steve phoned to engage an architect to renovate Mary's house two hours before the plane crashed.
4. Steve told Carole that the house was in escrow, when it is not.
5. Steve or someone who looks like Steve stopped by to see Bob's plane three weeks before the crash.

6. During the same timeframe Steve or someone who looks like Steve spoke with George about the plane's mechanics.

7. Steve watches the house and even sent his gardener over to make some unsolicited repairs after a storm.

8. Steve was orphaned at an early age and was raised by a wealthy aunt and uncle in San Francisco.

9. We don't know what he does for a living other than participate in investment focused partnerships.

The questions we came up with included:

1. What does Steve do for a living?
2. Was the crash an accident or intentional?
3. Was Steve the person who spoke with George about Bob's plane? If yes,
   a. Is he a licensed pilot?
   b. Does he own or lease a plane?
   c. If he flies small planes, why would he lie about it?
4. Why did Steve tell Carole the house was in escrow?
5. Is it possible that he would kill Mary and Bob for their house? Why?

As we tried to think of more questions for the list, I yearned to add another: "Was it a message from Mary and Bob the night my TV froze on the edition on "single-engine aircraft" of *How It's Made*? And if so, what were they trying to tell me?" But I had already lost Ross by confiding in him about my post-crash encounters with Mary and Bob and he knew me better than anyone else. I put the thought aside, knowing I couldn't afford to lose the respect and friendship of Kate and Nathan, too.

It was after eleven when we finished our lists and studied them for clues. "Almost everything we know could have some reasonable explanation except for calling an architect *before* the plane went down," Nathan said.

"I know," I sighed. "Maybe Gwendolyn's office got the date wrong, and we are going through all this for nothing."

"Well, we can't do anything more tonight," said Nathan. Patting his computer he continued, "I will give all of this information to our investigator and have her follow up for us. She should be able to tell us if Steve is a licensed pilot, what he does for a living, and if his pattern of behavior is to select a neighborhood and a house and then try to buy his way in. I will also have her follow up with Gwendolyn's office to confirm the time of Steve's call to them. I know she already has established a dialogue with the National Transportation Safety Board. I will call you tomorrow to give you a progress report."

Glancing at Kate while trying to stifle a yawn, he said, "Now I better say goodnight. I can show myself out."

Kate jumped out of her chair almost upending her half finished cup of coffee saying, "I'll show you out, Nathan." Both of them disappeared, walking toward the front of the house.

As I watched them leave the room I felt a pang of jealousy. They hadn't been out on a real date yet and they were already a couple—whether they realized it or not. I thought about Ross and the phone calls he hadn't made since our argument over my sanity. I missed him terribly. I wanted to call and tell him about our suspicions, but I feared he would just add paranoia to my list of mental maladies.

Feeling sorry for myself I poured a half glass of Merlot, found a piece of Godiva chocolate, and climbed the stairs to my bedroom where I planned on wrapping myself in Mary's afghan and sulking.

Chapter 29

When we met in the kitchen the next morning, it was apparent that neither Kate nor I had slept much the night before. Kate was the first to broach the subject, saying into her second cup of coffee, "My dreams last night were a Stephen King version of the last three months. I dreamt my mother was in the plane with Mary and Bob, and someone who looked like Steve was flying the plane singing Dylan's "Desolation Row" … then Carole, dressed in a skin-tight black and white outfit, was telling me to get out of the house immediately because the Foundation had sold it to her and she was anxious to redecorate … it ended with us at Carpaccio's for the memorial and Nathan introducing me to his wife."

While Kate's first two scenarios resonated with my own nightmares, the third one made me chuckle inside. I must not have entirely suppressed the giggle because Kate looked up sharply and demanded, "What? What's so funny?"

I was about to tease her about the Nathan dream, when I realized she had tears in her eyes. Kate's fatalism was contagious. As I reached across the table to take her hand, I felt like someone was grabbing all of my internal organs in their fist and squeezing, drawing me in on myself. Kate was right. Too much had happened. Too much was happening. Both Kate and I were on overload. We sat at the kitchen table for several minutes, still, waiting for the sadness to subside.

The noise of my cell phone ringing pierced our shared isolation like a pin popping a balloon in a small room. I didn't answer it, but it served to snap us out of our reverie nonetheless. When it stopped I looked at voice messages to see who had phoned. It was Steve. The call log indicated that he had left numerous messages since the night before. I turned the phone off. I wished for just an hour or two, I could turn my brain off, too.

At noon Kate and I met Joan at Carpaccio's to review the room set up and the music for the memorial—Kate was delighted when she learned we would be listening to a mélange of Mozart and Bob Dylan—and to sample a few of the treats that would be served. We went over the names of those who were coming, and Joan showed me a list of people who had requested to say a few words or propose a toast. The roll of would-be speakers was almost as long as the guest list. The finality of a memorial service hit me, and I started to emotionally fold. Fortunately, Joan's all-business manner and Kate's gentle calm prevented me from falling back into grief's black hole, and kept me focused on the tasks at hand.

With the final details for the memorial handled, Kate and I left Carpaccio's and returned to her mother's home. Kate had made arrangements for the Komen Foundation to take possession of the estate on May 3, just three days after the memorial, four days from now. Most of Dorothy's smaller possessions had been gifted, or boxed and moved to Kate's home. She had scheduled moving vans for May 1 to pick up the furniture and the larger items she was keeping. We planned to finish the work in Pacific Heights, and then move some of Kate's clothes and personal items to Mary's. We were almost ready to start going through Mary and Bob's possessions.

Sometime during the madness of the day's activities Kate realized if we were going to have a farewell dinner to say goodbye to Kate's childhood home it would have to be tonight. I suggested we invite one or two of Kate's mother's closest friends, like Joan Westin, but Kate declined. Thinking it might lift her mood, I proposed we invite Nathan.

Kate's response to this idea was to brush off some invisible dirt from her sleeve while shyly asking, "How about just the two of us, J? I know our friendship is only a few weeks old, but you are the only one left I truly consider *family*."

Feeling wetness in my eyes and warmth in my heart, I replied gently, "I feel the same way, though I hadn't articulated it, Kate. You are right, we *are* family." Then I told her to leave the evening's fare to me.

About nine o'clock, with the land lines and cell phones turned off, Kate and I sat down to an expertly made Caesar salad, a pile of fresh Dungeness crab, hot sourdough bread, and two bottles of 1997 Kistler Vine Hill Vineyard Russian River Valley Chardonnay.

After a number of toasts to Kate's ancestors, her parents, and almost every room in the house, Kate looked at me curiously and asked, "This is wonderful, but what made you choose these particular foods?"

Smiling to myself more than to Kate I responded, "Whenever Mary and I visited one another, this was what we would have our first night together. Only the wine would change."

Understanding the gesture Kate said, "Ah, a *family* tradition, I like that. I guess it's a good thing I like Dungeness crab." We toasted family and continued our meal.

Nathan picked us up at one o'clock the next afternoon. The memorial was scheduled to begin at two, and we wanted to be at Carpaccio's before anyone arrived.

As Nathan drove up Alpine Road he glanced at me in the rearview mirror and said, "Since we are all fairly confident that Steve will be there, let's talk about how you are going to handle him."

From the back seat I responded apprehensively, "Change fairly confident to 100 percent certain, as of a half hour ago he has left twenty-two voice messages on my cell since his call the night before last."

I saw Nathan's eyebrows arch in the mirror. "Twenty-two?"

After some debate all three of us concurred that less was more. I should make him believe my grief was so crushing—which wouldn't be a stretch—that my attorney has advised me not to make any decisions until after the memorial. Then I was to direct Steve to speak with Nathan.

While Kate and Nathan continued to give me advice I found myself drifting further and further away from them. Handling Steve would be nothing compared to hearing people who loved Mary and Bob memorialize them. I had scheduled the memorial three months after the crash to give me time to recover from my wounds. I had naively thought the time might also help me emotionally, but if anything my sense of loss and 'single-ness', a term most likely only a twin would understand, was even more unbearable. Like many people who have lost someone so close, I was trying to learn how to think shallowly, so that I didn't become a victim of my memories.

Exacerbating my angst was not having Ross in my life anymore. When Kate retired to her room after last night's dinner I had picked up the phone more than once to call him and beg him to come to the memorial. Each time I stopped, convincing myself that in the long run, the lack of trust would make our separation inevitable.

The sudden stopping of the car and Nathan saying, "We're here," brought me back to reality.

As Nathan helped me out of the car I heard Kate on the other side of the car say, "May I help you? Are you here for Mary and Bob's memorial? If you are, you're a bit early." Oddly I heard no response.

Straightening and turning toward Kate, I saw him. Ross was standing next to her, looking slightly awkward in an olive herringbone sports coat, powder blue button-down shirt, dark slacks, and hard shoes—a far cry from his Ski Patrol uniform. He had large, irregular bruises on his face and hands, a black eye, and he seemed to be holding himself protectively—as if he had broken ribs, but he looked wonderful to me.

Kate was still speaking to him, but he appeared not to hear her. He was staring at me. When I could find my voice I said in a whisper, "Ross."

Kate immediately ceased speaking and took Nathan by the hand. She whispered something in his ear and they quietly walked across the street toward Carpaccio's.

Ross didn't say a word; he just continued to stare at me. My heart was beating so fast I could hear the blood pounding in my ears. For several moments we stood frozen. Just as I thought I had regained enough composure to ask what had happened to him, Ross took me by the shoulders and said something. I was so aware of his touch that I missed his words.

"What?" I asked.

Looking at me so closely that I thought his eyes might be touching my very essence, he said, "I should have believed you, J. I am so sorry. I should have known if you said Mary and Bob were still here, then they must be. Can you forgive me?"

I could hear Ross's words but they weren't making sense to me. "I... I don't understand, Ross."

"I saw them, J," he said gently. "I saw Mary and Bob. They saved my life."

Chapter 30

While I was babbling, "You...you saw..." and, "...saved your life," Ross guided me over to his Honda Pilot and sat me in the front passenger seat. Then he climbed into the driver's seat and pointed to a bottle of cold water in the cup holder. After I took a few sips I replaced the bottle, looked in my purse for some Kleenex to wipe my eyes, then turned in the seat to face him. As I started to relax, my tears came in full force.

Seizing a moment of composure, I implored, "Tell me."

Ross closed his eyes as if playing the scene in his head. "I don't know if you have been paying attention to what's happening with the weather in Mammoth while you've been here, but after several days of spring sunshine, we had a series of unusually cold and heavy snowstorms last week. Then Friday the jet stream shifted and we hooked into a pineapple connection, giving us a big, wet snowstorm. So, of course, we have been doing a lot of early morning avalanche control, including this past Saturday morning.

"I was paired with Jeff. It looked like it was going to be a great morning. When the Snow Cat dropped us off at the top of Chair 22, the sun was just coming over the White Mountains and the clouds were moving off the top of Mammoth, creating a red glow over the horizon. It was beautiful." I could imagine the scene Ross was recounting; he had described it many times before. But I had to admit it always made me a little anxious. For all its beauty, he was telling me what it looked like right before he and his partner released potential avalanches. One of them would ski across the fall line from one anchor point to the next trying to release a slide, while the other watched. Then they would trade roles.

Now Ross was looking at me as he continued, "I took the first cut. I guess I must have misjudged it because one moment I was skiing across the snow then suddenly there was nothing beneath my skis. The snow in the couloir was sliding and there was nothing I could do about it but pray. I wanted to protect my head because the snow boulders that were sliding with me were the size of Volkswagens, but I was helpless. I don't know if I blacked out or if I just can't remember, but the next thing I knew I was completely buried in snow and ice and couldn't move. It was so dark I didn't even know whether I was upside down, I just knew I was going to die. Even with my transponder I was sure there was no way Jeff could get to me in time.

"Just as I realized I had used almost all of the little air that was in the snow pocket with me and panic was starting to set in, the black became gray and I could hear someone digging into the ice that entombed me. Suddenly there was a hole in the ice and fresh air wafted in. The hole continued to get bigger. When I had enough room to move my arms and get the snow out of my eyes, I expected to see Jeff. But it wasn't him. At first all I could see was the sleeve of an ugly, old, bright orange ski jacket."

The only ugly, old, bright orange ski jacket I had ever seen was Bob's. Mary used to try to buy replacements, but Bob refused to wear anything but his orange parka. The last time I saw it on Bob was the day of the crash, he was wearing it as he flew the plane.

"It was Bob. Mary was next to him and they were digging me out with their hands. I was certain I was either dead or hallucinating. But once the hole was big enough, they pulled me out, and I knew *it was them*, and I knew I wasn't dreaming. Neither of them spoke. They just helped me out and sat me next to the hole they had dug. Mary brushed some snow off my face and smiled at me, then they turned and walked away.

"Before I could call to them, I heard someone ski up behind me. It was Jeff. He was saying, 'Holy shit, you're alive! You *are* alive! Where is the couple that dug you out? I can't believe they found you. You owe them your life. Holy shit!' When I spun around to point to them, they had vanished."

I am not sure at what point during his story Ross took my hands, but as he ended his account we were holding on to one another as if we were in the middle of a violent windstorm and one of us might blow away. We sat that way in a dazed silence until we were interrupted by a knock at the window.

When I looked up I saw Kate looking concerned and a little protective. I had told Kate that Ross and I had broken up, but I hadn't explained the circumstances, since to do so was to tell her about seeing Mary and Bob. No wonder she was uneasy.

I opened the car door and said, "It's all right, Kate. We just needed to ..." I looked at Ross and he finished for me, "Clear the air," he said.

Kate's face relaxed slightly but she was still worried. She said a bit sternly, "Most of the guests have arrived and they are asking about you." I glanced at my watch. It was two-thirty. The memorial had started at two.

I turned the rearview mirror to check my make up and groaned; what make up remained was running down my face in streaks. While I made the necessary repairs, Kate introduced herself to Ross then asked me, "Does Ross know about Steve?"

I shook my head. "I haven't had a chance to tell Ross about anything that has happened in the last few weeks." Kate furrowed her brow at me again.

Before she could ask any questions we didn't have time to answer I turned to Ross and said in a rush, "There is so much we have to talk about. But for the present just know you will meet someone named Steve James; he lives next door to Mary's house. We think he might have had something to do with the plane crash, but we can't prove anything yet. We definitely don't want him to know that we think the crash might not have been an accident. So I am being polite, but keeping my distance from him as much as possible. Oh, I almost forgot. For some reason he is anxious to buy Mary and Bob's house and he keeps pressuring me to commit to selling to him." Looking at Kate I asked, "Did I leave anything out?"

Kate was looking at Ross who looked like I had sucker punched him. Trying to reassure him, I said softly, "It really is okay, Ross. Kate, Nathan, and I will explain everything after the memorial. For now we need to join the others." Then I climbed out of the car, straightening my clothes.

Ross looked more than a little concerned as we walked across the street to the restaurant. Before we reached the door he asked with just a little edge in his tone, "Who is Nathan?"

I smiled, explained he was my attorney, that he was in love with Kate—though I didn't know if he was aware of it— and he would meet Nathan in a matter of moments.

As trite as it sounds, as soon as we walked into Carpaccio's I felt the affection and friendship that filled the room. With Kate and Ross by my side I was embraced by

Mary and Bob's friends, colleagues, and neighbors. Most I knew. The few I didn't know introduced themselves and described what part of Mary and Bob's lives they had touched. After a few minutes I saw Kate fade into the crowd, moving toward Nathan, who was involved in a lively conversation with George. One of Kate and Nathan's assignments was to stay with George, who was going to see if Steve was the man he spoke with in Bob's hangar, and if so, to make sure George didn't try to exact any revenge or blow our cover.

Ross continued to stand next to me with his hand protectively on my back, nodding and smiling when he was introduced to someone new. As we made our way slowly through the throng, stopping to chat with each small cluster of mourners, Ross found a waiter and ordered two glasses of Merryvale Cabernet.

Between conversations I could occasionally hear a Bob Dylan tune or a Mozart piano concerto being played by a pianist on the baby grand piano situated toward the front of the room near the open windows. At one point during our journey through the room, Ross and I heard someone behind us say, "What a strange mix of music to play at a memorial." We smiled at one another—clearly the speaker really didn't know Mary or Bob.

Just before I was about to try to get everyone's attention, opening the floor to those who wanted to say something by offering a toast of my own, Steve rushed into the restaurant alone, looking a little disheveled.

As he spotted me and started his advance, I turned toward Ross and whispered, "Steve."

Without preamble Steve demanded, "J. I have been calling you for days. Where have you been?

Trying to hide my irritation and anxiety, I said in a controlled voice, "Steve, may I introduce you to Ross, my…"

I glanced at Ross thinking… boyfriend? Significant other? Then choosing a phrase that Steve had used to describe Carole when I first met her, I continued, "the love of *my* life."

Steve took a step backward as he looked up at Ross, who was about a half-foot taller. Ross extended his hand and Steve shook it dismissively with little more than a glance.

Then as Steve redirected his attention to me and was about to continue his barrage of questions, Ross asked Steve, "Did you know Mary and Bob well?"

Steve muttered something about being neighbors keeping his eyes on me while he responded, then asked if we could talk sometime after the memorial.

Before I could respond, Ross drew me toward him in an obvious show of possession, smiled at Steve and said, "I'm afraid J will be busy for the next few days. We have been apart for far too long. Perhaps she could call when she has some free time."

Looking defeated and angry Steve said stiffly, "I would appreciate it."

In the next moment his entire demeanor changed—from irate and demanding to calm and well mannered. Looking at Ross as if he had just been introduced to him, Steve took a business card out of his pocket and handed it to Ross. "Perhaps you and J would join me for dinner while you are in town. There is a terrific new restaurant just off Alpine Road. I hear they have the best martinis in the Valley."

Without waiting for an answer, he smiled at both of us and turned to leave. Before he was out of earshot I asked, "Steve, where is Carole?" Some of the anger returned to his face as he muttered, "She sends her regrets. She had a last minute crisis with a client." He moved swiftly toward the bar.

Chapter 31

I walked onto a makeshift platform next to the piano, thinking about how much Mary loved rituals. She had always found a sense of peace and order in them—more than most of our generation. It struck me as profoundly sad that my next words would start her final rite.

Those around me quieted as they saw me standing on the platform, and silence spread in ever widening ripples until it engulfed the room. I thanked everyone for attending, I handed my glass of wine to Ross, and took a sheet of paper out of my pocket. As I carefully unfolded it, cautious not to tear any of its well-worn creases, my throat started to constrict.

I began, "A little more than seventeen years ago I gave this toast at Mary and Bob's wedding…." I paused, as my nose involuntarily flared and my eyes stung, in an effort to hold back tears. "I decided these words were the ones I wanted to share with you this afternoon." With a tight hold on my emotions I looked at the paper to read, and then let my hand fall to my side. The words were etched in my heart. I quoted from memory,

"When Mary and I were little girls, I thought the term 'underprivileged children' referred to those kids who grew up without a twin. I still do." As I looked at my audience, I saw some smiles and some tears. I continued, "So it was with some apprehension that I learned Mary and Bob had decided to marry. Selfishly, I was afraid I might lose her. But quickly I learned Bob wasn't taking Mary away from me. He was making her happier than I think she has ever been. And at the same time, he was making sure I was a part of their life together. The three of us were family, in the truest spirit of the word."

Tears were running down my face as I took my glass of wine from Ross, held it at eye level and said, "To Mary and Bob. To Family."

As I stepped off of the podium, Greg Lee, one of Bob's closest friends and his business partner, climbed onto the dais. Unconcerned as he would have been under ordinary circumstances by the tears spilling out of his eyes, he held me for a moment then continued his journey on to the platform to memorialize his friends.

The stories, memories, and toasts went on for almost an hour. It seemed everyone had something they wanted to share. Periodically waiters circulated through the room with bottles of wine and boxes of Kleenex on their silver trays. Kate, Nathan, Joan, Ross, and I were sitting at a table next to the platform almost mesmerized by the flood of admiration and love being offered for Mary and Bob. It was as if you could feel the words more than hear them, and it was comforting.

One of the last to climb the dais was Jean McBride, Chairman of the Board of Hope For Our Children, a foundation that supports efforts that enrich the lives of vulnerable, abused, and neglected children in California. She was an imposing woman—blond, muscular, standing over six feet in her heels—but surprisingly soft-spoken. After she introduced herself, she explained that Mary had been an active Board member for many years, and Mary and Bob had been generous contributors. Then she glanced at me raising her eyebrows slightly, and I smiled and nodded.

Flushing slightly, Jean looked back at her audience saying, "J has given her okay for me to share some news she gave me only moments before the toasts started. I am pleased to announce that Mary and Bob munificently bequeathed Hope For Our Children $500,000." Collectively those in the room inhaled, and then the restaurant was filled with applause.

As Jean was about to step off the platform, Steve walked up to her, whispered something in her ear, while he handed her a slip of paper. As she looked down at the paper, Steve hurriedly left Carpaccio's. Annoyed by his rude interruption, I watched through the open windows as he headed toward his car, so I didn't notice Jean retake her position on the podium.

"Ladies and gentleman," she said a little unsteadily, trying to regain everyone's attention. "The gentlemen who just left…." Looking at the slip of paper she read, "Steve James." Still visibly shaken she continued, "He just made a donation to the Foundation in Mary and Bob's memory. He matched their bequest." She held up a check for $500,000 made out to Hope For Our Children.

It was past seven when the last of Mary and Bob's friends left Carpaccio's. Nathan, Kate, Ross, and I knew the four of us had a lot to discuss, but recognized we were all too tired to carry on a coherent conversation tonight. Agreeing to meet Nathan and Kate in the morning at Nathan's office, Ross and I decided to spend the night at the Stanford Park Hotel, which was just a few blocks from the restaurant.

My adrenaline was still high from Ross's unexpected appearance, the memorial, and Steve's donation to the Foundation. So after checking into our room, we walked across the street to the grounds of Stanford University and went for a walk. It felt good to be outside.

I told Ross the entire story, beginning with my first unplanned meeting with Steve when he thought I was a burglar at Mary's, his initial quest to buy Mary and Bob's home then settling for the house next door, his continuous offers to buy the house, running into Steve's architect Gwendolyn, Carole's belief that the house was already in escrow, and George's conversation with Steve at the hangar—George had confirmed it was Steve before he left the memorial. I also told him about an event I couldn't tell Kate and Nathan—when both of my TVs were stuck on the *How It's Made* episode on single-engine planes just before I left for the Bay Area. By the time I was finished, we had returned to the Hotel's softly lit lobby bar where we had coffee and brandy on a deep cushioned sofa.

After a few minutes of quiet Ross shook his head. "Why would he want Mary and Bob's house when he has a house next door? And why did he make a half-million-dollar contribution to the Foundation today in their names? It just doesn't make any sense."

We halfheartedly tried to come up with feasible explanations, but both of us were beyond tired.

As Ross put his arm around me, guiding me down the hall toward sleep, I realized how tonight was ending much differently than I had anticipated when I woke up this morning. Thanks to Mary and Bob, Ross was alive and he was back with me.

Unlike the torrid passion of most romantic novels, our lovemaking was gentle, slow, almost tenuous. As if we were reintroducing ourselves to each other. When the sky colored with the first hint of dawn, we finally fell asleep, sated by our homecoming. Perhaps this was why we both slept through the alarm we had set the night before. Ross was the first to awaken. Feeling the void left when he rose in search of coffee, I finally commenced the arduous task of opening my eyes. As I did my eyes lit on the time registered on the alarm clock just as the phone rang, both startling me out of my reverie.

"We're already a half hour late for our meeting, aren't we?" I said into the phone.

After a long pause Kate responded with a nervous laugh, "So are we."

Chapter 32

By twelve-thirty we were all sitting in Nathan's conference room eating deli sandwiches and drinking Arizona Ice Teas. The room could seat six comfortably, but no more. It had floor-to-ceiling bookshelves on three walls and a white marker board hanging on the fourth.

At the head of the small conference table sat Charlotte Carlisle, Nathan's investigator. She was in her late twenties, African American, slim with close-cropped hair. Her manner was businesslike and precise. It was her Abercrombie & Fitch low slung flare jeans sharing a peek of a flower-tatt on her flat stomach, floral patterned empire waist tank top, and flip flops that seemed out of context. Between bites of smoked turkey and alfalfa sprouts on sourdough, Charlotte prepared to present what she had learned about Steve.

With a glance at a small handheld computer she began, "Steve James is forty-one years of age. While alive his father was considered one of the wealthier men in California. He made his millions in real estate. Steve's parents were killed in a one-car accident when he was five years old. His mother was driving. Although newspaper articles that covered the accident cited poor weather conditions, the police report indicates that she was under the influence of multiple substances.

"After his parents died, Steve moved in with his maternal aunt and her husband who were living in a house Steve's

213

father had purchased for them. Although his aunt and uncle were not able to access Steve's vast inheritance, they had been nicely provided for in Steve's parents' will." Charlotte looked up to make sure everyone was still with her, took a bite of her sandwich, chewed it thoughtfully, swallowed, and then continued.

"What little I could piece together about Steve's childhood was unremarkable. His aunt and uncle used most of their newfound wealth to fund trips and parties, but usually included Steve in their activities. I spoke with two people who grew up with Steve. Both indicated he was more comfortable with adults than kids his own age, he was competitive, and always got what he wanted. One of his childhood acquaintances who also went to Stanford at the same time Steve did said…" Charlotte read from her notes, 'I am not sure if you will understand this, but Steve has always believed he is better than everyone else. Not in the manner of a snob. Steve genuinely considers himself to be more intelligent, more resourceful, more relentless, a better businessman … basically higher on the human being scale than everyone else. This superiority is reflected in how he communicates with people, how he treats them, and definitely why his way is the only way that matters.'" Charlotte glanced up again to see if anyone had a comment. After a pause Nathan signaled for her to continue.

"Steve graduated with a bachelor of science in business from Stanford University with honors and went on to complete an MBA. He has never married, and from what I can learn most of his relationships with women are brief. I was able to find a woman he dated a few years ago for a month, who said, 'Steve always made me feel I wasn't quite good enough—you know, not pretty enough, not smart enough.' Another woman he dated for a brief time told me she broke up with Steve because he had a temper, especially when things didn't go his way."

"Steve is quite wealthy. He seems to have acquired his father's acumen for real estate and has tripled his original inheritance, which he received when he turned twenty-two. From the information I was able to obtain, I would estimate his net worth at just shy of half a billion dollars. He owns commercial and residential properties all over the state with the greatest concentration of his real estate holdings in San Diego and here in San Francisco." Charlotte looked up from her notes. "I have a list if you are interested." Nathan said he was and Charlotte pulled a file folder from her purse took out a few sheets that were stapled together, and handed them to him.

Nathan glanced through the list. "With all of this property why would Steve want Mary and Bob's house?"

Treating Nathan's question as rhetorical, Charlotte went on, "He also owns several toys including a small airplane...." Charlotte scrolled through her electronic notes. "A Cessna Turbo Skylane." There was a collective gasp in the room. Charlotte looked up, curious about the reaction her last piece of information had evoked.

"Are you sure about the airplane?" I asked quietly. "It was my understanding Steve wouldn't be a passenger in a small plane, much less fly one."

Charlotte responded confidently, "I'm not sure where you got the impression Steve didn't like small planes. He has been a licensed pilot for almost fifteen years, and the Skylane is just the latest in a string of small aircraft he has owned."

Thinking she had cleared up a misconception, Charlotte smiled. "That's as much information as I could get in the timeframe you requested."

"Good work, Charlotte," praised Nathan, also a little shaken by the revelation. "What about the National Transportation Safety Board investigation? Were you able to learn anything from them?"

Charlotte scrolled down her computer. "I spoke with Kevin Anderson, who is head of the investigation team for the crash." Looking at me, she said, "I believe you met with him about a month or so ago." I nodded. "He said pretty much what we expected—the investigation is proceeding... no cause has been discovered to date... it may be several months before an opinion or determination can be rendered... the usual cause of private airplane crashes is pilot error or an equipment malfunction... if we have reason to suspect foul play, please contact him."

Nathan thanked her for the report. Charlotte slipped her computer into her purse, picked up the rest of her lunch, and left us to discuss what we had learned.

As soon as the door closed behind Charlotte, we all started speaking at once. It wasn't until Nathan stood up, holding his hands out in a Messiah-like pose, that we quieted down.

In a sober tone he said, "What we have is a lot of circumstantial information. We have nothing to prove the crash was not an accident, much less that it was deliberately caused by Steve." Nathan's proclamation was followed by a vigorous and emotional debate.

This time it was Kate who brought us back to order by walking to the whiteboard on the wall of the conference room. "We need more information. Let's discuss how we are going to get it."

She wrote Carole on the whiteboard, as she said, "Carole's receptionist has left two messages asking me when I want to meet with Carole again. The only rub is that Carole wants to meet at my boyfriend's house so she can get a feel for the place."

Kate looked uncomfortable. I told Ross about the boyfriend's-house ploy she had used when she met with Carole.

When I finished Nathan said, "Well, that's easy. Meet Carole at my house. It's in Pacific Heights, and it needs lots of work. Maybe Carole will actually come up with a few good ideas."

Kate accepted Nathan's offer with only a modicum of embarrassment, and wrote on the white board after Carole's name, "schedule meeting at Nathan's house."

"I will try to schedule an appointment with her tomorrow. Do we have specific questions I should ask her?"

After a little discussion, Kate added under Carole's name, "Why is Steve so interested in Mary's house?" When the conversation about Carole concluded, Kate excused herself to go to Nathan's office and phone Carole's receptionist to schedule the meeting.

"Steve invited J and me to have dinner with him before I leave town," Ross said. "He keeps pressuring J to meet with him, and I would be much more comfortable if I were there." Looking at me, he said, "I think we should take him up on his invitation, and see what we can learn. We could tell him tomorrow night is our only free night."

Nathan concurred, reminding us not to forget to see if we could discover the motivation behind Steve's contribution to the children's foundation. Ross took the business card Steve gave him out of his wallet and left to join Kate in Nathan's office to make a call of his own.

When we were alone, Nathan turned to me with a look of concern. "J, as your attorney I must tell you it is extremely unlikely anything will come of our investigation. Even if we get answers to all of our questions, they won't prove a crime was committed. If Steve really did cause the crash, we need either a confession or concrete proof he tampered with the plane just to get the police to consider it wasn't an accident. And neither appears forthcoming. Once we have exhausted all of these efforts, we are all going to have to go back to business as usual, and accept the fact we have no recourse. Do you think you can do that?"

While I knew what Nathan was saying was true, it was still difficult to hear. I had to hold back tears. "Honestly, I don't know if I can, but I will try."

As he began to pick up the litter from our lunch, Nathan said distractedly, "If only Mary and Bob were here so they could tell us what happened."

Standing to help him clean the table, my tears abated and I almost smiled as I thought, "Perhaps they can."

Chapter 33

Nathan and I finished cleaning up the detritus from our lunch, and Kate and Ross returned to the conference room after scheduling their respective appointments. Kate had scheduled her meeting with Carole for five the following afternoon at Nathan's house, and Ross had told Steve we would meet him for a seven o'clock dinner the next evening at the Parkside Grille. With the arrangements made, Nathan and Kate debated whether Nathan should be at the meeting with Carole. Kate said she thought it was a bad idea, and the discussion ended.

Ross's and my deliberations were much more dynamic. They spanned the time from our last moments in Nathan's office, through checking out of the Stanford Park Hotel and moving back to Mary's home, through the next morning's run, through our afternoon's gardening in Mary's yard. We were still debating the best strategy to use with Steve as we showered and dressed for our dinner with him.

Ross wanted to confront him. I wanted to finesse him. Ross was concerned about my safety, so he wanted to put Steve on notice—to let him know we were watching him. I had to find out if Steve had caused the airplane crash, and if he had, to make sure he paid for it. So alerting him to our suspicions was the last thing I wanted to do. Unfortunately we spent so much time disagreeing about strategy that we failed to identify questions to elicit what information we needed from Steve for our investigation to proceed.

Just as Ross finally acquiesced to my more subtle strategy, the house phone rang. I answered it while Ross finished shaving. It was Kate. She was phoning from Nathan's. Her meeting with Carole had just ended.

"Aside from telling me Nathan's house needs a complete remodel, Carole said two things of interest. First, she told me that when she confronted Steve about lying that the house was in escrow, he told her the deal to purchase Mary's house would be finalized in the next few weeks."

"You are kidding," I blurted. "What can Steve be thinking?"

"I suggested that Carole give you a call just to make sure there is a deal. I even gave her your cell number. I hope that was all right. The way Carole sounded I expect you will get a call tonight or tomorrow."

"It was a brilliant thing to do, Kate," I assured. "What was the other point of Interest?"

I could almost hear Kate smile over the phone. "Carole wanted to know if I would like to meet her for dinner this evening. She told me Steve had to break their date for the evening because of an unanticipated business problem."

"I suppose this means Steve is going to put a full court press on me to sell the house tonight," I whined. "It will be interesting to see how he plans on pressuring me with Ross present." After a brief silence I asked, "Are you having dinner with Carole?"

Kate answered, "No. I told her I had a date."

"Do you?"

"You bet I do," she said.

Steve had told Ross he would be coming from a business meeting in the East Bay so he would meet us at the restaurant. Ross and I pulled into the parking lot of the Parkside Grille ten minutes early, and took a moment to sit in the car and enjoy the scenery. The Grille is set in a forest of redwood trees. If you didn't know any better you would think you were in a remote rural area instead of four miles from the 280, which provides freeway access from San Francisco to San Jose. Sitting next to Ross as we listened to the Jays squawk, and inhaled the musty fragrance of the woods, I felt homesick for Mammoth Lakes.

As we were getting out of the car, Steve's black Range Rover pulled into the lot. He immediately saw us and parked next to Ross's Honda. There was an awkward round of handshakes and embraces. While the three of us walked toward the restaurant door, I thanked Steve for the incredibly generous contribution he made at the memorial to the children's foundation in Mary and Bob's name. He seemed slightly abashed by my gratitude, saying it was the least he could do, and held the door open so we could enter.

The restaurant décor was high-end mountain lodge. We were led through a high-ceilinged room with an open kitchen to an impeccably set table next to a window. Even though it was almost completely dark outside, Steve insisted Ross and I sit on the side of the table that afforded the best views. The hostess took our cocktail orders. Before she could retreat, Steve asked when Bill would arrive. The hostess told him Bill was already at the restaurant, just attending to last-minute changes for a small banquet being held later in the evening.

Steve insisted, "When he is finished, please have him come to our table to meet my guests." Then, either noticing the hostess's reaction or realizing how boorish he had sounded, he backed off. "Sorry. I had a rough day. Would you please ask Bill when he has a moment if he would stop by our table?" The hostess nodded and hurried away, while Steve explained that Bill was a good friend, as well as the owner of the restaurant.

We made small talk through martinis and an appetizer of baked organic goat cheese with grilled focaccia bread, a bottle of wine, salads, and steaks. Relaxed by the drinks and superb cuisine, conversation started to come more easily—especially for Steve, who proved to be a skilled raconteur. He chatted effortlessly about his various community-fund raising efforts, turning a mundane alumni dinner for Stanford University he had chaired into a sidesplitting satire. Steve listened as well as entertained. He sounded genuinely interested when he asked us what it was like to live in the Eastern Sierra. The only time he lost his poise was when we first sat down and I asked if Carole would be joining us. He muttered something about Carole having to meet with a difficult client, and then changed the subject. Steve's brief breach of composure notwithstanding, by the end of the entrees I was beginning to question our suppositions about him even though I thought I knew better.

Just as the waiter started to clear the table, Ross's cell phone chimed. He looked embarrassed as he excused himself to go outside and answer it. I knew Ross detested people who spoke on their cell phones in restaurants, theaters, bars, and golf courses. He appeared to be mortified that with a simple cell chirp he had just joined the ranks of the rude.

Before Ross was out of sight, Steve's demeanor turned serious. "J, we *have* to talk. I want to buy Mary and Bob's house. Hell, I *need* to buy the house. I know I sound crazy, but for some reason it has become a minor obsession with me. Just name your price. We can close the deal *tonight*."

I'm not sure if it was the martinis and wine, or the easy conversation that had caused me to let my guard down, but the abrupt shift in Steve's manner left me at a loss for an appropriate response. After an awkward pause I uttered, "I'm just not ready to make a decision yet. I need some time."

I could see the blood rise in Steve's face and his lips begin to form the words of an angry response when he looked beyond me and his expression shifted back to pleasant and benign. Sensing motion behind me, I realized it was Ross who retook his seat beside me and apologized for the cell phone interruption. Steve rose and announced that he had ordered a special dessert and wanted to let our waiter know we were ready for it. He hastily left the table.

Ross glanced curiously at the abrupt departure, but he made no effort to discover what happened between Steve and me while he was outside on his cell phone. In fact, we barely looked at one another while Steve was gone, fearing Steve might sense some sort of conspiracy when he returned. Within a few minutes he was back with a broad smile on his face as if our exchange about the house had never happened. Once again he was the affable, charming gentleman he had been when the evening began. Two waiters followed him to the table. One held a silver tray with a bottle of Veuve Clicquot and three champagne flutes on it. The other carried a tray of tapas-sized desserts—crème brulé, chocolate cake, marzipan, strawberry tarts, chocolate mousse—every decadent sweet one might hope for.

After Steve's failed appeal to convince me to sell Mary's house to him, I thought he would want to end the evening early, but it was clear with the arrival of the champagne and desserts he had not yet finished playing host. Once the flutes were filled, Steve toasted new friends then focused most of his attention on Ross. He asked Ross what it was like to be a professional ski patroller, and entreated him to talk about his more harrowing experiences. Then Steve shifted the discussion to a comparison of ski resorts, comparing U.S. resorts to Europe, South America, and New Zealand.

It was after eleven when Ross asked the waiter for the check, only to find Steve had taken care of it at the beginning of the evening. Ross retrieved my knee-length black down coat from a hook in the entry while Steve said good night to Bill. The three of us walked into the chilled night air toward our cars parked side by side.

When we reached the cars Steve gave me a good night hug, whispering surreptitiously in my ear, "You know you don't want to move from Mammoth, so call me as soon as you decide to sell the house." Then he turned to shake hands with Ross.

As Ross and I watched Steve drive off in his Range Rover, I was more confused than ever.

Chapter 34

I was grateful Mary's house was only a few minutes away; it had been a long evening. As Ross drove I told him about Steve's latest press to buy Mary's house, and my bungled response.

After listening to my account, Ross commented thoughtfully, "It's like he is two different people. If you hadn't told me about him before I met him, I'd say he is a genuinely nice guy."

"I know, most of the time this evening I kept thinking I was crazy to have ever suspected him of causing the crash. He's so... so charming... so nice."

Ross nodded. "None of the pieces of this puzzle fit."

For the next few minutes we were silent as we both tried to make sense of the evening. Finally we acknowledged how tired we were and decided to table any more discussion of Steve until morning.

We passed Steve's house just before taking the turn up Mary's steep driveway. Steve's car was parked and he was walking toward his front door. He saw us drive by and gave us a friendly wave. I felt as if I were in the Twilight Zone.

As Ross pulled the Honda into the garage I suddenly remembered the cell call Ross had received during dinner and asked about it.

His face clouded as he answered, "I have to go back to Mammoth tomorrow. Three patrollers are out with flu, the

Mountain is short staffed, and they are expecting a big crowd for the final week of the season. I'm sorry, J. I know I told you I would try to stay through the week."

I tried not to show my disappointment. "Don't worry, I have a lot to do here," I said pointing to the house. "Kate and I are going to start sorting though Mary and Bob's things." Then stifling a groan as I looked around the interior of the garage crowded with boxes of tools, mountain bikes, skis, and other assorted sports equipment, I added, "If you were staying I would just have had to put you to work out here."

Ross and I awakened early the next morning and decided to go for a run up a section of Alpine Road long ago closed by landslides. The fog fall was receding back over the mountains toward the coastal town of Pescadero at a quicker pace than normal, which portended an unseasonably warm day. As we reached the bottom of the trail, it appeared that everyone in the community was out to celebrate the warm weather. The trail was crowded with mountain bikers, hikers, dog walkers, and runners, turning the trail into an obstacle course. By unspoken agreement we ran faster than usual, enjoying the single-minded effort, focusing all our energy on the run instead of the conundrum of Steve or Ross's impending departure.

At the end of our run, Ross challenged me to a race up Mary's driveway. I was about to claim exhaustion, but changed my mind when I saw Steve out of the corner of my eye coming out of his house—I wasn't ready to find out who he was today.

I was nearly at the first switchback in the driveway when Ross realized I had accepted his challenge. I beat him to the top of the driveway by mere inches. Instead of complaining about my illegal head start, he accepted defeat like a gentleman.

When we reached the front of the house we took our dusty running shoes off and placed them under the wrought iron bench next to the front door, a practice Mary had always insisted upon in an effort to keep her light gray Berber carpet clean. I grabbed a couple of cold bottles of water from the refrigerator, as we passed through the house, out to the deck facing the mountains. A well-worn teak bench with a faded blue cushion was our destination. We settled in to chat before it was time for Ross to leave.

Ross began our conversation in a tight, worried voice. "At the risk of sounding chauvinistic, I don't want you to meet with Steve while I am gone. In fact, I would prefer it if you would let Nathan handle all of your research until I return. The Mountain can return and help. Will you do that for me?"

I was touched by his concern. "I do have to let it go for a little while. It's time for me to concentrate on getting the estate in order. And... and I guess I have to...." A sob caught in my throat and I couldn't finish. Ross took me in his arms and held me. When I was finally able to finish my sentence I said softly, "...have to make some decisions about the house."

Ross tightened his grip on me, responding, "You don't need to make any decisions now if you aren't ready..."

He was cut off by the ringing of the house phone. I reluctantly moved out of Ross's embrace and walked into the house. "I better get that. The land line hardly ever rings, so it may be important." I went into the kitchen, grabbed the portable phone, and as I made my way back to the bench and Ross, said hello.

It was Carole and she was all business. "This is Carole Nelson, Steve James' ... uh ... girlfriend. I need to know if you are in escrow to sell your house to Steve or if you have verbally agreed to sell your house to him."

Even though I should have been expecting the call, I was taken aback by Carole's directness. My mind racing for a response, I blustered, "My house?"

My response gained Ross's interest. He studied me closely. It also elicited a prompt response from Carole, who demanded, "Yes. It's a simple question. Are you selling your house to Steve?"

Standing up, straightening my spine as if Carole were questioning me in person, I articulated each word as I answered, "No, Carole. I have not agreed to sell my house to anyone. I have not even decided whether I will ever sell the house."

I heard Carole's quick intake of breath. "Thank you. I will not bother you again." Before I could respond she hung up.

As I turned the phone off Ross asked, "Carole?"

I told him what Carole had asked, and her words before she hung up.

"I don't like this." He stood and started to pace. "It's a bad time for me to be leaving. You shouldn't be here alone with Steve next door. Perhaps you should come back to Mammoth with me, and we can return when the Mountain closes."

I grabbed Ross's hands so he would stop pacing. "Don't you think you are overreacting a little bit? Kate was going to move in this week anyway to help me go through Mary and Bob's things. I will just ask her to come a few days early. Mary and Bob's alarm system is state of the art, and Nathan just had all the locks re-keyed and the alarm code changed. We should be fine. Besides, if Steve did cause the crash, it took a lot of planning. He's not going to do something crazy. That just doesn't seem to be his style."

Without a better solution, Ross acquiesced. He went into the house to shower and pack while I phoned Kate to see if she would come to stay with me a few days early.

I dialed Kate's cell.

"You will never guess where I am!?" She answered. "I'm at the Old Course at Half Moon Bay. Nathan and I are playing golf."

"Lucky you! I have always wanted to play that course. I didn't know you're a golfer."

"I'm not. Nathan is teaching me." Whispering, she added, "It's fun, but I suck at it."

"The reason I am calling: Ross needs to go back to Mammoth this afternoon, and I was wondering…"

Interrupting, Kate said, "I'll have Nathan drop me off at your place when we finish golfing. Tomorrow you can drive me home to pick up some clothes and my car. Oops. Just a minute."

I heard Kate and Nathan talking in hushed voices in the background. Kate returned, speaking quickly. "We'll pick up dinner on our way. I have to go. Apparently cell phones aren't permitted on golf courses."

Before I could thank her, she disconnected.

Chapter 35

I went into the bedroom where Ross was packing. I told him Kate's plan to begin her stay this evening, which made him look only slightly less worried. I assured him we would keep the alarm system on, and showed him the canister of pepper spray I had put in my pocket, proving I had means to defend myself. He pretended to relax.

It took Ross only a few minutes before he had the Honda packed and ready to go. I was able to delay his departure for another ten minutes by insisting I prepare him a picnic basket for the road. Inevitably I could think of no more delays. After our long absence it was difficult to part, even for a week. Mammoth seemed like a million miles from Portola Valley. He promised to call every night and I promised to stay safe.

Back inside the house after Ross's car was out of sight, the void seemed unbearable. I had an overwhelming need to talk to Mary, tell her what was happening, and seek her advice. Since that was not an option, I moped around the house until I realized I hadn't showered after my run.

As I entered the guest room to shower, I made a mental list of what I needed to accomplish before Nathan and Kate arrived, which included making up the guest room for Kate, and more significantly, making up Mary and Bob's room for myself.

I had been staying in the guest room. Actually, I had always thought of it as my room. The thought of moving to

Mary and Bob's room added another layer of emotional discomfort.

I tuned my iPod to the Rolling Stones *Forty Licks* CD and went into a cleaning frenzy, hoping the Stones and the work would fill the void in the house, at least for a while. I moved my belongings to the master bedroom, changed the linens in both bedrooms, cleaned the guest room and guest bath, and vacuumed the entire house. I found some late-blooming daffodils in the yard, cut and placed them in a vase in the guest room. Just as I finished sweeping all the decks, Kate and Nathan arrived. Nathan was carrying bags from P.F. Chang's. Kate was carrying a putter. Both were in high spirits.

"How did the golf game go?"

As Nathan set the bags down in the kitchen he said in an unusually proprietary manner, "It's hard to believe Kate never played before. With just a few lessons and a little practice, She's going to be a great golfer."

Kate burst out laughing, "Great golfer? I almost killed that poor man who played with us. If you hadn't yelled duck, he would probably be in the hospital right now!"

While I started going through the bags of food, I asked about the Ping putter still in Kate's hand. Nathan explained he had bought it for her at the course, so she could practice her putting.

"You know, putting is one third of the game," he said authoritatively. They continued to talk golf and tease one another while I made us manhattans, and set the table for dinner.

Over a meal of Harvest spring Rolls, Peking Dumplings, Egg Drop Soup, Moo Goo Gai Pan, and Lo Mein, I told them about Ross's and my dinner with Steve the night before. They seemed as disconcerted by Steve's Jekyll and Hyde as Ross and I were. Kate asked if Carole had phoned, and I filled them in on both the content and the tone of the conversation. Finally, I told them of my promise to Ross that I would discontinue researching the situation until he returned. Nathan seemed a little relieved with this final bit of news; he was still scheduled to meet with Kevin Anderson, of the NTSB in a few days and there really weren't any new avenues to pursue in the meantime.

When I insisted on doing the dishes and cleaning up the kitchen to give them a few moments alone to say goodnight, Kate smiled gratefully and led Nathan out onto the deck. About fifteen minutes later as I was finishing up my chores, Nathan came back into the kitchen, and reminded me to set the alarm as soon as Kate was inside. Promising to call the next day, Nathan took Kate by the hand to go to his car. As they were walking down the stone steps I smiled to myself as I heard him say he was going to call the Pro at his Golf Club in the morning to see what kind of golf clubs he would recommend for her.

Moments later when Kate returned we walked through the house to close the windows and lock the doors. When we reached the guest room, she asked, "Can you still arm the alarm if I leave the door to the small deck off my bedroom open? It's awfully warm and still tonight."

"Certainly," I responded. "In fact, I was thinking about leaving the windows open in the master bedroom. Steve thinks Ross is going to be here the rest of the week, so he shouldn't be a problem." We went to the alarm pad by the front door, where I made the adjustments. Then I showed Kate how to arm and disarm the system. I also made sure she memorized the code.

Once the alarm was set we poured ourselves some wine from an open bottle of Sterling Cabernet and sat at the kitchen table to make a plan for the next day. We decided to begin on the ground floor, and work our way through the house, numbering each room in the order we wanted to follow. I opened the small half closet next to the front door to show her the boxes, tape, markers, and other supplies I had purchased for our task.

It was almost one in the morning when Kate and I finally said good night. As I went through my regular night cleansing rituals, I could hear the guest shower running. Once again I realized what a gift Kate was. I didn't think I could handle the mystery surrounding the crash and Steve, much less going through Mary and Bob's possessions, alone.

Just as I was about to get into bed, I heard Kate coming up the stairs to the master bedroom, saying softly, "J? J are you still awake?"

I walked toward the top of the stairs. She asked if I had some contact lens solution. I went to the bathroom, found my back-up bottle and gave it to her. Did she need anything else? She said she was fine, and started towards the stairs.

I followed her to the stairs and hugged her. "Kate. Thank you. If you weren't here, I am not sure what I would do."

She hugged me back. "Mary knew. She left us each other," and turned to walk down the stairs.

Watching her move down into the darkness, I cautioned, "Kate. There are no lights on downstairs. Do you want me to walk down with you?"

"I'm fine," she replied. "There's enough ambient light in the house, it's not necessary." As I turned to go to bed, I heard her say "Good night, J."

Chapter 36 — Steve

After my last attempt to speak with Carole, I knew what I had to do. I just couldn't believe she was making me do it. I thought it might take a few days; I just had to wait for the boyfriend to go back to Mammoth—which was only a week away. Then this afternoon I saw him drive by the house with his duffel in the back of his car. Later Janet had a few more visitors, but they left around eleven. Good. It was time to take back control.

It was an unusually warm evening for spring. As I walked up the driveway using my penlight to navigate the turns, I couldn't help but think about how my life had gone from perfect to crap in the matter of a few months. And, it was all because of this bitch, Janet.

I met Carole by chance at the Mill Valley Art Festival. We were admiring some kiln-formed glasswork by Cathe Howe, and quite naturally began a conversation. When we found out we were both collectors of her work, something clicked. By that evening we were dining together, by the end of the weekend we were sleeping together. I had always been successful with women, though sometimes I thought it was because of my money and position. But Carole was different. It was evident from the beginning that she wanted me as much as I wanted her. It was the first time in my life I felt like I was with an equal.

And beautiful! When Carole walked into a room, everyone—men and women alike—noticed. It wasn't just her great body, eyes the color of cobalt glass, or her natural platinum blond hair, it was the way she carried herself—demanding to be admired. To top it all, she wasn't interested in my money or position. She was a successful interior designer with money and a reputation of her own.

I suppose the end was set into motion on that weekend in January when I asked Carole to marry me. My plan for proposing to her came to me one day when we were sitting side by side on stationary bikes at the Health Club. Carole loved to work out and soon after we had started dating—if one could call it just dating—she convinced me to join her Health Club and work out with her. It was hard at first; I had never been much of an athlete. I had always preferred more cerebral pursuits. But she pushed me. And soon I actually began to enjoy it.

So I waited until the first warm day in January, and then put my plan into action. I had bought us two road bikes—a Le Mond Versailles for Carole and a Salsa Campeon for me. I surprised her with the bikes in the morning, and then told her I had planned the entire day, beginning with a ride up Alpine Road. She seemed pleased. My intent was to ask her to marry me on the ride, and then we could go into Palo Alto to lunch and buy a suitable engagement ring. I knew she would want to pick out her own ring—she had definite style preferences. After purchasing a ring befitting my fiancée, we would finish the day off with a celebratory stay in the suite I reserved at the Stanford Park Hotel.

As we neared the end of Alpine Road, I stopped at the bottom of one of the residential streets. When she fussed that she wasn't tired yet, I told her I wanted to talk to her about something. We laid our bikes on the curbside, and she started strolling up the street looking at all the houses. When I caught up with her, I took her by the hand, and asked her to marry me. That's when she pointed to a large house on the top of the hill and said casually, "Steve, I will marry you when you buy me that house."

Although it wasn't the answer I had hoped to hear, it wasn't the one I feared either. So I said, "Give me a few weeks, and it will be yours." I suggested we go pick out an engagement ring. She demurred, saying that she wouldn't accept an engagement ring until the house was in escrow.

We spent the rest of the day in the Stanford Park Hotel suite properly celebrating our almost-engagement.

The following Monday I drove to Carole's house, as I now thought of it. I was sitting in my car at the end of the driveway, formulating my pitch, when a man and woman on mountain bikes came riding down the driveway. When they saw me there, they stopped and asked if they could help me. I said, "Actually, if you are the owners of this house, perhaps you can." I introduced myself, and they did the same. Mary was a fit, attractive brunette, and though of medium height, she gave the illusion of being taller. She had an incredibly warm smile that made me believe I would be successful in my quest. Bob, on the other hand, was aloof. Tall, dark, athletic, and quite comfortable with himself, he just stood there watching Mary and me talk—tapping his foot as if to indicate they should be riding not talking.

But I had their attention, so I plunged forward. I offered to purchase their home. I told them they could name their price and if it were semi-reasonable, I would pay it. While Bob gave a short derisive laugh, Mary smiled, thanked me for the offer and said they would never sell. She said goodbye and they rode off.

I was angry. I was mortified. I was motivated. I was not giving up.

I returned the next week with local listings and comps from a Real Estate Broker. When I knocked on their door, Mary answered. Before she could say anything, I told her that I would top the highest sales price in the area by a million dollars. She looked a little taken aback by the number, but then smiled at me as if I were a homeless man begging for a dollar and politely said that she and Bob were not interested in selling—not for any amount of money.

The next day, I spoke with the man who lived just down the hill and next door from Mary's home, and made the same offer—though I reduced the incentive by a half million dollars. The owner, John Hathaway, said he would have to discuss it with his wife and would call me in a day or two. By the end of the week I owned their home. In a month I had moved in.

When I showed Carole the house I had purchased, she said it was nice, but she wasn't going to marry me until I bought her the house she wanted. After a little fast thinking on my part, I told her that I was in negotiations with the owners of the house she wanted. I also told her we could live in this house while the renovations she was sure to want were completed, and then this house would eventually be used as the guesthouse for our estate.

A few days later I called on Mary and Bob once more. This time Bob answered. Before he could tell me to get lost, I said, "I just wanted to apologize if I was a little pushy. I really love this neighborhood. I also wanted to let you know that I just became your new next door neighbor." When Mary joined Bob at the door, I explained that I had just purchased the Hathaways' home, and since we would be neighbors, I hoped we could also become friends.

When I moved in I had them over for a glass of wine. Mary reciprocated by inviting me over for dinner. Gradually I got to know them, their home, and their habits. I also learned that their only relative was Mary's twin—the bitch.

Arranging for the plane "accident" was easy. Since Bob and I had almost identical planes, figuring out how to take a Turbo Skylane down was fairly simple—at least for me. To make matters even easier, Bob's own airplane mechanic unwittingly gave me easy access to the plane and even shared Bob's maintenance schedule with me.

Once the plane crashed, it was only going to be a matter of time. While I was surprised that Janet hadn't died with Mary and Bob, it hadn't worried me. She would have to sell the house. According to Mary, she had tried to get Janet to move closer, but Janet refused because she loved living in Mammoth. I was sure she wouldn't want to leave Mammoth now to live in her dead sister's house.

I thought everything was going perfectly, then Janet accidentally ran into the architect walking around the grounds of her home, and the whole thing went to hell. The bitch started asking questions. Worse yet, she refused to put the house on the market. I told her she could name her price. But she still wouldn't sell. She said she needed time to think about it.

I thought I had Carole convinced I was in negotiations to buy the house, but the bitch told Carole she had never agreed to sell the house to me and didn't know if she ever would put the house on the market. That's gratitude for you. Didn't I make a half-million-dollar donation to that organization for kids Mary and Bob liked so much? Didn't that mean anything?

Now Carole wanted nothing more to do with me. She called me a liar. She said she knew all along I was weak and ineffective. She was no longer taking my calls, and had the audacity to refuse delivery of the gifts I sent over to placate her.

When I reached the house, I quietly lifted myself to the second story deck off the guest bedroom. Just as I had anticipated, the sliding door had been left open, letting fresh air into the room, as it had been since the bitch arrived in Portola Valley.

It was about two a.m. and all the lights were out, but my eyes had adjusted to the night on the walk over. I took my gun out of my pocket and silently slid the screen door open. As I approached the bed, I heard someone coming from the kitchen toward the bedroom. I looked down and saw that the bed was empty. The bitch must have gone to the kitchen for some water. As I waited just inside the doorway for her to walk into the bedroom, I heard a woman walking toward me and yelling, "Good night, J."

The woman who was walking into the room wasn't Janet. Fortunately, she didn't turn on the light. Before she could see me, I hit her on the side of her head with the butt of my gun. She went down with a loud thud and a sickening snap.

Moving toward the kitchen, I heard Janet shouting, "Kate! Kate is something wrong? Kate?!" Then Janet appeared at the foot of the third floor stairs, rushing toward the guest room. When she saw me she abruptly stopped. All she wore was a long blue t-shirt and a pair of white athletic socks. Noticing the gun in my hand that was pointed at her heart, her face shifted from concern to a mixture of fear and anger. "What are you doing here?" She demanded. "What have you done to Kate?"

Chapter 37

Just as I was getting into bed, I heard a crash downstairs. I knew I should have insisted Kate turn on some lights as she returned to her room. There are too many obstacles in an unfamiliar house. Not bothering to put on a robe over Ross's blue t-shirt I used as a nightgown, I ran downstairs to see if Kate had hurt herself, while trying to remember where Mary kept her first aid kit.

As I reached the bottom of the stairs I became more concerned; I couldn't hear Kate. I yelled, "Kate! Kate, is something wrong? Kate?!" But I still heard no reply.

Then I saw him. At first I wasn't sure who it was. I just knew it was a man with a gun pointed at me. But Kate was right. With the help of the ambient light I could see. And what I saw was Steve.

My first reaction was fear; it was followed quickly by cold, hard anger. "What are *you* doing here?" I demanded. "What have you done to Kate?"

After a moment of unnerving silence, Steve started screaming, "You bitch. It's all *your* fault. None of this would have ever happened if it weren't for you. Why didn't you just die in the crash with your worthless sister?" His face was red, his gun hand was shaking, his teeth were clenched, and he was spraying spittle while he shouted.

I knew it was only a matter of time before he would lose the little control he had left and shoot me, so I asked in the calmest voice I could muster, "What is this all about, Steve? Is it about the house?"

But it was as if he couldn't or wouldn't hear me. He just kept shouting, "It's your fucking fault she left me. It's your fault that woman is dead. It's *your* fault..."

Woman is dead. Who did he mean? Carole? Kate? Had he shot Kate? No, I would have heard a gunshot. But I hadn't heard anything from her, from her room. Where was she? Oh, God. He couldn't have killed Kate. If he killed Kate it was my fault.

Steve was still yelling at me. I could no longer hear his words, just the sound of his rage. He looked like he was ready to explode. Any moment now he would pull the trigger and that would be it. I had no place to hide, no way to protect myself.

Then for one incredible moment he just stopped, frozen in place. The sudden quiet almost knocked me over. He was looking at me differently. No. He was looking past me.

As he continued to stare I thought I heard a stirring from the guest room hallway, but I couldn't be sure. Steve heard nothing. He was fixated on something behind me.

As I watched, Steve straightened. He held his gun more steadily and said in a controlled, even, almost quiet voice, "What are *you* doing here?" I wanted to turn and see who Steve was addressing, but I couldn't take my eyes off him or the gun.

With Steve's next words, I didn't have to wonder anymore. "You are dead. I took down your plane. I killed you." Mary and Bob came into my periphery view as they walked to my right toward the front door, Steve's eyes following their every movement.

Steve had quit speaking; he was transfixed. I was afraid to move, not wanting him to refocus on me. Mary and Bob just continued to smile at Steve, saying nothing, all the while advancing slowly to the door.

Suddenly, in one explosive moment George—how did George get here—leaped from the guest room hall with Kate's new putter in hand. Before Steve could react, George slammed the putter into the back of Steve's head, taking him down with one stroke.

Once we made sure Steve was unconscious, George taped his hands and feet with tape from my packing supplies, while I went in search of Kate.

I turned on the lights. Kate was lying at the entrance to the guest room hall, crying weakly, blood dripping from the side of her head, one leg bent at an impossible angle.

I crouched on the floor next to her, gently placed her head in my lap, and pleaded softly, "How badly are you hurt? Kate, please tell me you are going to be all right."

Kate looked at me, her hazel eyes almost transparent, and whispered, "I saw Mary and Bob. They were here." Then she fell limp.

I stayed on the floor with Kate's head in my lap, making deals with God, as I heard George call 911. I remained that way until a Paramedic led me to the living room, seating me on the sofa so they could work on Kate.

I was unable to move, speak, or cry while the house filled up with more paramedics and police. Someone put a blanket around my shoulders. I was vaguely aware of people trying to speak to me, but I couldn't make out what they were saying. I was drowning in grief and guilt.

Moments or hours later, still seated on the couch, the scene around me came back into focus. The house was still crowded with people. George and Nathan were on either side of me, holding my hands, quietly talking to one another. As clarity returned, so did an overwhelming sense of sadness.

When first Nathan, then George glanced at me, I could see in their faces they knew I was back.

As they started to speak, I held up my hand to quiet them, and said in the steadiest voice I could muster, "It's my fault. *I* killed Kate."

"No, J, you didn't," Nathan said gently. "Kate is going to be all right. She has a concussion, and her left leg is pretty badly broken, but she will recover. They just took her to Stanford Hospital." He studied me closely. "Do you understand what I am saying?"

"Kate's going to be okay?" I whispered.

"Yes, J," George said. "Kate will be fine." As their words penetrated my fogged brain, I let go and began to cry.

The next several hours went by in slow motion. Paramedics examined me. Once they were gone, two police officers separated George and me, and questioned us individually about the evening's events. With Nathan at my side, I tried to recount the events of the evening, being as specific and detailed as possible.

Near what turned out to be the end of the interview, the officer questioning me asked "Who are Mary and Bob? When did they arrive? And, do you know where they are now?"

As I was trying to come up with a response, Nathan, who had stiffened considerably at the questions, interjected, "Mary and Bob owned this house. They were killed in a plane crash in late January of this year. Why are you asking about Mary and Bob?"

Ignoring Nathan's question, the police officer looked at him incredulously. "Are you sure they are deceased?"

I felt Nathan start to rise in anger; I placed my hand on his arm. "Officer, Mary was my twin, Bob was her husband, my brother in law. Mary and Bob were friends and clients of Mr. Hadley. I was in the same plane crash that killed my twin and brother-in-law. We are certain they are deceased. Why would you ask about them?"

The officer, whose name I forgot as soon as he had given it to me, looked to be in his late twenties and confused. He looked around the room as if looking for some assistance, then focused on me. "As my partner and the Paramedics were taking Mr. James into medical custody he regained consciousness. He kept asking where Mary and Bob were."

Shaking my head I responded, "George must have hit Steve with that putter harder than we thought."

Chapter 38

The sun was rising by the time the last of the police left the house. As soon as they were gone Nathan suggested I try to get some sleep, then announced George would stay with me while he went to the hospital to see how Kate was doing.

Before he finished his sentence I grabbed my purse saying, "You're not going to see Kate *without me*."

Nathan looked like he had expected my reaction as he suggested, "Then you might want to dress in something a bit more presentable."

I realized under the blanket that still covered my shoulders I was dressed for bed in Ross's blue t-shirt—which was now stained with Kate's blood—and a pair of my running socks.

I was about to run upstairs to change, when on a hunch I took Nathan's car keys out of his hand, then trotted up the stairs. "Just in case you were thinking of leaving without me." As I made my way to the master bedroom, I heard Nathan suggest to George *he* might want to clean up *too*.

Moments later my face was washed and I was dressed in a pair of jeans, a black cotton turtleneck, and sandals. Nathan and George still looked dubious, until I held up my brush and a hair clip. "I'll comb my hair in the car. Let's get going."

We walked into the hospital entrance twenty minutes later. Looking more like street people than visitors, the receptionist's initial greeting was chilly. Nathan, who looked the most respectable, took the lead and asked for Kate Richards's room number. Still uncomfortable with our rough appearance, the receptionist asked if we were family.

I pointed to George saying, "This is Kate's uncle, I'm her sister…" and gesturing towards Nathan, "He's her fiancé." Unenthusiastically the receptionist directed us to the nursing desk on Kate's floor.

When we arrived at the next nurse's station, we went through the same explanation and introductions, though the reception was a bit warmer. Once Kate's nurse was located, she told us Kate was resting, but had periodically asked to see Nathan and me. When the nurse explained only one family visitor could go into the room at a time, and only for fifteen minutes every hour, I almost cried, certain Nathan should be the first in the room.

Simultaneously Nathan and I pointed at each other saying resignedly, "You go first."

Kate's nurse must have heard the angst in our voices. "If you promise not to excite Kate, you may both go in for this first visit. After that you must take turns." Looking at George with a raised eyebrow she said, "You are all right with waiting, aren't you?

He nodded and headed into the small, windowless waiting room next to the nurse's station. "Give her a hug for me."

As we entered her room, Kate appeared to be sleeping. She was as pale as the bandages that swathed her head, her left leg was in a large white cast, and there was bruising on the left side of her face. As I took it all in, I was unable to stifle a sob. At the sound, Kate's eyes fluttered open and they landed on Nathan who was standing at the foot of her bed. Up until that moment he had successfully controlled his emotions.

Appearing heavily medicated, Kate gave Nathan a blurry smile. "Did you see Bob and Mary too?" Then she closed her eyes and drifted back to sleep.

Nathan looked beaten as he whispered, "She's hallucinating. Do you think I should go speak with her doctor?"

I walked toward him until we were face to face, gripped his hands, and said quietly, "She's not hallucinating. I will explain later. It's only fair I explain to both you and Kate together, but not until Kate is coherent enough to understand and not in front of George. You are going to have to trust me."

I took a chair from beneath the window, moved it next to Kate's bedside, and sat down, placing my hand gently on hers. When I glanced back at Nathan I was surprised to find he didn't look startled by my disguised revelation, he was actually smiling to himself as if the final piece of a puzzle had just fallen into place.

In a few moments Kate opened her eyes again. This time she looked at me. She said haltingly, "J, you're okay. I kept asking, but no one could tell me anything."

Just as I cried, "I'm so sorry, Kate. This is all my fault. Steve wanted to hurt me, not you. It should have been me."

After a moment of trying to soothe one another, we fell silent—holding each other's hands, comforted by each other's presence. Some minutes later, Nathan and a nurse lightly nudged me awake. Still clinging to one another we had both fallen asleep, my head lying on the bed next to our clasped hands.

When we returned to the waiting room, Nathan asked George to drive me back to the house and make sure I went to bed. "Take my car. I'll take a cab back to your house, J. I'm just not sure how long I will be," said Nathan. Too tired to protest, I told Nathan where the spare house key was and gave him the alarm code, and followed George out of the hospital.

As George half guided, half carried me to Nathan's car I asked wearily, "How did you know?"

"What do you mean?

"How did you know we needed help? Why did you come to the house?"

George stopped and looked at me. "Because you called. Don't you remember?" Without waiting for me to reply he continued, "At first I wasn't sure it was you. I mean it sounded like you, but all you said was, 'I need help.' But then I saw Mary and Bob's number on caller ID, so I hopped in Bob's Mosler and drove like hell."

I was about to say it wasn't me, but I caught myself. "I guess so much happened so quickly I just don't remember. But I am so glad I did, George. You saved Kate's and my lives. I will never be able to repay you." George's cheeks colored while he awkwardly grasped my arm and guided me to the car.

"George, You need to go home. You look as exhausted as I feel. I promise I will go right to bed."

He looked troubled. "I don't know, J. Won't you feel uncomfortable staying here alone?"

"Not anymore, thanks to you. Just come in with me for a moment."

The house was a mess, but I knew just what I wanted and about where it should be. I walked over to Mary's desk, where I had all of Mary and Bob's important documents stacked. Thumbing through them, it took me a moment before I found what I was looking for. I took out a document, signed it, and handed it to George, kissing him on the cheek as I did so.

"What's this?" he asked as he fumbled around his pockets for his reading glasses.

"It's the pink slip to the Mosler. She's all yours now. It's not enough, but I am hoping it will make you smile."

"I can't take the car," George stammered. "It's worth way too much."

"Is it worth more than Kate's and my lives?" I countered. "George, you are the only person I know who can really appreciate it." I added with a bit of unintentional irony, "Besides, Bob would probably haunt me if I gave it to anyone else." I kissed him again on the cheek and sent him home.

I had one more thing to do before I went to bed. I called Ross's cell even though I knew he was at work and wouldn't be able to answer it, and left a voice message. "Ross, a lot has happened here since you left. I am on my way to bed, and as soon as I wake I will call and tell you everything. The Cliff's Notes version is that Steve has been arrested, Kate is in the hospital with a compound fractured leg but otherwise all right, I am fine, Mary and Bob helped save the day with a little assistance from George, and Nathan is taking care of all of us. I love you."

Then I worked my way through the debris, climbed up the stairs to the master bedroom, dropped onto the bed, pulling the forest green afghan around me, and fell asleep with all my clothes on.

Chapter 39

By noon the next day, I had spent a total of ninety-five minutes on the phone with Ross, a world's record for him—he generally averages about ninety-five *seconds* on a phone call, and that is when he is feeling chatty. During most of that time I tried to convince Ross he didn't need to leave his job and rescue me. Eventually he yielded, on one condition. At Ross's request Nathan moved into my guest room to keep an eye on things. I suspected the house's close proximity to the hospital played a significant role in Nathan's eager willingness to do Ross the favor.

In the late afternoon I was scheduled to review and sign my statement at the police station. Nathan accompanied me as my attorney. When we arrived we were diverted to a small room for some additional questions. The additional questions concerned my call to George. The police officer who met with us introduced himself as Officer Cooke and was a double for the *Today Show's* Matt Lauer.

As soon as I sat down, he asked, "Why did you call George Carter instead of 911?"

Still exhausted by the events of the night before and the subsequent questioning, I responded in a tired voice, "I don't remember calling George, though I am glad I had the presence of mind to do so."

As if my answer was the wrong one, Officer Cooke leaned a little closer to me and questioned, "But why George and not the police?"

"I don't know, Officer," I answered, slightly irritated.

He was angrily circling something with his pen over and over on a pad of paper he had placed in front of himself when he sat down to begin the interview. "It doesn't make sense," he insisted.

Nathan intervened, "Is this a problem, Officer? Janet has been through a great deal in the past few months. She was in a plane crash, the same crash that took the lives of her twin sister and brother-in-law. Then someone she initially thought was a friend and neighbor not only turns out to have probably caused the crash, but breaks into her home and attempts to kill her—after, I might add, he physically assaults her house guest. It's less than fifteen hours later, during which time Janet has had little chance to recover, and you are badgering her about why she called a friend instead of you?"

"It just doesn't make sense," Officer Cooke repeated less forcefully than before.

"Well, Officer Cooke, Mr. James' attempt to kill my client doesn't make any sense either. If you will get Janet her statement, she will review it and sign it," Nathan said dismissively.

Officer Cooke picked up his pad of paper and left without a word, returning moments later with my statement.

Nathan and I were leaving the police station thirty minutes later. Once we reached Nathan's car, I turned, facing him to thank him for his assertive handling of Officer Cooke, when he gave a slight smile and said, "I am assuming it wasn't you who phoned George for help." Then he opened the passenger door and helped me in without waiting for a reply.

The next few days took on a routine. I would hear from Ross before he went to work; twice a day Nathan and I would go see Kate; I would spend about three hours going through and packing things from the downstairs closets while Nathan went to his office to work for a few hours; Nathan and I would have a late dinner; I would call Ross before I went to sleep.

Kate was asleep more than awake during our first few visits, but soon the ratio changed. She became increasingly coherent and for longer periods of time. Eventually she told us what happened that night from her perspective—which wasn't much. She remembered saying goodnight to me, sensing some movement in her bedroom, then darkness. She said when she regained consciousness she was lying on the floor of the hall. She could hear Steve yelling at me, but couldn't see him because she faced in the wrong direction. When she started to turn she realized that besides an injury to her head, her leg was broken. She was just able to turn sufficiently to see Steve's back.

"You will probably think I am loony, but for a moment I thought I saw Mary and Bob. Just as I was trying to turn to get a better look, someone else came in through the door of the deck, and I passed out again. The next thing I remember I was riding in an ambulance."

That was yesterday's conversation. Now that Kate's pain medications had been reduced and she was conscious most of the time, I was ready to tell to Kate and Nathan about Mary and Bob. As Nathan drove us to the hospital, I shared my intentions with him. He just nodded at my pronouncement.

Interestingly enough since our first visit to the hospital when I told Nathan Kate wasn't hallucinating, he had made no mention of my statement nor asked questions. Then he just assumed when Officer Cooke was questioning me, that it wasn't me who had called George for help. His calm acceptance had started to unnerve me, until I remembered he had lost his twin brother on 9/11. Perhaps he was having his own visits.

As we walked into Kate's room, one of her doctors was walking out. When I saw Kate, I could sense her excitement about something. "What is it, Kate?" I asked.

"The doctor just left, he said I can go home tomorrow." Upon uttering these words, you could see her exhilaration fade. "I guess I don't really have a home at the moment," she said dismally. "The Foundation now has mother's home; I haven't been in my own place for a couple of months. I'm not even sure what shape it's in…"

"Of course you could just come home to Mary's," I said with a grin. "All we have to do is figure out how to get you up the stone steps. Everything you need is on the main floor, and I will be there…." A glance at Nathan's face and I amended, "We will be there to make sure your every need is taken care of."

Awkwardly Kate sat silent; this wasn't the reaction I was expecting. Then I got it. "Oh Kate," I murmured "How stupid of me. You're uncomfortable going back to the house. The last time you were there you were almost killed. I'm sorry."

Looking down at the pale blue linens that covered her, she whispered, "That's not it, J. Of course I want to go home with you. I'm just not used to people taking care of me."

Nathan drifted to her side, lifted her chin, and said softly, "Get used to it."

We spent the next several minutes trying to determine the best method for getting Kate up the steps. It wasn't until a young nurse came in and heard our conversation while she was replacing Kate's IV bag, that our problem was solved.

"It's simple," she said. "Take Kate in the same way you took her out. We can make arrangements with the ambulance company." There were objections from Kate, who found the idea of returning in an ambulance a little embarrassing, but eventually the matter was settled.

We had spent so much time discussing how we were going to get Kate safely ensconced in the house, I was afraid she might be too fatigued to have the conversation I had originally intended for the visit. But Kate was beaming. So I momentarily looked at Nathan, who gave me an almost imperceptible nod.

I took the chair next to Kate's bedside, while Nathan closed the door and then sat in the chair on the other side of the bed. I took a deep breath. "There is something I have wanted to tell you both for a long time now, but I was afraid you wouldn't believe me." I took another deep breath. "The night Steve broke in... Kate, you did see Mary and Bob."

Chapter 40

Kate inhaled so deeply I stopped to make sure she was all right.

As I poured her a glass of water, Nathan asked almost reverently, "When was the first time you saw them, J?"

Even though I had already witnessed evidence of Nathan's complete acceptance of my visions, it still surprised me. Was there a world of post-death visitations I had never heard of?

"Nathan, you are not surprised at all. Did you see your twin brother after he died?"

Staring off to a space only his, Nathan responded with great sadness in his voice, "No. Ever since his death I have fantasized he would check in with me in some manner. I guess I have never quit believing that it *could* happen."

Listening to our exchange while she took a few sips of water, Kate interrupted, "I don't understand? Are you saying Mary and Bob are still alive? And what does this have to do with Nathan's brother?"

Nathan took Kate's free hand. "No, sadly Mary and Bob *are* dead. What I think J is trying to tell us, is Mary and Bob's spirits have been showing up to give her a helping hand now and then." Looking at me he asked, "Aren't you."

I took a deep breath, nodded, and began my tale. I told them about seeing Mary in the hospital during the first few days after the crash. How the doctors, nurses and Ross had convinced me that seeing Mary was a result of the painkillers and my grief.

"It wasn't until several days after I returned home that I received the first indication Mary hadn't left…"

Then I launched into a litany of each encounter beginning with the Godiva chocolate next to my glass of wine; Mary saving me from the shopping cart Lynn Ratonne had shoved at me in the grocery store parking lot; my new computer being mysteriously set up with "Oscar" as the password; waking at Mary's to find the green and blue afghan around my shoulders; and, the episode of *How It's Made* on single-engine airplanes being stuck on both my TV sets when I was trying to watch a movie.

Nathan and Kate had listened quietly with only an occasional sigh or intake of breath. But when I mentioned the single-engine airplane episode, Nathan interrupted, asking me to give them the details of the incident.

When I finished he said, "I wish I had known about that when it happened. We would have focused on the crash and Steve sooner."

Cognizant of Kate's injuries and how close she came to dying at Steve's hands, my eyes filled with tears. "I'm sorry. I didn't think anyone would believe me. When I told Ross, he thought I was hallucinating. I was afraid you and Kate would think I was crazy, too. I don't think I could have handled that."

"*I'm* sorry," Nathan said. "That was a thoughtless thing to say, J. I would have done exactly what you did had I been in your shoes." There was a long and awkward silence while I tried to quell my tears and Nathan searched for words to make me feel better.

Kate broke the tension. "What made Ross finally believe you?"

As I related Ross's account of the avalanche, both Kate and Nathan listened spellbound. When I finished Kate whispered, "Mary and Bob saved his life." Then looking at me, her eyes glistening, she continued with awe, "It wasn't my head injury. I really did see Mary and Bob." Fearing my tears might return if I responded aloud, I just smiled at Kate and nodded.

We talked a little longer until Kate started to look fatigued. As had become Nathan's and my custom, I left Kate's room for the last half hour of the visit to give them some time alone. While they visited, I made arrangements for an ambulance company to pick up Kate and take her to Mary's house the next day.

Kate's homecoming went smoothly. Nathan and I rearranged some of the furniture on the main floor of the house, so by the time Kate arrived her movements were unimpaired by obstacles. As soon as the ambulance company delivered her to the house, I uncorked a bottle of champagne, and Nathan produced a dozen white and peach roses. Kate entertained us with snippets of the exchange between the ambulance driver and the attendant as they made their way up the driveway, which she admitted she listened to while keeping her eyes tightly closed. Apparently they spent several minutes idling on the street in front of the house trying to come up with an alternative to driving the ambulance up the steep driveway. Finally they realized there were no reasonable alternatives, and powered up it as quickly as they could.

For dinner I prepared Petrale Sole in a lemon butter caper sauce, roasted red potatoes, and steamed asparagus. Nathan picked up a blueberry tart from a local bakery for dessert. During dinner he gave us an update from the district attorney's office. Steve's attorney had arrived only moments after he was summoned to the police station, but was unable to convince Steve to stay quiet. Apparently Steve told anyone willing to listen—including the emergency medical personnel who arrived on the scene to take care of Kate, as well as the plethora of police he encountered at the house, in the patrol car and at the police station, "Mary and Bob are supposed to be dead. I killed them."

Clearly amused by the situation, Nathan said, "The lead detective told me at first they thought Steve was going for an insanity defense because he was so insistent about what he saw. Now the police psychologist thinks it was a combination of guilt, adrenaline and anger—coupled with the fact he was attempting to kill another member of the family—that made Steve hallucinate. They think they have enough evidence of premeditation to beat any attempts at a plea of insanity. It also sounds as if the police are now working closely with the NTSB team investigating the crash. The list of charges against Steve just keeps growing."

Kate listened to Nathan's report intently. "Do you think they are still here? Or do you think now that Steve has been arrested they moved on?" she asked.

Even though I had been wondering the same thing since the evening of Steve's assault, the question still froze my heart. "I think they probably moved on," I whispered so softly that I had to repeat it. As I said the words the second time I felt like I was losing Mary and Bob all over again. Kate saw my distress and tried to comfort me, but I assured her it was fatigue, not grief, weighing me down.

Dishes done, I poured myself a glass of Cabernet, said goodnight to Kate and Nathan, and went upstairs to get ready for bed. I was tired. The kind of bone weary fatigue that happens when your heart is broken, and all you want is to be in your own home with your best friend's arms around you. It was time to focus on the future.

I curled up in the large forest green upholstered chair and decided I wouldn't leave it until I had a personal plan of action. It was two a.m. before I crawled out of the chair. But I felt much better as I stripped off my clothes and got into bed. I knew what my next steps would be.

When I walked into the kitchen the next morning, Kate and Nathan were reading the newspaper while indulging in fresh strawberries and English muffins. I helped myself to some of the berries and popped a muffin into the toaster.

"I have made some decisions," I announced. As they raised their heads to hear my news, I motioned to Nathan that he had blueberry jam on his cheek, while I took my muffin out of the toaster and joined them at the kitchen table.

"First, I have decided to go home for a few days. I miss Mammoth, and most of all I miss Ross." Kate smiled approvingly while Nathan looked uneasily around the room. "You two don't have to go anywhere. Actually, I was hoping you would hold down the fort until I return.

"This leads me to my second decision. When I return, I have decided to put the house on the market, though I have also decided it will be the buyers not the price that will determine whom I sell the house to. I could never sell the house to someone like Steve." I looked Nathan. "You can do background checks for me, can't you?"

Nathan smiled and nodded as Kate asked, "Are you sure you want to sell the house? Perhaps you should think about it a little longer."

"No, I'm sure. In an odd way Steve was right. I don't want to move from Mammoth. And this house needs to be cared for; its charm and energy would fade if it were used as a second home."

As I got up to toast a second English muffin, I got my first surprise of the day when Kate asked, "Would I do? I mean, if you are really going to sell the house, and if you wouldn't mind a friend living in it, could I buy it?"

I don't know who was more shocked, Nathan or me. The idea of Kate buying the house made my heart soar. By selling the house to Kate a little of Mary and Bob would still be present, and yet Kate would make the house her own. Maybe Mary and Bob had never cared about Steve being caught; perhaps their mission had been to make sure the house they had worked on and lived in for so many years found the right owner.

When I recovered from my initial shock, I went over to Kate, carefully threw my arms around her shoulders and said, "Absolutely."

Chapter 41

Breakfast turned into a mini-celebration, Kate and I both excited about all the possibilities that opened by selling the house to her. After our initial burst of enthusiasm, Nathan grew a little ill at ease with the excited chatter.

I finally asked, "Is something troubling you about this, Nathan?"

He nodded uncomfortably saying, "Given Kate's and my er... relationship... perhaps you should find another attorney, at least to advise you during the sale of the house."

Kate grew quiet. I smiled. "I don't think that's necessary, but I don't want to make you uncomfortable. Why don't you draft a proposal, and then work out the details with my accountant. Remember, even before Kate offered to buy the house, I said the decision would be based on the buyers not the price."

Nathan acquiesced, still looking uncomfortable, so I added, "If you feel there is a conflict after you speak with my accountant, I will let you find someone else to represent me in this real estate transaction."

Nathan smiled. "Agreed!"

Back in good humor, Nathan left to water the budding roses along the driveway and sweep the decks. After he left, Kate and I resumed our animated conversation, focusing more on Kate and Nathan's blooming relationship than the sale of the house.

Two hours later I was ready to drive back to Mammoth. While I packed the car, Kate hobbled around the kitchen making me a lunch for the road comprised of a smoked turkey sandwich, potato crisps, carrot sticks, a slice of blueberry pie, and a couple of bottles of chilled water. Now I was set to drive home with only one stop to fuel my car. I was surprised at how much easier it was to leave the house this time. I was sure it was the knowledge that its new owner was already enjoying the beauty and solitude the house offered with someone she loved.

As I drove onto the 280 North, I thought about the third decision I had made the night before. Not to let the inheritance from Mary and Bob significantly change my life. I loved Ross, living in Mammoth, my friends in Mammoth, my work, and road trips. I had never really needed anything I couldn't buy, sometimes I just couldn't purchase the object of my desire as quickly as I would like to. Usually the wait made the purchase more rewarding. It was a lifestyle that fit me.

The trip went quickly. Before I knew it I was sailing through Sacramento, then skirting South Lake Tahoe, turning onto Highway 395 in Minden/Gardnerville, and cruising down 395 to Mammoth.

Unfortunately throughout the most of the trip I fretted about the fact that Mary and Bob had most likely left my universe forever. I had just started to get used to their unorthodox appearances when I needed them. Now I felt like I had lost them all over again. I knew if I wasn't vigilant, grief from their absence could overwhelm me in the coming months. I was comforted in the knowledge that Ross, Kate, and Nathan would be there to help me through the rough patches.

By the time I reached the eastern side of the Sierra my cell signal returned. My phone beeped, indicating a missed call. It was Ross. The message he left momentarily lifted my spirits, though it was phrased oddly. He said, "Looking forward to seeing you at Nevados for dinner at six-thirty. Love you." I hadn't called to let him know I was driving home today. Finally I assumed he called the house and Kate or Nathan had told him I was on my way home. I guess I should have told them that I wanted to surprise Ross. Though Nevados is one of my favorite restaurants in Mammoth—eating there at any time was a special treat. And, the knowledge Ross had made a reservation to celebrate my homecoming was heartwarming.

Glancing at the clock in the Subaru I realized I would make it into town just in time. I hoped Ross wouldn't mind that I was going to show up travel-worn in jeans and a black cotton turtleneck—my de facto winter/spring uniform. I drove into Nevados parking lot just as the clock indicated six-thirty. I dabbed on some lip-gloss and ran a brush through my hair. Then I rushed into the restaurant and literally ran right into Ross who had been standing at the door watching my arrival. As he held onto me trying to break my fall, I grabbed hold of him and took him down with me. Laughing as hard as we were, Tim, the restaurant owner, helped us both up while we received hoots and applause from the regulars at the bar.

When we were both standing on our own, Tim led us to our table saying, "I hope I got everything right. I had a difficult time finding the candy. This is what you requested, isn't it?"

Tim had taken us to the corner table, where there was a vase of daffodils, a bottle of Merryvale Cabernet, and a box of Godiva chocolates.

I looked at Ross in wonder, "What a perfect homecoming. You thought of everything!"

Ross glanced at Tim uncomfortably, then back at me in confusion. "J, I don't know what you're talking about. When Tim phoned to confirm the reservation I assumed you..." he trailed off as we both looked at Tim.

Tim shook his head a little bewildered. "J, your assistant phoned this morning and made the reservation."

"My assistant," I repeated.

"Yes, Mary. I took the call myself. She said you were celebrating a special occasion, but she didn't say what it was. Was it a prank?" he asked, somewhat alarmed.

Ross and I locked eyes at the mention of Mary. I could see in him the same flood of warmth that was engulfing me. "No, Tim. It wasn't a prank. I was just a little confused for a moment. Sorry."

We sat down. Tim opened the wine and asked if we wanted it to breathe in the bottle for a while. We declined, asking him to go ahead and pour the cabernet.

When Tim left to take care of his other customers, Ross raised his glass for a toast. He said quietly, "To Mary and Bob."

Thoughts of the crash and all that had transpired since flooded in, making me realize my life would never be the same. As I raised my glass to touch Ross's, the final realization—Mary and Bob were still watching over me.

I answered Ross's toast in a whisper, "To Mary and Bob."

About the Author

Terry Gooch Ross lives in Mammoth Lakes, California. She loves Ross, cross-country skiing, running, living in the mountains, and of course, Mary.

CPSIA information can be obtained
at www.ICGtesting.com
Printed in the USA
BVOW06s0327200217

476532BV00007B/41/P

9 781621 419488